The Adventurer's Guide to Treasure (and How to Steal It)

By Wade Albert White

The Adventurer's Guide to Successful Escapes

The Adventurer's Guide to Dragons
(and Why They Keep Biting Me)

The Adventurer's Guide to Treasure
(and How to Steal It)

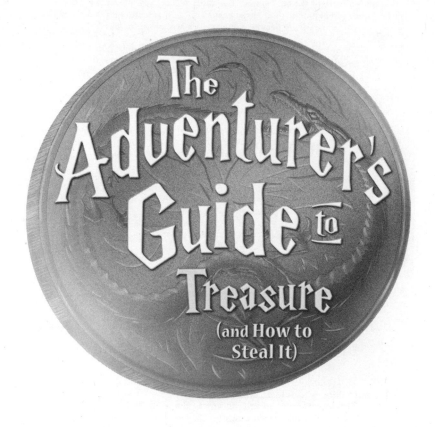

The Adventurer's Guide to Treasure
(and How to Steal It)

WADE ALBERT WHITE
Illustrations by **MARIANO EPELBAUM**

LITTLE, BROWN AND COMPANY
NEW YORK BOSTON

Text copyright © 2019 by Wade Albert White
Illustrations copyright © 2019 by Mariano Epelbaum
Spot art on page 283 © photocell/Shutterstock.com

Cover art copyright © 2019 by Mariano Epelbaum. Cover design by Karina Granda.
Cover copyright © 2019 by Hachette Book Group, Inc.

Little, Brown and Company
Hachette Book Group
1290 Avenue of the Americas, New York, NY 10104
Visit us at LBYR.com

First Edition: January 2019

Little, Brown and Company is a division of Hachette Book Group, Inc.
The Little, Brown name and logo are trademarks of Hachette Book Group, Inc.

The publisher is not responsible for websites (or their content) that are not owned by the publisher.

Library of Congress Cataloging-in-Publication Data
Names: White, Wade Albert, author. | Epelbaum, Mariano, 1975– illustrator.
Title: The adventurer's guide to treasure (and how to steal it) / Wade Albert White ; illustrations by Mariano Epelbaum.
Description: First edition. | New York ; Boston : Little, Brown and Company, 2019. | Series: Adventurer's guide ; 3 | Summary: "Anne, Penelope, and Hiro are tasked once again with an impossible quest to save the world, leading them on a mission to defeat the supreme leader of pirates, rescue dear friends, and solve the riddle of Anne's mysterious heritage." —Provided by publisher.
Identifiers: LCCN 2018009912| ISBN 9780316518444 (hardcover) | ISBN 9780316518451 (ebook) | ISBN 9780316518482 (library edition ebook)
Subjects: | CYAC: Pirates—Fiction. | Identity—Fiction. | Doppelgèangers—Fiction. | Magic—Fiction. | Adventure and adventurers—Fiction. | Humorous stories.
Classification: LCC PZ7.1.W448 Adx 2019 | DDC [Fic]—dc23
LC record available at https://lccn.loc.gov/2018009912

ISBNs: 978-0-316-51844-4 (hardcover), 978-0-316-51845-1 (ebook)

Printed in the United States of America

LSC-H

10 9 8 7 6 5 4 3 2 1

*This book is dedicated to
Dr. Henry von Klickenbeard III, Esq.,
a mad scientist I made up just now,
because even fictional people
deserve to have a book dedicated to them
every once in a while.*

———◄•►———

- CONTENTS -

Arrr, 'Tis a Prologue

At Saint Lupin's Completely Ordinary School Where Nothing Unusual Ever Happens, Most Especially Not Illegal Quests That Destroy Famous Landmarks and Get Your Questing License Suspended, no students are taught about pirates. They are not taught how to identify pirate clothing, how to eat pirate food, or how to talk like a pirate. They do not bathe themselves by dangling from the mast during a thundershower, and they do not learn how to tie unnecessarily complicated knots. They also never have long philosophical discussions with their parrots. This lack of education, incidentally, is not at all consistent with the advice given in the popular educational manual *How to Prepare Your Students to Detect and Repel an Imminent Pirate Attack*.

Understandably then, this leaves the school wide open to invasion. And in that spirit, it is widely recognized that there are three ways for pirates to raid an institute of higher learning:

1. Simply walk in through the front gates (it's not like anyone's guarding them).

2. Try bribing any zombie sharks that might be in the moat (this rarely works, however, since the sharks don't understand how bribes work; they're zombie sharks, not loan sharks).

3. Disguise your pirate ship as one of the monthly supply ships, forge the necessary permits to get past any security checkpoints, drop off half the crew at the docks so they can infiltrate the academy on the ground, and then attack from the air. This is needlessly complicated but also a lot more fun.

P.S. Make sure you have a plan to deal with the school dragon.

First Day

A nne was leaving Saint Lupin's.

Leaving it in the hands of other people, that is. She was temporarily stepping down from her position as Rightful Heir of Saint Lupin's and starting her life as a full-time student. After months of renovations, the school was finally up to code and ready to open its doors. Despite the suspension of the school's questing license, there was still a full slate of subjects to choose from, albeit with some changes. For example, Old World Mythology had been crossed out in the student handbook, and someone had carefully written "Survey of Everything Not Related to Quests" in fancy script in the margin. "Fighting Styles of Forest Rodents" had been changed to "Rock Painting 101," and "Modern History of Ancient Dragons" was now listed as the "Fine Art of Holding Your Breath." These changes were in compliance with special orders from the Wizards' Council forbidding the school from teaching its students anything whatsoever to do with adventuring.

There was only one problem: There were no students.

Or more accurately, there were no *new* students, because in addition to restricting the subjects that could be taught, the council had also frozen enrollment.

Anne walked along the twisting corridors of the Manor toward her first class, flipping through her handbook as she went. She was familiar with the Saint Lupin's campus, of course, having grown up there. But for most of her life it had been an orphanage, and on a scale of one to ten—ten being beyond fabulous and one being the worst place imaginable to live, even worse than places that served boiled cabbage and stale pine cones every night for dinner—she would have rated it a negative eighty-seven. So despite the restrictions that had been placed on the school, she was still excited for the start of term. This would be her first time in a proper classroom. In preparation for the big day, Anne had braided her hair and donned her favorite yellow tunic, because it seemed to make her brown skin glow and it matched her bright yellow eyes.

Anne was the only person she knew of who had yellow eyes. She'd never known her family and never had a place to call home. It had long been her hope that becoming an adventurer would help her discover her true origins. So far she had managed to uncover two important clues: On her first quest she had learned that she was connected to something called Project A.N.V.I.L., and on her second quest she had been told to find someone called the Lady of Glass, who apparently could reveal everything to her. Although helping with the school's renovations had kept Anne occupied these past several months, she remained determined to discover the truth about who she really was and where she came from.

Walking beside Anne were the two other students at Saint Lupin's. Penelope Shatterblade was a large girl with pale white skin, long red hair, and blue eyes. She and Anne had grown up together at the orphanage. Penelope wanted to be an adventurer, too, but had been rejected by every single quest academy. When she was only two years old, her parents had led a quest that went tragically wrong, resulting in their own deaths as well as the deaths of several others. Now her family name was considered a curse. The other student was Hiro Darkflame, an average-sized boy with beige skin, brown eyes, and long black hair tied back in a ponytail. The ponytail covered a tattoo on the back of his neck of a serpent swallowing its own tail. It was the symbol of the secret branch of the Wizards' Council where his parents worked, and it indicated he was expected to follow in their footsteps. He was a brilliant student and aspiring wizard, but unfortunately his magick spells always had unintended consequences that usually resulted in something blowing up.

Since the council had confiscated their quest academy cloaks with the words CAUTION: STUDENT ADVENTURER printed on the back in bold black letters, the three of them wore patchwork cloaks made from the purple, yellow, and black curtains taken from several empty dormitory rooms. Their handiwork left something to be desired, but with the school also in financial straits after their last quest, they had been unable to afford official replacements.

Hovering along behind the three students was a black

fire lizard named Dog. He was two feet long from tail to snout and had black scales and wings and bright green eyes. Usually he spent his days curled up in a basket in the corner of the main office, but the teachers had requested that Anne bring him along as an unofficial fourth student to boost class enrollment.

Hiro was reading a letter as they walked along the corridor.

Penelope yawned and rubbed her eyes. "Why do classes have to begin so early?"

"Early? It's eight o'clock in the morning," said Hiro, not looking up from his letter. "If they had let me make the schedule, we could have started classes by seven. Maybe even six."

"Be thankful they didn't let you, then," said Penelope. "Because if it was six o'clock right now, I'd have to thump you just on principle." She glared at Anne and Hiro. "And what is it with you two and the whole reading-while-walking thing?"

Anne lowered her handbook. "Sorry. I was trying to see what classes are available."

Hiro held up his letter. "And this just arrived this morning. It's a letter from my mother. She wants me to attend Take Your Student to Work Day tomorrow. She and my father are keen to get me working for the Wizards' Council as soon as possible." He didn't seem overly thrilled at the prospect.

"Hey, maybe your mother will take you into the council archives and show you all kinds of classified material," said Penelope.

Hiro rolled his eyes. "Knowing my mother, she definitely will."

Anne noticed a second, lighter piece of paper sticking out beneath the letter. "What's that?"

Hiro shrugged. "I haven't bothered to look at it yet. It's just another newspaper clipping. She's constantly sending me articles that allude to missions she and my father have been involved with. The articles never mention the two of them directly, of course, but I'm expected to read between the lines."

"You shouldn't ignore your mother," said Penelope, and she snatched the clipping out of his hand.

"Hey, give that back!" said Hiro.

He made a grab for the paper, but Penelope held it away from him and started reading the article aloud. "Wow, listen to this: 'Yesterday morning a quest medallion was stolen from the Pyrate Museum. The medallion in question is none other than the famous Darkflame

Medallion, acquired following the Battle of the Great Rift.'"

"What?!" exclaimed Anne and Hiro together.

"I didn't know your family owned a quest medallion," said Anne.

Hiro frowned. "Neither did I."

"And what's the Battle of the Great Rift?"

"I've never heard of it."

"Well, as long as the thief who stole the medallion doesn't bring it anywhere near Saint Lupin's, we should be fine," said Penelope, handing the article back to Hiro.

Anne, Penelope, and Hiro had already gotten caught up in two quests that year, and as much as Anne liked adventures, she was perfectly happy not going on another one until they had received a lot more training.

"It wouldn't matter anyway," said Hiro, scanning the clipping. "The article says the quest was attempted over a century and a half ago. The medallion's made of gold, though, so they think the thieves probably just want to sell it or something. There's even a picture of it here at the bottom." He showed them the picture, but it was too grainy to make out in any detail. The medallion was sitting in its own case among several other cases displaying other artifacts.

11

Hiro tucked the papers into his cloak. "I'll have to ask my mother about the article. I'm surprised she didn't say anything about it in her letter."

They continued on their way.

Anne flipped to the back of her student handbook and checked the printed schedule. "Do either of you know what our first class actually is? My handbook only lists a time and room number."

Hiro shrugged. "When I checked last night, the professors were still working out the final details. I think the Wizards' Council dropped some last-minute regulations on them."

"*More* regulations?" said Penelope. "Pretty soon they're going to require students to attend a class on council regulations just to understand them all."

Hiro flipped through his copy of the handbook. "That might actually have been one of the regulations."

They arrived at the assigned room, a large ballroom at the end of a seldom-used corridor with piles of dusty furniture stacked along one side. Prior to becoming an orphanage and then a quest academy, the school had been a private estate. That meant the campus had all sorts of interesting spaces, such as the vast library Anne used to sneak into, to "borrow" books for herself and Penelope.

Dog zipped through the large double doors ahead of them. Two chandeliers hung from the ceiling, and seven tall windows lined the back wall. Anne followed him in and stopped short. Two people were already inside.

The first was an old man with a long, wispy beard. He was standing behind a podium, but he appeared to be fast asleep. His light brown skin had a wood-grain pattern, and he wore faded yellow and brown robes. This was Sassafras, the school's professor of magick. Curiously, there was a platypus poking out of the sleeve of his robe where a left arm should be.

The second person was a girl Anne didn't recognize. She had yellowish-tan skin and bright pink hair down to her jawline. The dark wooden chair in which she was seated had two large wheels attached at the back with two smaller wheels in the front. Two heavy iron rings hung from the arm of the chair that was facing them, and Anne suspected the other arm had a matching set. What they were for, however, she couldn't begin to guess. The girl's feet rested on footboards, and her legs were wrapped in a dark green blanket. A leather pack rested on her lap. The girl was staring intently at the ceiling and didn't notice them. Dog glided over to her.

"Do you know that you have a habit of stopping in doorways?" Penelope said behind Anne.

The girl flinched at the sound of Penelope's voice and turned in their direction. Anne stepped into the room followed by Penelope and Hiro.

"Sorry if we startled you," said Anne. "We weren't expecting anyone else to be here yet."

The girl smiled shyly. "That's okay. I got distracted admiring the architecture. This is a beautiful campus."

Anne glanced up at the ceiling. She'd never paid much attention to it over the years, probably because for most of her life she'd had to focus her energy on simply making it through the day. Now that she looked, she had to agree the scrollwork was impressive. The morning sun pouring in through the windows was certainly picturesque, if a little bright.

Dog nuzzled against the girl's arm, and she patted his head obligingly.

"Who are you?" Penelope asked, somewhat abruptly.

"My name is Marri Blackwood," the girl replied. "I'm a new student. In fact, I was beginning to worry I might be the *only* student."

Penelope folded her arms across her chest. "Are you a dragon?"

Anne understood why Penelope would ask such a question. The last new student slated to attend the school, a boy named Valerian, had turned out to be a half-dragon and not entirely trustworthy at first, although they had eventually become friends and worked together.

Marri's eyes widened. "A d-dragon?"

"Because if you are, you might as well tell us now," Penelope continued. "We're good at figuring that stuff out. For example, I see that Dog is quite interested in you, and he's not interested in anybody. It makes a person suspicious as to why."

Marri reached into her pack and brought out two biscuits. "He probably just smelled these. They're leftovers from my breakfast." She offered one to Dog, and he snatched it out of her hand and gulped it down in one swallow.

"Are you here to steal Anne's gauntlet, then?" asked Hiro.

Anne owned a special gauntlet that marked her as a Keeper of the Sparrow. When she wore the gauntlet and inserted a prophecy medallion into the slot on the cuff, it would activate a quest that she and her adventuring group were obligated to undertake. On both of their previous quests, people had tried to take the gauntlet away from Anne.

Marri looked from one to the other. "I—I don't know what you're talking about. I'm a transfer student. I just came here to study. Honest." She reached into her pack again and dug out two small wooden tokens.

Anne walked over and read the inscription on the first token. "Pie artisan?"

Marri blushed. "I know, it's not exactly the greatest adventuring role. It's what I drew from the Bag of Chance."

Anne smiled at her reassuringly. "You're not alone. I was supposed to be the thief of the group, but I drew a blacksmith token instead." She brought out her token to show Marri. As always, it felt unusually cool to the touch.

Anne squinted at the second token Marri was holding. It contained only four letters. "What does A-C-T-P stand for?" she asked.

"Adventure Career Training Program," said Marri. "That's the program that allows me to study abroad for a semester." She pointed to the still-sleeping wizard. "Professor Sassafras brought me in here and told me this is where we'd be having our first class."

"It is," said Anne. "And you'll have to excuse our behavior. We were told no new students would be enrolling, so we were taken a little off guard when we saw you in here." She extended her hand. "I'm Anne. This is Penelope and Hiro."

Penelope and Hiro also held out their hands, albeit more cautiously.

Marri shook each of their hands eagerly. "Oh, I already know who the three of you are," she said. "In fact, I'd be surprised if anyone on the Hierarchy hasn't heard about you and your adventures by now. Did you really defeat the dragon queen all by yourself?"

Marri was referring to their previous quest. Anne had been forced to fight the queen of dragons after the queen had taken possession of a giant metal dragon body.

"That's...not quite the way it happened," said Anne.

"Sure it is," said Penelope, and she slapped Anne on the shoulder. "Anne's just being modest. She totally slayed that dragon. And before that she finished a Level Thirteen quest."

Anne frowned.

"Sorry, I didn't mean to pry," said Marri. "It's just, I've never met anyone famous before."

"That's okay," said Anne. "You're not prying, and

for the record, I'm not famous. I was simply in the wrong place at the wrong time."

"Twice," muttered Hiro.

Marri glanced at Anne's left hand. "I'm surprised you're not wearing it now. Your gauntlet, I mean. I guess I assumed you would keep it with you at all times."

Anne shook her head. "Because of the temporary restrictions placed on the school, we're not permitted to carry any quest-related items around campus. The gauntlet is stored in a safe place."

Marri looked disappointed.

"So where are you from?" asked Hiro.

"The outer tiers," said Marri. "A little place called Riverhold."

"I don't think I've heard of it," said Anne.

"It's a pretty cold and desolate place, to tell you the truth. In fact, if there's a bright center to the Hierarchy, Riverhold is on the tier that it's farthest from."

"There *is* a bright center to the Hierarchy, in fact," said Hiro. "It's called the BGFM."

Marri smiled. "I know that. I was just making a little joke."

"Oh."

The Hierarchy consisted of millions of tiers—giant

floating islands—that circled a pulsing sphere of magickal energy known as the Big Glowing Field of Magick, the BGFM. Saint Lupin's was on its own tier, approximately four miles in diameter, with the school situated at the center. Most of the tiers were packed together in tightly layered rings that orbited around the BGFM's equator, but there were also smaller clusters of tiers drifting around the poles and elsewhere—the outer tiers.

"So, why did you transfer to Saint Lupin's?" asked Penelope, a hint of suspicion remaining in her voice. "It's not like we're the top-ranked academy, especially with our current suspension."

Marri coughed and stared awkwardly at the floor. "I, um, had some trouble getting into the other academies. It's...kind of a long story."

Anne's heart went out to Marri. She knew only too well the difficulty of trying to get into a quest academy and the toll a growing pile of rejection letters could take. One of the things Anne liked so much about Saint Lupin's was how accepting it was of students, no matter their background.

"Excuse us for a moment," said Penelope, and she pulled Anne and Hiro into a huddle. "Should we believe her?" she whispered.

"Why wouldn't we believe her?" Anne whispered back.

"Our overall track record with new students joining the group hasn't exactly been stellar. We've been on two quests so far and a new student joined us for each one. It was a total disaster both times."

"Hey, I was one of those new students," said Hiro. "What's wrong with me?"

Penelope began checking off her fingers. "You blew up the original quest academy, set fire to the royal palace, caused an avalanche that nearly buried a small village—"

"How was the avalanche my fault?"

"Because I said so."

"You're exaggerating things," said Anne. "There's nothing wrong with Hiro, and technically we weren't even an official group until he joined us. And there was nothing wrong with Valerian, either, for that matter."

Penelope crossed her arms. "You mean Valerian the half-dragon thief who stole your gauntlet and unleashed a giant metal dragon on the entire Hierarchy?"

"The giant metal dragon wasn't his fault. And he fought on our side in the end."

Hiro held up a finger. "Can I say something?"

"No," said Anne and Penelope in unison.

"Look," said Anne. "I'm not saying there haven't been . . . challenges . . . but we have to give Marri a chance. We can't judge her before we even get to know her. And you and I both know there are many reasons why quest academies might unfairly reject a prospective student."

Penelope scowled at this, but Anne could tell she had won her over.

"Fine," said Penelope. "But if she turns out to be a half-rhinoceros, half-carnivorous jellyfish, I'm going to say I told you so."

Before they could pursue the matter further, Sassafras let out a loud snort. His eyes popped open, and he gripped the podium with his bony fingers. "And that's why you should never stare directly into the eyes of a basilisk pumpkin." He adjusted his spectacles and looked at the group of them. "Why are you all standing?"

"Er, we only just arrived, Professor," said Anne. "Class hasn't started yet."

Sassafras rubbed his eyes. "That's a relief. I hate it when I sleep through the beginning of a lecture— especially when it's my own." He gestured to Marri. "I see you've met our newest student. We explored a little bit of the grounds on our way here, but I trust you three will give her the grand tour after class."

"Certainly," said Anne.

"Good. Then everyone take your places, please, and we'll get started."

Anne, Penelope, and Hiro all took seats near Marri, and Sassafras began pacing in front of the class.

"So, normally this would be Magick 101, but due to the suspension we've had to make a few adjustments," said Sassafras. "So, welcome instead to a class that is sure to be of tremendous value to you no matter your chosen vocation, equal parts fascinating and dangerous, a subject no person who considers themselves to be a true student of the humanities can do without: Introduction to Flower Arranging. In this class, we will study the nature of various plants and flowers and, er, how to arrange them."

Penelope's hand shot up.

Sassafras stopped his pacing. "Yes, Ms. Shatterblade?"

"Aren't these substitute classes kind of pointless? I mean, I know you're not allowed to teach us anything about quests, but how is arranging flowers going to help us?"

"Well, you never know when an obscure bit of

knowledge might come in handy. And there's more to flower arranging than meets the eye." He picked up a small object from the top of the podium. It was a twig. "For instance, does anyone know what this is?"

Anne gasped. "It looks like the branch Mr. Shard used on our first quest!"

Penelope squinted at it. "I think you're right. Whenever he tapped it, it grew into a bridge."

Sassafras nodded. "Very good. They're called everlasting branches. Quite rare. And the dead ones do make useful bridges and such in a pinch. But the live ones have even more peculiar properties." He set down the first twig and picked up a small plant pot. The pot contained another twig, but this one had a tiny purple flower growing from it. "For instance, if you simply hold a live one and concentrate, it will shape itself into the thing you most desire at that moment."

Sassafras held out the twig and closed his eyes. The twig began to lengthen and widen, with branches shooting off to the side. It grew so big that Sassafras had to set it on the floor. The twig had transformed itself into a bed with a group of purple flowers arranged as a pillow.

"Just what I needed," said Sassafras. He snapped the bed off from the original potted twig and handed the pot to Penelope. "Now it's time for you students to have a turn. Ms. Shatterblade, why don't you try first?"

Penelope took the pot in both hands and held it out. The twig lengthened and flattened into a long blade, and a branch formed itself into a hilt.

"Excellent work," said Sassafras, snapping off the sword and handing it to Penelope.

Penelope gave it a few swings. "Good balance. Too bad it's not the real thing."

Penelope was officially the fighter of their adventuring group, but first-year students were only permitted to carry wooden practice swords.

Sassafras handed the pot to Hiro. "You next, Mr. Darkflame."

Hiro cleared his throat and held the pot in a slightly trembling hand. At first the twig began to expand into a long ornate quarterstaff, like those often carried by full wizards. Before it finished transforming, however, it shook violently and exploded in a shower of sawdust, causing everyone to flinch and the platypus to duck inside the sleeve of Sassafras's robe.

"Whoops!" said Sassafras, snatching the pot away. "That can happen sometimes with magick users. Ms. Blackwood, how about you try next?"

Marri took the potted twig apprehensively. She closed her eyes, and the twig began to grow. It twisted like a vine, with delicate branches shooting off and curling around one another. When it finished, the twig had transformed into a small model of a three-masted airship. There appeared to be a symbol on one of the sails, but Anne couldn't quite make it out. She wondered why Marri's greatest desire at the moment was for an airship.

"That's so cool!" said Penelope.

"Yes, you definitely have the knack for it," said Sassafras, and then he turned to Anne. "And now, last but by no means least."

Anne took the pot and closed her eyes. The pot quivered slightly, but nothing seemed to be happening. Anne opened one of her eyes and peered down at the twig. It hadn't grown in the slightest.

Sassafras placed a hand on Anne's shoulder. "Not to worry. Sometimes it takes a while to get the hang of it. Give it another try."

Anne sighed. None of the others had needed a second try. Even Hiro had made it change (before it exploded).

"Sorry to interrupt, but is that a supply ship?" asked Hiro.

Everyone looked out the windows. A medium-sized airship was rising over the nearby forest, its sails fully unfurled. It didn't appear to be leaving, though. If anything, it was slowing down. Numerous figures could be seen running about on its deck.

Sassafras squinted. "It could be a supply ship. I can't be certain, though, because there's a large patch on the sail covering the symbol."

"That's weird," said Penelope. "And anyway, supply day was last week, wasn't it?"

Back when the Matron ran Saint Lupin's, a supply ship only stopped by once every year. Ever since Anne had become the Rightful Heir, however, and the campus required major renovations, the supply ships had been stopping by once per month.

The ship slowly rotated until it was parallel to them. A dozen portholes opened along the side, and a long black barrel extended from each porthole.

"What is it doing?" asked Anne.

Penelope walked to the back of the classroom and pressed her nose against the window. "It's hard to make out, but I think those are cannons."

"On a supply ship?"

There was a puff of gray smoke from one of the black

barrels in the center. Seconds later, a loud crack split the air and rattled the windows.

Penelope nodded vigorously. "Yep, they're cannons all right. I wonder who they're shooting at?"

A high-pitched whistling grew louder and louder.

"I think they're shooting at us!" yelled Hiro.

Before anyone could move, the wall in front of them exploded in a flash of blue light.

TAKEN FROM THE HANDY PAMPHLET
*CAPTAIN BLIGHTROT'S TIPS FOR HOW TO
TALK LIKE A PIRATE:*

1) Call everybody "Matey."

2) Randomly threaten to make people walk the plank.

3) When in doubt, just keep yelling "Arrr!"

The Battle of Saint Lupin's

Anne lay on the floor of the ballroom covered in debris. Her ears were ringing, and she fell into a brief coughing fit from all the dust in the air. The explosion had shattered two of the windows and collapsed a portion of the wall and ceiling. Dog flew over and began licking her cheek. She sat up unsteadily and checked to see if anyone was injured.

"Why is a supply ship shooting at us?" yelled Hiro, who was lying facedown on the floor with his arms shielding his head.

"Maybe Jocelyn asked for an extension on the school's credit, and this is their way of saying no," Penelope said as she brushed herself off. She crawled over to one of the unbroken windows and raised her head just enough to see outside. "They took the patch off the sail. I can just make out the symbol. It looks like a giant letter O with a giant letter X under it. O-X spells *ox*."

Hiro scrambled over and took a peek. "Actually, I think that's the symbol for poison."

"Cows are trying to poison us!"

"By shooting cannonballs at us?"

"Haven't you ever heard of lead poisoning?"

Marri and her chair were covered in bits of plaster. Anne scrambled over and helped her remove the worst of it. Marri did the same for Anne, picking pieces of plaster from her hair and brushing the dust from her shoulders.

"Are you hurt?" asked Anne.

Marri shook her head. "Just a little shaken."

"It looks like they're coming around for a second pass. We need to get out of here!" said Penelope. "Where's Sassafras?"

Anne quickly scanned the room. The middle of the floor was covered in shards of glass, pieces of broken window frame, and chunks of plaster, and everything was coated in dust. There was no sign of their teacher.

"Maybe he went for help," said Hiro.

"And left us to fend for ourselves?" Penelope said skeptically. "He's absentminded, sure, but even Sassafras wouldn't abandon four students in the middle of an attack."

"Well, he's definitely not here."

Another high-pitched whistling filled the air.

"Everybody out!" shouted Anne.

Dog shot into the air, and the four of them rushed for the exit, but another explosion rocked the room with yet another accompanying flash of blue light. The shockwave threw Anne off her feet again, and she skidded across the floor and slammed into a wall. The back of her head throbbed in pain. Clutching her head with one hand, Anne placed the other against the wall for support and rose on trembling legs. Heavy particles filled the air. The second blast had taken out three more windows at the far end of the room and collapsed half the ceiling. Penelope and Hiro had landed next to Anne. Marri had been tossed against the wall as well, but had managed to keep her chair upright.

"Is anyone hurt?" Anne called out, trembling.

Marri was coughing but gave her a firm nod and a thumbs-up.

Some of the flying glass from the windows had slashed Hiro's arm, and it was bleeding. Penelope tore a strip off the inner lining of her cape and quickly wrapped it around the wound.

"That's good enough for now," said Hiro, his voice shaking. "We need to leave."

Anne scanned the debris with rising panic. "Where's Dog?"

As with Sassafras, there was no sign of the fire lizard anywhere.

"He's probably off hiding in the dungeon by now," said Penelope.

Anne felt sick at the thought that Dog might have been wounded. "But he was right here a second ago."

"I'm sure he made it out," said Hiro. "And we should, too."

A piece of ceiling came crashing down beside Anne and she jumped.

"Let's go!" she said.

Marri struggled to maneuver the wheels of her chair over the debris, so Hiro helped her out. Penelope followed close behind, and Anne brought up the rear. She paused at the threshold to scan the room one last time for any indication of Sassafras or Dog. Finding none, she exited. Everyone moved quickly down the corridor. Rounding a corner, they all breathed a little easier, although they were still completely confused as to why anyone would be attacking the school.

As they stood there catching their breath, a short man with ruddy cheeks came running up. The top of his head barely reached Anne's shoulders. He wore a rusty breastplate and helmet and was armed from head to toe with multiple knives, axes, and swords.

"Captain Copperhelm!" Anne shouted. A great wave of relief washed over her at the sight of a teacher.

"What in the blazing sun is going on here?" Copperhelm barked. "And why are you all cowering in a huddle? Sassafras is supposed to be teaching you how to make a nice bouquet, not how to blow up the school!"

Anne shook her head. "It wasn't Sassafras. One of the supply ships is attacking Saint Lupin's."

"Or it might be poison cows," said Penelope.

"Sassafras and Dog are missing," added Hiro.

Anne pointed toward the ballroom. Copperhelm started off in that direction, but there was another crack of cannon fire, and moments later a third explosion shook the building, although this time farther away. Instead of ducking or running back, however, Copperhelm marched resolutely down the hallway until he reached the door. Anne was so worried that another attack would strike directly where he stood that she thought her heart might beat out of her chest. Copperhelm surveyed the ballroom for several long heartbeats before returning.

"That's not a supply ship," he said. "Or cows. I just caught a glimpse of it, but it's definitely a skull and cross-bones. That means pirates."

"We're being attacked by pirates?!" exclaimed Penelope. "That is so cool!"

Copperhelm glared at her.

Penelope's cheeks flushed. "I mean, it's cool except for the part where it's totally not cool at all. That part is bad. Very, very bad."

Copperhelm placed a heavy hand on Anne's arm. "They're attacking another part of the school right now. Get your team out of here. Head into the forest and hide in one of the mines. I'll see to the defenses."

"But Sassafras—"

"Your first responsibility is to see to the safety of your group. We'll all keep an eye out for Sassafras, and if you do happen to see him, tell him to meet me at the main gate."

"Okay," said Anne, her heart pounding.

"By the way, who's this?" he asked, jabbing a thumb in Marri's direction.

"The new student."

Copperhelm tipped his helmet to Marri. "Welcome to Saint Lupin's. Try not to get blown up if you can help it." With that, he ran back the way he had come, moving at a much faster pace than Anne would have thought possible for someone of his stature.

Wheels were already turning in Anne's head, and she took a calming breath. She was scared, no question, but Saint Lupin's was the closest thing to a home she had ever known, not to mention she was its Rightful Heir, and she wasn't going to hide when it needed her most. She also didn't like the idea of running from a fight when other people were out there putting themselves at risk. Fear gave way to quickly rising anger. How dare someone attack their school!

"You heard Captain Copperhelm," said Hiro. "We need to head for the forest."

Anne shook her head. "There's something else we need to do first."

"There is?" said Penelope.

Hiro's eyes widened. "You're going to try to fight them, aren't you?"

"We can't just abandon our friends," said Anne determinedly.

"I'm all for fighting, but we don't have any weapons," Penelope pointed out.

"I have an idea about that."

Hiro groaned and shook his head. "Ideas are bad. Bad, bad, bad."

Penelope grinned. "Are you thinking what I'm thinking?"

"I am if you're thinking of the Knights of Saint Lupin's," said Anne.

They were referring to three walking suits of armor called the iron knights. In reality, the knights were Old World power suits that could be controlled by a human pilot. They were originally the property of the Matron, the former headmistress of Saint Lupin's, but Anne had come into possession of them when she became the Rightful Heir of Saint Lupin's at the end of her first quest.

"But Captain Copperhelm gave strict orders to head directly for the mines," Hiro persisted.

"The knights are working in the mines, so technically we'll be following his orders," said Anne. "I'll need my gauntlet to control the knights, though, and that's currently being stored in the school's armory. So we just need to make a little detour first."

Hiro crossed his arms. "Have I mentioned how much I hate detours?"

Anne turned to Marri. "We'll take you with us to the mines, but you can stay hidden there. You only just started at the school, and we can't expect you to risk yourself for us."

Marri met Anne's eyes with a determined look. "I became part of this group the moment I arrived," she said. "What kind of a team member would I be if I let everyone else face all the danger?"

Anne nodded, and the four of them set off down the corridor in the same direction as Copperhelm. When they reached the main lobby, everything was relatively quiet, although shouts drifted in through the windows along with what sounded like the clink of metal on metal. The unmistakable smell of gunpowder hung in the air. Instead of heading out the front entrance, they turned and made their way along a short corridor that led to a large oak door. Anne pushed it open, and the four of them proceeded inside.

The room was lightly furnished. Weapon racks lined the walls, all of them empty. There was a single bed along the back wall, a bookshelf stuffed with books and scrolls, and a massive sword leaning in the corner. There was also what looked like a ten-foot-tall metal statue of a man with three arms in the middle of the room.

Marri gasped when the statue turned its head to look at them.

"Marri, Rokk. Rokk, Marri," said Anne.

Rokk was an Old World robot. They'd met him during their first quest, and he had traveled with them ever since. Unfortunately, during their second quest he fell under the control of the Copper Knights and attempted to kill the dragon queen. The Wizards' Council tried to have him deactivated, but Anne used what little influence she had to keep him at Saint Lupin's.

"Um, hi there," said Marri, looking somewhat alarmed by his presence.

"Greetings," said Rokk. "My sensors have detected several explosions nearby. Is there a problem?"

"You could say that," said Anne. "Saint Lupin's is being attacked by pirates. I need my gauntlet so we can operate the iron knights. And Captain Copperhelm could probably use your help with the school's defenses."

Rokk picked up the sword in one hand. With another hand, he reached under the bed and pulled out a rectangular wooden box with an orange ribbon tied around it. Anne tore off the ribbon and opened the box. The inside was lined with crushed blue velvet, and nestled there was a brown leather glove covered in strips of overlapping metal. Her gauntlet. She pulled it onto her left hand.

"You might also find this useful," said Rokk, selecting a single red-covered book from the shelf with his third hand.

Anne immediately recognized *The Adventurer's Guide*. She had discovered it in the library the day before her thirteenth birthday, the day before her first quest. The book often provided clues about how to complete their quests. Unfortunately, it had been stabbed with a sword, and now much of the information it provided came out scrambled. Since it was yet another adventure-related item, Anne had been forced to store it along with the gauntlet.

Several shouts echoed down the hallway.

"It's the pirates," whispered Hiro.

Penelope tiptoed into the hallway for a moment, then quietly returned and eased the door shut. "It sounds like they've entered the main lobby."

"Is there any way to lock this door from the inside?" Anne asked Rokk.

"Negative," said Rokk. "Additionally, it would only be a matter of time before they broke it down."

"I have something that might help," said Marri. She reached into her leather pack and pulled out a cloth bag. From the bag she removed a small blue object. It was less than an inch in diameter and many sided.

"What's that" asked Penelope.

"An icosahedron."

"A what?"

"It means a dice with twenty sides," said Hiro.

"Oh."

"What does it do?" Anne asked hopefully. She welcomed anything that could help them against the pirates.

Marri carefully picked up the dice between her thumb and forefinger and held it toward Rokk. "Could you look at this, please?"

Rokk leaned over, and a green beam of light shot out of his eyes and swept over the cube.

"Curious," said Rokk. "If I'm not mistaken, that is a—"

Marri muttered something under her breath, and a blue ray shot out of the dice and struck Rokk in the chest. For a moment, he was surrounded by a nimbus of light. Then he disappeared, along with everything he was holding.

Hiro gasped.

"What happened?" shouted Penelope. "Where did he go?"

Marri held up the cube. "Don't worry. It's supposed to do that. Your friend is fine. He's merely been shrunk and placed inside the dice."

Anne stepped closer. Indeed, there was a tiny Rokk peering out from one of the faces of the dice and looking very surprised (or at least very surprised for a robot).

"But how does that help?" asked Anne.

"Simple," said Marri. "With that robot and his giant sword out of the way, it's much easier for me to do this."

Before Anne could ask what "this" was, Marri reached beneath her chair and pulled out a short sword. She pointed it at Anne.

Anne blinked several times to make sure she was seeing things correctly. "What are you doing?"

In a flash, Penelope yanked her wooden sword out of its scabbard and leapt forward, but with a quick flick of her wrist, Marri disarmed her. The wooden sword clattered across the floor and under the bed. Hiro pulled his

Special Order Spell Catalog out of his cloak, but with another swish of her blade, Marri sliced the catalog in half.

Anne started for the door, but Marri had anticipated the move and wheeled her chair back to block the way.

"Don't make this harder than it has to be," said Marri. Gone was the shy new student. Her voice was commanding. "Fighting would be foolish. You don't have any weapons."

"Don't count on it," said Anne, and she held up her gauntlet. "Activate Three-Handed Sword of the Guardian."

A giant sword appeared in the air above her. It looked identical to the sword that had been sucked into the dice along with Rokk. Anne reached up with the gauntlet and grabbed it. It looked impossibly heavy but was in truth quite light, and Anne had no difficulty wielding it. She had never been formally trained in sword fighting, but she was hoping the mere sight of the massive blade might be enough. Marri certainly looked concerned.

At that moment, the door burst open and four burly individuals—two men and two women—barged in. One of them had a peg leg, another had a hook instead of a hand, and two of them wore eye patches. They all wore pieces of mismatched leather armor and carried long knives, and each of them had a badge pinned to the chest with a unique number on it. The four pirates spread out and pointed their blades at Anne, Penelope, and Hiro.

"We've beaten the scurvy dogs and secured the grounds, Captain," said a pirate with the number nineteen on his badge. He dropped what looked to be another two dice into her cloth bag.

"*Captain?*" said Anne, and she stared at Marri anew. "Who are you?"

Marri dug out her two tokens again and pressed them together. They merged into a single larger token, and the letters from PIE ARTISAN and ACTP swirled around until they spelled something completely different: S. PIRATE CAPTAIN.

"I knew it!" said Penelope.

"What does the *S* stand for?" asked Hiro.

"Senior," said Pirate Nineteen. "It marks her as one of the highest-ranking pirate captains in the Hierarchy."

Anne swallowed and gripped the hilt of her sword firmly.

"Everything all right here, Captain?" asked a pirate with the number twenty-two. She was staring intently at the massive blade in Anne's hand.

Marri looked pointedly at Anne. "Well?"

43

Anne looked left and right. There were five pirates, and Penelope and Hiro had both been disarmed. There was no way Anne could protect both herself and her friends against such odds.

"Deactivate sword," said Anne through gritted teeth, and the Three-Handed Sword disappeared.

Marri turned to Pirate Twenty-Two. "Take the gauntlet."

The pirate sheathed her knife and walked over to Anne. Reluctantly, Anne removed the gauntlet and passed it to her.

Marri stared at Anne for a moment. There was a glint of anticipation in her eye. Earlier Anne had mistaken it for the excitement of starting at a new school, but now she saw it was something more sinister, and it made her nervous. Finally, Marri turned her chair around and headed out the door.

"Bring them," she ordered, her tone firm and resolute.

And the pirates led them out.

THE STORY OF THE INCREDIBLE SHRINKING MACHINE

Once upon a time there was an incredible shrinking machine.

It shrank things.

That's pretty much the whole story.

Marauders, Raiders, and Buccaneers

The pirates escorted Anne, Penelope, and Hiro back to the main lobby. From there they proceeded down the long corridor to the headmistress's office. The hallway was lined with the statues of the former headmistresses and headmasters of Saint Lupin's. As always, Anne felt a lingering sense of disapproval as she passed them, perhaps from a mildly guilty conscience for all the times she'd snuck around where she wasn't supposed to. As the group approached the office door, the sound of breaking glass came from inside the room.

The office was octagon shaped. There were three tall stained-glass windows and in the center a great oak desk. Along the walls, floor-to-ceiling shelves held thousands of glass domes, each displaying a unique quest medal-- lion. A pirate wearing the badge number fifty-three was moving swiftly along the shelves, plucking off the glass domes and tossing them aside, and deftly sweeping each medallion into a burlap sack.

"Hey, that's our stuff!" shouted Penelope.

Anne started toward the pirate, but their four beefy escorts blocked the way.

Yet another pirate stood off to the side holding an orange-and-white cat who was struggling to get free. Her Royal Highness Princess Fluffington Whiskers of the Mousetrapper Clan—or Princess Whiskers, as she liked to be called—was technically the headmistress of the school. The cat sank her claws into the pirate's bare arm, and the pirate released her with a yelp. Princess Whiskers landed gracefully on the floor and immediately sprang at the pirate closest to Anne. The pirate shrieked and tumbled into one of the shelves, and Princess Whiskers bounded onto the desk. She arched her back and hissed.

"And a hiss hello to you, too," said Marri. She held up another one of her dice and captured the feisty cat midpounce in a flash of blue light.

Anne was too furious for words. The only thing keeping her from flying at the "captain" was the meaty hand of a pirate three times her size on her shoulder. She remained where she was, trembling with outrage. Marri moved behind the desk while the other pirates guided Anne, Penelope, and Hiro to a spot on the floor where an X had been painted long ago.

Pirate Twenty-Two laid Anne's gauntlet on the desk, but Marri didn't reach for it. Instead, she waited patiently until Pirate Fifty-Three finished going through the quest medallions. He dropped the last medallion into the sack with a clink and then headed out the door. Anne surveyed the damage with gritted teeth. Every medallion was gone, stolen, including a special copper medallion bearing the image of a dragon that had been on display on the desk. That was the medallion from her second quest. She had never managed to recover the silver medallion from her first quest, but if she had, no doubt it would be gone as well.

"Those medallions belong to me," said Anne, doing her best to hold her emotions in check.

"Not anymore," Marri replied. "They fall well within standard pirate looting rights."

"Are you at least going to tell us what this is all about?" Penelope asked impatiently.

"All in due time."

Marri sat there with her hands on her lap, studying them but otherwise unmoving, as though waiting for something to happen. Soon the sound of approaching footsteps echoed down the corridor, and moments later two more pirates entered, each carrying one end of a wooden chest bound in thick iron straps and secured with a chunky iron lock. They set the chest down with a thump and stepped back.

"Thank you," Marri said to them. "Now we can—"

Another commotion arose from the corridor, and a woman with dark brown skin and a head of voluminous black hair burst into the room wielding a rapier. Her name was Jocelyn, and she was for all intents and purposes the actual headmistress of the school. She was meticulously dressed in black pants, a red vest, and a white blouse. Her normally warm brown eyes carried a glint of steel.

"Marauders!" shouted Jocelyn. "Raiders! Buccaneers!"

"Personally, I've always liked the term *swashbuckler*," Marri said calmly.

"Well, I hope you like dungeon cells, too, because that's where I'm going to put you," Jocelyn continued. "How dare you attack this school! I am Lady Jocelyn Abigayle Daisywheel the Third, and I demand that you—"

A blue ray struck her and she disappeared. Marri dropped yet another dice into her cloth bag.

"Hey, you release our teacher right now, you... you...pirates!" yelled Penelope, her cheeks reddening with anger.

Even Hiro looked livid.

Anne slipped out of her captor's grasp and leapt forward, but before she even rounded the corner of the desk, Marri held up yet another one of her dice and Anne came screeching to a halt. She wanted to rip those dice out of Marri's hand, but there was no point getting herself trapped as well. She would have to bide her time until the right opportunity presented itself. The pirate who had been holding her guided her back to the X.

"As I was saying," said Marri, "now we can discuss why I've come here and what you're going to do for me."

"Why would we do anything for the likes of you?" asked Penelope.

Marri upended the cloth bag on the desk and dumped out seven dice. They each had a different number of sides. The first contained a tiny Rokk. The other six held Sassafras, Dog, Copperhelm, Princess Whiskers, Jocelyn, and Nana, the school's black dragon. They all appeared to be in a state of suspended animation. The flashes of blue light during the pirate attack hadn't been from the cannons. They had been from Marri capturing people. And by the looks of it, Anne, Penelope, and Hiro were the only ones left.

"Let them go!" shouted Hiro. He tried to rush forward, too, but the pirate holding him was too strong.

"I will release them. You have my word on that," said Marri. "But first you need to complete a task for me."

"Why should we take your word for anything?" asked Anne.

Marri stared at her with a grim expression. "Because you have no other choice."

She reached into the pack on her lap and pulled out a medallion—a gold medallion. The light reflected off its highly polished surface, nearly blinding them. Marri set it on the desk next to the gauntlet with a heavy *thunk*.

"I recently acquired this," she said. "It's called the Darkflame Medallion."

Penelope gasped. "*You* stole it from the museum. Hiro, they have your family's medallion!"

Hiro stared at the medallion. "Why did you take it?"

"It's what we do," said Marri matter-of-factly. "We seek out the medallions from failed quests."

"But why?" asked Anne.

"To claim their treasure, of course. When someone fails a quest, the treasure usually gets left behind." She shrugged. "Pirates like treasure. And I happen to know that the treasure for this quest is worth a fortune."

"But prophecy medallions can't be reactivated," said Hiro. "Once a quest has been attempted, you can't access them again, regardless of whether or not the quest was completed."

"I'm not trying to reactivate it. I only need the information inside it, to point me in the direction of the treasure. And for that, all I need is the gauntlet that originally activated the medallion—and a little ingenuity."

"What makes you think it was Anne's gauntlet?" asked Penelope.

"Simple deduction," said Marri. "I know that the gauntlet that activated the quest ended up at Saint

Lupin's. Yours is the only gauntlet here. Add to that the fact that the youngest son of the Darkflame family is a member of your group, and there's really only one possible conclusion."

"And if you're wrong?" asked Anne.

Marri ignored the question. Instead, she motioned to the two pirates who had carried in the chest, Pirate Sixty-Six and Pirate Seventy-Five. Pirate Sixty-Six produced a rusty key and inserted it into the lock on the chest. There was a loud click, and the lock snapped open. The pirate pulled off the lock and lifted the lid. An eerie silver glow came from inside the chest. Holding a pair of tongs in her thick leather gloves, Pirate Seventy-Five reached into the chest and lifted out a small vial containing a viscous black liquid that seemed to be moving of its own accord.

Anne felt Hiro tense beside her.

"What is that?" asked Penelope.

"This substance is a relic of the Old World," said Marri, her eyes glistening. "No one alive today knows how to manufacture more. It is extremely rare to find it in its liquid state, and this single vial is worth more than the entire Saint Lupin's tier."

"And what are you going to do with it?" asked Hiro.

For all that he didn't really care for quests or adventure of any kind, he was fascinated by anything to do with the Old World. Although this time Anne noted a hint of concern in his voice.

Still using the tongs, Pirate Seventy-Five carried the vial over to the desk. She removed the stopper and tipped the contents into the circle on the gauntlet where a medallion was normally placed.

"Hey, what are you doing?!" Anne shouted.

She struggled to get free again, but this time the hand gripped her tightly. She watched helplessly as the dark substance pooled into the medallion slot.

As the black liquid oozed out of the vial, Marri dug a small leather pouch out of her pack and pulled a small crystal shard out of it. She held the shard between her thumb and forefinger with great care. It glinted in the sunlight that streamed through the windows.

"Is that a dragon stone?" asked Anne.

"A piece of one, yes," said Marri. "We're attempting to modify the gauntlet's GPS."

"What?!" Anne exclaimed.

Marri dropped the shard onto the pool of black liquid. As soon as it made contact, there was a blinding flash of light and a familiar rainbow-colored form appeared above the desk. It was Jeffery, the magickal holographic sparrow who lived in the gauntlet and acted as the General Pathfinder Sparrow for any quests that were activated. His form expanded and contracted randomly, exploding into bursts of colors and re-forming, deforming and seeming to melt, bursting into flame, and then becoming a pillar of ice. This was all accompanied by an unbearably shrill screeching. Anne cried out with every transformation, but after several heart-stopping moments Jeffery returned to his normal size and disappeared. The black liquid and the piece of the dragon stone were also gone.

Marri closed her eyes and raised her fists in a sign of victory, and several of the pirates in the room hooted and hollered.

Anne nearly collapsed against the edge of the desk. "What did you do to Jeffery?"

"I believe the Old World term is *hot-wired*," said Marri. "Presuming the shard and the black liquid worked together as planned, we have just modified a part of his code. He should now be able to access any medallion this gauntlet has previously activated."

"But what if they didn't work as planned?" stormed

Anne, struggling against her captor. "What if all you did was hurt him?"

"I guess there's only one way to be certain," said Marri. "Put it on."

Anne fell completely still.

This wasn't at all what she'd been planning for her first day of classes. She would do whatever it took to free those who had been imprisoned, but it was clear Marri and her pirates currently had the upper hand. That didn't mean they knew everything, though. If Anne gave the impression of cooperating, they would give her possession of the gauntlet. The gauntlet would allow her to control the iron knights, presuming she could signal them from this distance. It was a long shot, but right now it was her best hope.

Anne walked resolutely over to the desk and picked up the gauntlet. It felt the same as ever. She looked one last time at the blue dice lined up on the desk, took a deep breath, and slid her hand inside.

Marri handed her the gold medallion. Anne took it in her free hand but hesitated. Everything was happening so fast, and she needed a moment to think. She turned the medallion over several times. Anne had never held anything made from gold before, and she found it surprisingly heavy. There was something else, too: The medallion bore the image of a dragon—the Sign of Zarala. It had been on the medallions from Anne's first two quests as well. Given how those quests had gone, she did not take it as a good omen.

"The sooner you insert it, the sooner we can finish this," said Marri.

Steeling herself, Anne placed the medallion over the inset of the gauntlet and gave it a gentle nudge.

The medallion slid into place with a soft click.

And then it exploded.

THE ADVENTURER'S GUIDE TO QUESTING GAUNTLETS SAYS THE FOLLOWING ABOUT HOT-WIRING YOUR GPS:

The GPS in your gauntlet is a finely tuned piece of magickal engineering. In order for the GPS to perform its many varied tasks, it has been connected directly to the space-time continuum. The wizards who created this link spent countless hours of study and preparation, rehearsing the required spells hundreds of times and working in an environment of complete silence—except, of course, for the obligatory yellow rubber ducky.

But sure, if you want to mess around with it in your spare time, go right ahead. It's only all of existence at stake.

4

The Gold Medallion

For the third time that morning, Anne found herself flying flat on her back. The heat from the gauntlet was almost unbearable, but unlike the last two times when a medallion had attached itself to her gauntlet, she was not entirely unprepared. She squeezed her eyes shut and took deep, steadying breaths until the pain subsided. When she opened her eyes again, she was relieved to find Jeffery perched on her chest and peering down at her.

"For the record, whatever you did to the gauntlet just

now, it was a very bad idea," he said. "My head feels all wonky."

"Tell me about it," said Anne, but she ignored her own aching head and inspected the gauntlet for damage. Other than being a little singed, it didn't look too worse for wear, which was a relief. The gold medallion also seemed to be intact. It hadn't actually exploded as it had seemed in the moment, but some sort of shockwave had definitely been released.

Penelope and Hiro rushed over and knelt next to Anne, and Jeffery fluttered up to the edge of the desk.

"Are you okay?" asked Hiro.

Anne nodded slowly. She had expected something to happen, but the blast still shocked her. Penelope quickly checked Anne over from head to toe.

"Do medallions always blow up like that when they attach?" asked Penelope as she bent Anne's arm back and forth to see if it was working properly. "It nearly knocked Hiro and me off our feet, too."

Anne managed to sit up. "No. They weren't pleasant, but that was definitely a first."

Penelope leaned in closer and whispered. "Anne, take a look." She opened her hand so only Anne could see.

Nestled in the palm was the blue dice containing Nana. "I swiped it during all the commotion."

Anne was about to respond, but Marri wheeled her chair around to the front of the desk, and Penelope pulled back her hand.

"Is she injured?" asked Marri.

Penelope glared at her. "She's fine, no thanks to you."

Marri turned her attention to Jeffery. "What happened? Is the medallion damaged?"

"Why, hello, strange person whom I've never met before," said Jeffery.

"This is Captain Marri Blackwood," said Anne, not bothering to disguise her annoyance. "She and her pirate crew carried out a brazen and unprovoked attack on Saint Lupin's. They damaged several of the buildings and imprisoned all the teachers inside some magickal dice. And all for the stupid treasure inside that medallion."

"Gotcha," said Jeffery. "Also, glad to see this situation isn't in any way tense or awkward." He tilted his head as though he were listening to a faraway voice. "Anyway, the medallion is fine. And so is the gauntlet, thanks for asking. Also, you'll be happy to hear that the quest has been successfully reactivated. It's a Pirate

Treasure quest, which I suppose makes sense given the present company."

"What did you say?" asked Marri. She reached over and grabbed Anne's gauntlet, nearly yanking her off the floor. "Reactivated? Nothing we did to the gauntlet should have reactivated the quest. Are you sure?"

"Only about a thousand percent sure," said Jeffery.

Marri released the gauntlet and pressed her hands to the sides of her head. "Oh, this is bad. This is very, very bad."

"I thought you said you didn't want to reactivate it," said Anne.

"I didn't even think it was possible. I only wanted the location of the treasure."

"What does it matter if it's activated or not?" asked Penelope. "You can find the treasure either way, can't you?"

Marri turned to them with a wild look in her eye. "You don't understand. If he finds out, he's going to be furious."

"If who finds out?" asked Hiro.

Marri swallowed. "Octo-Horse Pirate."

The other pirates in the room shifted their feet nervously, and their eyes darted toward the door as though expecting something extremely unpleasant to come charging in at any moment. Anne had never heard the name Octo-Horse Pirate, and by the blank looks on both Penelope's and Hiro's faces, neither had they.

"Octo-who-what?" asked Penelope.

"Octo-Horse Pirate," Marri repeated. "Half octopus, half horse, all pirate—or at least that's what it says on his business cards. He's the supreme leader of all the pirate factions. He gave me the mission to steal the gold medallion from the museum, but I was supposed to take it directly to him. I wasn't authorized to access it on my own."

"Then why did you?!" Hiro cried.

Marri glared at him defiantly. "I have my reasons." She looked back to the medallion. "But if the quest has been reactivated, then he'll find out what I did, unless... unless..."

Hiro groaned. "I hate it when people say 'unless.' Nothing good ever comes from it."

Marri spoke with resolve. "We'll complete the quest."

"*We?*" said Anne incredulously. "You're the one who started this."

Marri ignored her and continued. "If we finish the quest and bring back the treasure, then it won't matter that we accidentally reactivated it. Surely he'll overlook that one little mistake."

Anne cut in more forcefully this time. "First of all, *we* didn't accidentally reactivate anything. That was entirely *you* and your merry band of thieves here. Second of all, if you think we're going to help you complete some quest after what you just did to our school, you're dreaming."

Marri pointed to the dice on the desk. "If you ever want to see your friends again, you'll help me complete the quest. That's the price of their freedom. And yours."

"Or maybe we'll just free them ourselves!" shouted Penelope.

She was holding the dice containing Nana over her head. Before any of the pirates could react, she threw the dice at the floor. It shattered in a little puff of blue light.

Penelope looked disappointed. "Well, that was a bit anticlimactic."

Anne looked around. "Where's Nana?"

"Right here," said a tiny voice by her ear.

Anne turned her head. Hovering in front of her nose was a tiny black dragon the size of an overgrown bumblebee.

"Nana?" said Anne, not quite believing her eyes. "Why are you so small? Turn big again!"

"I'm trying to, but it's not working."

"That's what happens when you break someone out of the dice instead of releasing them properly," said Marri.

"Sorry, Nana," Penelope said sheepishly.

Before Nana could say anything more, Pirate Twenty-Two reached over and caught the miniature dragon between two halves of a hollow metal sphere. It clicked shut.

"Hey, let her go!" yelled Anne.

But the pirate dropped the sphere into a leather bag hanging from her belt.

"As you can see, smashing the dice isn't going to work," said Marri. "Your only option is to cooperate and go on the quest."

Anne was near the boiling point. Pirates had invaded her school, kidnapped her teachers and friends, experimented on her gauntlet, and were now demanding she do their bidding and go on a quest for them? She looked to Penelope and Hiro. Normally she would ask for their advice, but in the current situation that wasn't possible. Anne couldn't think of anything to do but stand there in silent defiance.

"Fine," said Marri. "Be that way. I'll solve the quest on my own, then, and you and your friends will remain my prisoners indefinitely." She pointed at Jeffery. "Where is the treasure?"

"How am I supposed to know?" said Jeffery.

"Because that gauntlet originally activated the gold medallion. You're the GPS, so you should remember the details."

"Hey, I've never seen this medallion before in my life."

Marri pounded a fist on the arm of her chair. "You're lying! The procedure with the black liquid only works on the gauntlet that originally activated the quest. It worked, so this has to be the right one."

"Jeffery is no liar," said Anne with an edge to her voice.

Jeffery looked from one to the other. "Look, I don't know what you people did to my gauntlet, or why it reactivated the quest, but I remember every medallion that's ever been inserted in that slot, and this isn't one of them—well, until now, of course."

Marri glared at him but seemed to accept what he was saying.

"Fine, we'll figure out that part later," she said. "Give us the quest riddle."

"Actually, I'm still feeling a bit weird, so if we could wait a while—"

"Now!"

Marri's eyes were twin orbs of fire. Jeffery looked helplessly to Anne, and she gave him an almost imperceptible nod. There was no point in having Jeffery suffer needlessly, and if history was any lesson, the quest riddle would present its own difficulties.

"Yes, ma'am," Jeffery said to Marri.

He perched on the edge of the desk and sang out in a lilting tempo:

Walk the halls of castle high,
Wake the rose that never bloomed,
Hand to it the legend's power,
Free the worlds betrayal doomed.

"How do you wake a rose?" asked Pirate Nineteen.

"And what does it mean by *worlds*?" asked Pirate Twenty-Two. "Isn't there just the one?"

"What legend?" asked Pirate Seventy-Five.

Penelope grinned. "It wouldn't be a proper quest riddle if it wasn't impossibly cryptic. Best of luck with it, though."

"Enough!" shouted Marri. She closed her eyes and massaged her temples. "What level is the quest?"

Jeffery tilted his head. "Hmmm, as far as I can tell, it's a Level Q quest."

"What's Level Q?"

"I don't even want to know anymore," muttered Hiro.

Jeffery hopped onto Anne's gauntlet and gave the medallion a kick. "Stupid quest medallions with their bizarre levels."

"Never mind that," said Marri. "There's really only one thing that matters: How much time is there to complete the quest?"

"Hmmm, as far as I can tell, you have fourteen hundred and forty days," said Jeffery

"Well, at least there's plenty of—"

"Whoops! Did I say days? I meant minutes."

Marri's eyes widened. "But—but that's only one day!"

"Yep. And actually, you have slightly less than that," said Jeffery. "Someone started the quest but then paused it after less than an hour."

Anne stepped forward. "Marri, listen to me. You need to release Jocelyn and the others right now. You'll never manage this on your own. I'm not even sure we could. But they have years of questing experience. They can help you."

Marri shook her head. "I already told you: If you want your friends released, you'll have to complete the quest yourself."

"We have absolutely no reason to believe that you'll stick to your word," said Anne.

"And I have no reason to believe you would complete the quest otherwise."

"Did it ever occur to you to ask?"

Marri gave her a sharp look. "Pirate captains don't ask. They give orders and expect to be obeyed."

Anne wanted to tell her what a fool she was being, but it was obvious Marri had made up her mind. Marri swept the dice into her bag and then wheeled herself toward the door. The pirates carrying the chest followed her.

"Bring them!" she snapped.

The remaining pirates, the four who had escorted Anne, Penelope, and Hiro into the office, led them toward the front entrance with Jeffery flying above them. Anne and the others trudged down the long hallway, boots echoing on the broken tile, hearts heavy at the prospect of becoming prisoners of this pirate crew. The pirates pushed them out the front door—

—where everyone came to a stumbling halt.

The sky was filled with airships. Each had a seven-pointed black star on its mainsail, which marked them all as Wizards' Council ships. Several had come along-side the pirate ship. On the ground, five dragons spread out in a rough semicircle facing the front doors of the Manor. As Anne and the others stood on the steps, two dozen fireballs landed in the middle of the court-yard, and two dozen wizards in various-colored robes appeared out of the smoke and dust.

A wizard in a red robe with yellow trim walked up the steps and stopped in front of Anne. "Are you Anvil, Keeper of the Sparrow and Rightful Heir of Saint Lupin's?" he asked.

"Yes!" said Anne, hopeful that perhaps the Wizards' Council had taken note of the pirate attack and had come to save them. Her relationship with the council had been rocky thus far, but perhaps this would mark a turning point.

The wizard took a small notebook from his pocket and flipped it open. "Good. My name is Lieutenant Formaldehyde. I'm with the Wizards' Council. As I'm sure you're aware, this school is currently under sus-pension and therefore not permitted to undertake any quests. We've been monitoring this tier for any signs of illegal quest-related activity, and at precisely nine thirteen this morning we registered the activation of a prophecy medallion. Therefore, it is my duty to inform you that you are in direct violation of Sections 102 and 304 of the Questing Regulations."

"Three guesses what that means," said Penelope.

Anne's brief moment of hope melted away. Back down in the yard, a tall man pushed his way to the front. He had tanned white skin, a square jaw, and dark wavy hair that was graying at the temples. He wore gray pants, black leather boots, and a charcoal tunic with a midnight-black cape slung over one shoulder. A crow was perched on his other shoulder.

Anne recognized him immediately.

It was Lord Greystone, the Minister of Questing.

"It means you're all under arrest," he said.

ACCORDING TO THE WIZARDS' COUNCIL,
THERE ARE FIVE LEVELS OF ILLEGALITY:

1) Illegal

2) Mostly illegal

3) Illegal for kittens

4) Not really illegal, but we'll pester you about it anyway

5) Not illegal (but still illegal)

5

Flight from the Council

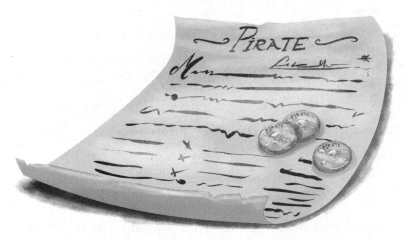

The Wizards' Council airships were enormous. Each one was filled with armed soldiers and had at least a hundred cannon ports on each side. Wizards either adopted defensive stances or shouted random orders at nobody in particular in an effort to look important. The dragons seemed restless—as in ready-to-shoot-flames-at-the-least-sign-of-trouble restless. They were snapping at one another as well as the wizards.

"Is getting arrested just a thing that happens to us

now?" asked Hiro. "Because it seems to happen to us a lot."

"Er, why are there so many of you?" Anne asked the lieutenant as Greystone was making his way up the steps.

"Lord Greystone has familiarized us with your adventuring history," said the lieutenant. "We felt it best to come prepared."

When Greystone reached the top of the stairs, he ignored Marri and the other pirates and focused solely on Anne, Penelope, and Hiro.

"I'll make this quick," he said. He pointed first at Anne. "You will surrender your gauntlet to the council and be forever barred from attending another quest academy or going on any official adventures. And that's presuming you don't end up spending the rest of your life in a dungeon cell, which you most certainly will if I have anything to say about it. Furthermore, under the conditions of your suspension, all proceeds from any and all quests in which you have participated in the past are now forfeit. This includes, but is not limited to, the Saint Lupin's tier itself."

Anne opened her mouth to protest, but Greystone pressed on and turned next to Penelope. "Ms. Shatterblade, after you are finished with whatever other punishment the council decides is appropriate, your family name will be completely wiped from all records, and you yourself will be exiled from the Hierarchy, never to return. We're going to rid ourselves of the name Shatterblade once and for all."

All the color drained from Penelope's face. For once, she seemed to be at a complete loss for words.

Finally, Greystone turned to Hiro. "As for you, Mr. Darkflame, your parents have been notified of the situation. They are currently away on a secret mission, but they will return as soon as possible. If it were up to me, you would suffer the same fate as your two companions here, but no doubt your family connections will shield you from the worst of it. Nevertheless, my advice to you is to get as far away from these two as possible, as soon as possible. At the very least, you can expect a black mark on your permanent record, which I assure you will be brought up every single time you apply for a position at the Wizards' Council, because I'll be there to make sure it gets brought up."

Marri raised her hand as if to interrupt, but one look from Greystone and she decided better of it.

Greystone stepped back and surveyed the three of

them together. "The three of you will be taken from here directly to a council holding cell, where you will await trial. With any luck, you will be found guilty and spend several years in a hard-labor camp. Regardless of that, however, I'm pleased to say that I won't have to concern myself with any of you much longer."

At that moment, one of the council dragons reared back and let out a tremendous roar. The roar was accompanied by a huge red fireball, which struck the airship directly above it and punctured the hull. Seconds later a huge explosion rocked the airship, blowing a sizable hole in the hull and setting one of the masts on fire. Soldiers ran about on deck trying to put out the flames.

"I told them gunpowder and dragons don't mix," growled Greystone. He turned to the lieutenant. "Formaldehyde, I'm leaving you in charge here while I sort out that mess."

Greystone hurried back down the stairs.

A squadron of soldiers surrounded the dragon that had released the fireball and tossed ropes around its neck to calm it down. That turned out to be a bad idea. The dragon bit through the ropes and swept several soldiers from their feet with its tail. Meanwhile, the other four dragons became agitated at seeing their companion mistreated. Soldiers started to run in all directions as wizards shouted contradictory orders and proved generally useless.

Amid all the chaos, a rainbow-colored blur dropped out of the sky and landed on Anne's shoulder. It was Jeffery. Thankfully, the lieutenant was distracted by all the commotion and didn't see him.

"Where have you been?" whispered Anne.

"Oh, nowhere in particular. But hey, did you know dragons are extremely ticklish behind the knees?"

Anne surveyed the burning airship and the chaos on the ground.

"That was you?" she asked.

"I figured a big enough distraction might give you the opportunity to sneak away."

Anne pointed to the lieutenant. "We can't sneak anywhere with a council wizard standing right in front of us."

"Or maybe you could," said Marri, joining them. She held out her hand. In her palm were three tokens, each with PIRATE engraved on it.

"Who are those for?" asked Penelope.

"The three of you," said Marri. "If you officially join my crew, I can get you out of here."

"And let us guess the price for your generosity."

"You know what I want."

Anne pursed her lips. They were between a proverbial rock and a hard place. They could either stay and be imprisoned by the council, or go with Marri and her crew and help them complete the quest, with no guarantee of what would happen to them afterward.

"If we agree to join your crew, wouldn't that mean we'd have to follow your orders?" asked Anne.

"Yes," said Marri. "But you would also receive a share of any treasure we find."

"Sounds good to me!" said Penelope, and she reached for one of the tokens.

Anne moved to block her hand, but Hiro beat her to it.

"Can I have a word with my friends?" he asked.

"Certainly," said Marri. "But don't take too much time. If we're not gone before Greystone gets back, you're going to be out of luck. Not to mention, the clock on the quest is ticking."

She moved back and gave them space.

Anne, Penelope, and Hiro formed a huddle.

Hiro spoke first. "I just want everyone to know what's

at stake. If we do this, if we become pirates, everyone needs to understand that there's no going back. Not to adventuring, not to the academy, and not to working anywhere else in the Hierarchy. Once a pirate, always a pirate. Those are the rules. And we would absolutely have to obey orders, for as long as Marri wanted us on her crew. We don't get to choose when we're done."

Hiro's tone was serious and sharp. Anne had never heard him speak like this.

"It's not like we have a load of options," said Penelope. "If we stay here, I'll get exiled and Anne will be barred from adventuring. When you look at it that way, what have we got to lose?"

Anne studied Hiro. He was trembling, and she thought she understood his concern.

"If you do this, you won't ever have a chance to join the Wizards' Council?" she asked.

Hiro shook his head.

Anne's heart went out to him. No doubt he was thinking of his family and everything they were expecting from him. "Maybe you should take some time and think it over. Greystone said your parents might be able to get you out of this. That's something to consider."

Hiro lowered his head, and Anne could see that he was struggling. It was Penelope, though, who placed a hand gently on his shoulder.

"It's okay, Hiro," she said. "We understand. Maybe it would be best if we parted ways."

The silence stretched on for several more seconds, but finally Hiro looked up.

"No," he said. "We're a team. You've both stuck by me when I needed you. One way or another, we're finishing this together."

Anne's heart leapt for joy, and Penelope slapped Hiro on the back so hard that he nearly fell over.

"Awesome!" said Penelope. "Now I don't have to put you in a headlock."

"So, we're all agreed, then?" asked Anne, looking to each of them. "We're becoming pirates?"

Penelope and Hiro both nodded.

They broke their huddle, but before Anne took one of the tokens, a thought occurred to her. It wasn't right that Marri was calling all the shots. She needed them as much as they needed her.

"Before we accept your offer, we have one condition," said Anne. She knew she was taking a risk, but it was necessary.

Marri raised an eyebrow. "And that is?"

"You have to join our adventuring group. For real this time."

"And you have to give back all our quest medallions," added Penelope.

Marri frowned. "And why should I do either of those things?"

"Because if we join your pirate crew, you would have authority over us. But I'm the official leader of our group, so if you join us, it would even things out. Neither of us would have the upper hand."

Penelope nodded. "And giving back the medallions would be a sign of your good intentions."

"We're pirates. We're not especially known for our good intentions."

Anne crossed her arms and waited.

Marri eyed them skeptically. "I'm not sure you're in a position to negotiate. I could just leave you here for the council, and then you would have nothing."

"Yes, but then best of luck explaining to Octo-Horse Pirate about activating the quest. From everything you've told us about him so far, I don't think that's something you want to do."

Anne could tell Marri wasn't entirely convinced, and

the pirate captain took her time answering, no doubt looking for some way she could turn the deal more to her favor. Anne said nothing and simply waited.

Marri sighed. "Fine, I'll join your group."

Anne nodded, and she and Penelope and Hiro each took a pirate token from Marri's hand.

"You'll need to sign this," said Marri, bringing out a piece of parchment. "It's a standard pirate agreement. Things like fulfillment of contract, shipboard duties, your percentage of any loot taken, insurance against lost limbs—"

"*Lost limbs?!*" Hiro exclaimed.

"—and what we would write on your tombstone in case you get eaten by a sea monster. You know, the usual."

"Er, just out of curiosity, what *would* you write on our tombstones?" asked Penelope.

"Here lies Penelope. She was eaten by a sea monster."

"Okay. Just checking."

The three of them signed the parchment. Marri rolled up the contract and stuffed it into her pack.

"Jeffery, is there anything we need to do to make her an official part of the group?" asked Anne.

"Nope," said Jeffery. "Telling me is enough. I'll simply log it in my files."

Anne turned back to Marri. "Looks like we're good to go, then."

"Good. Follow my lead," said Marri. She approached Lieutenant Formaldehyde. "Is there a problem here, lieutenant?"

The lieutenant checked his paper and frowned. "Who are you?"

"Marri Blackwood, captain of the *Blue Daisy*. My crew and I are here on official pirate business. Since this matter about a quest doesn't have anything to do with us, I assume that my crew and I are free to go."

The lieutenant looked back to the yard, no doubt wanting to consult Greystone first, but the Minister of Questing was nowhere to be seen.

"Lieutenant?"

The lieutenant straightened his robes. "Ah, yes, of course. That's fine. You may leave."

"Thank you."

Marri started down the ramp next to the stairs, and Anne and the others followed.

"Wait a minute," said the lieutenant. "You're free to go, but those three have to remain here."

Marri stopped. "But they're part of my crew."

Anne, Penelope, and Hiro all showed him their pirate tokens.

"Er, well, I didn't realize—"

"You did say this matter didn't concern us, correct?"

"Yes, but it does concern *them*."

"That's fine," said Marri. "They can stay, but my crew and I are leaving."

"That's fine."

They all started off once more.

"But—"

Marri stopped again. "But what?"

"But how can they go and stay at the same time?"

"Well, I guess that's for you to figure out. Greystone left you in charge, and I'm sure he expects you to be able to deal with such a trivial matter. Just explain it to him the way I explained it to you, and I'm sure he'll understand."

The lieutenant looked perplexed but nodded. "Okay, then. And thanks."

"I can't believe that really worked," said Anne when they were out of earshot.

"It won't work for long. Eventually either he'll figure out he's been duped or Greystone will return. At best I figure we have ten minutes. Fifteen if we're lucky." She spun her chair to the other pirates. "Let's move!" she barked, and Anne was surprised by the sudden tone of command in her voice.

Marri continued down the ramp and rolled into the yard. Everyone else followed at a run. As they approached the hovering pirate ship, several ropes were lowered, including one that split into four smaller ropes, each with a metal hook at the end. The pirates grabbed the ropes and immediately started climbing. Marri took the rope with the hooks and expertly fitted them into the four rings attached to the arms of her chair.

"See you up top," she said, and she gave the rope three tugs. It went taut and she immediately began to ascend.

Anne, Penelope, and Hiro each grabbed a dangling rope and were pulled up to the waiting airship as well. When they reached the top, pirates were rushing in every direction—not in a panic, but with a sort of efficient urgency.

"You three can join me on the upper deck for now," called Marri.

They followed her up a ramp at the back of the main deck to a smaller deck. Several other pirates were going about their tasks. One stood in front of a giant wooden wheel, no doubt used for steering the airship. Another stood beside him holding a clipboard.

"This is Mr. Locke, first mate aboard the *Blue Daisy*," said Marri, indicating the pirate with the clipboard. "If he gives you orders at any time, you should obey him instantly." She turned to Locke. "Time to be on our way."

"Aye, Captain," said Locke. He barked out several instructions, which resulted in an increased flurry of activity. Moments later, the airship lurched forward. It slid between the two considerably larger warships hovering on either side of it and sailed out over Saint Lupin's.

From this vantage point, Anne could see the full extent of the damage the pirate attack had caused. The ballroom lay in ruins, and one of the dormitories had been flattened. There were several breaches in the outer walls. With everyone either taken prisoner or under pirate contract, there would be no one to watch over Saint Lupin's while they were away. It saddened Anne to see the school in such a state. Perhaps back when the Matron was running things, Anne wouldn't have cared, but so much had changed since then. Anne vowed to complete this quest as quickly as possible so that at the very least Jocelyn and the others could return and make repairs and begin classes properly. But then Greystone's words flashed in her mind. She'd be fixing Saint Lupin's up for someone else....

As the ship left the skies over Saint Lupin's, they entered a large fog bank.

Marri pressed her lips together. "We're not going to outrun them for long, even with this cover. We need a destination. Preferably our first quest location."

Hiro's eyes actually brightened at this. "Does this mean we get to do research? Oh, if only we had worked things out earlier, we could have used the library at Saint Lupin's. I've been working on IDs for everyone. I've also been updating the card catalog. Do you have any idea how out of date it was?"

"If we're going to a library, I'd be happy to help," said Jeffery. He acquired information from books by eating them, and it was a constant struggle to keep him from consuming every piece of writing in sight.

"We don't have time for that," said Marri. "But I was under the impression you have access to a special book that might be able to provide us with a clue. I believe it's called *The Adventurer's Guide*."

Anne's eyes narrowed. "How do you know so much about us?"

"I have my sources."

Anne frowned. "Well, the last time I saw that book, Rokk was holding it."

Marri searched the cloth bag and handed the twenty-sided dice to Anne.

"Handle it carefully," said Marri. "You saw what happened with the other one."

Anne studied the dice. Rokk was still suspended, but as she turned the dice over in her hand, she noticed that his body flopped with it. She kept turning the dice until she found a tiny red-covered book floating next to him.

"It's in there," said Anne. "It was damaged during our first quest, though, so it doesn't always provide reliable information."

"It'll have to do."

"Three ships astern and closing fast!" came a shout from the crow's nest.

Anne looked behind them but could barely make out three dark forms in the distance through the fog. The council ships couldn't use their cannons from this angle, but if they pulled even with the *Blue Daisy*, then Marri and her crew (not to mention Anne, Penelope, and Hiro) would be in serious trouble.

"Let us worry about the ships," said Marri. "You concentrate on figuring out where we need to go."

Anne squinted at the tiny guide. "I can't make out the title."

Locke reached into his pocket and pulled out a piece of circular glass with a wooden frame around it. "Use this. If you look through the glass at something, it makes it appear larger."

Anne held the glass over the dice, and indeed everything appeared much larger. The title on the cover read *The Adventurer's Guilt from Slaying Monster Cranberries*. She tapped the dice gently, and the title changed to *The Adventurer's Guide to Defending Your School from Pirates*.

"A little late," Anne muttered.

She nudged the dice a second time, and the title of the book changed once again. Now it read *The Adventurer's Guide to Lost Castles of the Hierarchy*. Anne tipped the dice on its side until the book opened to the first page. She read the tiny paragraph of text that appeared there.

"Here we go," she said. "It says: 'Castle Stormwind, otherwise known as the High Castle, sits atop the central peak of the Cerulean Mountain Range. It is famously the site of the last siege of Uz the Magnificent.' "

"The High Castle could be the 'castle high' mentioned in the riddle," suggested Hiro.

"If so, that's not much help," said Marri. "High Castle is a popular name. I can think of at least a dozen places called that. And besides, the riddle is ancient. Chances are whatever place it's referring to isn't even called that anymore. But it might be on the map."

"What map?" asked Anne.

Marri brought out a tube and pulled a rolled-up piece of parchment from it. She unrolled the parchment across her lap. It was a map.

"This was on display at the museum next to the medallion," said Marri. "But I'm unfamiliar with the symbols on it."

"Enemies to port! Number unknown!" came another call. "Also, to starboard!"

Anne looked off both sides. The council ships were closer now and she could see them more clearly. They had opened their cannon ports, and a moment later there was a crack of cannon fire and the whistle of an incoming cannonball. The shot fell short, though, and passed well below them.

"Steady," said Marri. "Nothing to worry about yet. They're just guessing."

Eventually they would find their mark, and Anne returned to the map with a new sense of urgency. "Where's the legend?" she asked.

Without the legend, deciphering the map would be difficult, if not downright impossible.

"Wait a minute!" said Hiro. He dug his mother's letter out of his cloak pocket and unfolded the newspaper clipping. "Listen to this: 'Taken along with the medallion was an ancient treasure map. Also from the same collection, but untouched, is a jade cylinder seal known as the Legendary Seal of Uz.' Cylinder seals were an administrative tool invented thousands of years ago," Hiro explained. "They're cylindrical, of course. Usually only an inch or two long. A person could use them for almost anything: a signature, a magick spell—"

"Or the legend of a map?" asked Anne.

"*Hand to it the legend's power,*" said Penelope. "The power of the legend is to unlock the map."

Anne turned to Marri. "Where's the seal?"

Marri looked crestfallen. "Still in the museum. There were many artifacts locked in separate cases. We didn't think they were important."

"We're going to need that seal."

"But the museum is crawling with extra security because of the theft."

"Fog clearing ahead, Captain," said Locke.

"Ship closing in on the port side!" hollered Hiro.

"Probably hoping to board us," said Marri. "Deploy countermeasures."

One of the pirates picked up a small canister and placed it in a slingshot attached to the portside railing. A second pirate aimed and fired. The slingshot sent the canister flying through the air. It hit the main deck of the council ship and exploded in a puff of green smoke.

"What was that?" asked Penelope.

Marri grinned. "Stink bomb. Nonlethal, but definitely unpleasant."

"Coming in from both sides now, Captain," said Locke.

"They're trying to squeeze us."

Anne scanned the skies and spotted a cluster of tiers. "What about through there?"

"Good eye," said Marri. "Twenty degrees to starboard, Mr. Locke."

Locke conveyed instructions to the helmsman and

the airship steered in among the tiers. They were tightly packed, and the hull scraped along the port side as they squeezed through. The larger council ships tried to follow, but they entered the gap at the same time. They collided with a crunch. One of them tried to veer away but slammed into the side of a tier. Its center mast tore free and went spiraling over the side. The other council airships were forced to stop. Only two of the ships thought to drop below the tiers to keep up.

Marri surveyed the path ahead. "We're almost in the clear. Prepare the engines."

"Engines?" said Anne.

Marri ignored Anne's question and pointed to the stern. "Let me know when the flaps are fully opened and secure."

Anne moved to the railing at the stern. Directly below, two doors were being winched open. Once they were locked into place, two metal tubes were extended, and a pirate holding a torch stood next to each. One of the pirates waved at her.

"They're signaling ready!" shouted Anne.

The gap between the tiers widened, leaving plenty of room for several ships to sail side by side. The two warships rose and began to close.

"Now, Captain?" said Locke.

"Not yet," said Marri.

The bows of the warships pulled even with the stern of the *Blue Daisy*, one on either side.

"If those ships get into a position where they can use their guns..." said Hiro.

"Now, Captain?" said Locke.

"Hold!" said Marri.

As the warships continued to gain on them, Marri pointed to a row of seats along the stern railing. "You'd better straps yourselves in," she said to Anne, Penelope, and Hiro.

Anne saw that other pirates around the ship were either buckling themselves into similar seats or heading belowdecks. Even Marri clicked the wheels of her chair into slots on the deck. Anne, Penelope, and Hiro ran over and sat down. Each seat had several straps, but they were all tangled. Anne pulled at two of the straps, trying to free them. As she was fighting with her seat, the *Blue Daisy* passed the end of the tiers.

"Captain?" asked Locke.

"Now!" shouted Marri.

"Light the engines!"

Several "Ayes" were shouted back in reply. Anne glanced back, and the pirates holding the torches lowered them.

The warships were directly next to them now, one on each side. Anne could see council soldiers standing next to the cannons on both ships, and heard voices from either side yelling "Ready! Aim!..."

Anne had barely clicked the buckle of her second strap into place when the *Blue Daisy* shot forward like the ship itself had been fired out of a cannon. Behind them came the report of cannon fire as the two warships sent forth their volleys, but the *Blue Daisy* was well out of harm's way. The cannon fire from each of the ships slammed into the hull and sails of the other, toppling masts and blowing railings apart. Both ships immediately lost speed, and one of them began to drop.

The *Blue Daisy* continued to accelerate, and the entire ship began to vibrate. Then it became enveloped in a green bubble of energy, not unlike the inside of a fireball. The straps bit hard into Anne's shoulders. She tried to tighten them, but one of the buckles released. The force of the acceleration dragged her out of her seat. She grasped at the other strap.

"Anne, hang on!" yelled Hiro.

Penelope reached toward her, but it was too late. Anne lost her grip and was torn out of her seat by the sheer force of the wind. She flailed her arms in a desperate attempt to grab anything that would keep her on the ship, but there was nothing within reach. She tumbled end over end and slammed into the railing at the stern.

And everything went black.

ACCORDING TO *THE ADVENTURER'S GUIDE
TO DREAM INTERPRETATION*, THESE ARE
THE TOP THREE DREAMS AND THEIR
MEANINGS:

1) Dreaming about being chased represents anxiety (probably due to being chased).

2) Dreaming about death represents change (for example, the change between breathing and not breathing).

3) Dreaming about flying represents a desire for control. (Either that or your medallion is malfunctioning because of recent damage and is giving you nightmares, but really, how often does that happen?)

6

The Pirate Haven

Anne was no longer aboard the airship. She was standing in a long gray corridor. Or rather, she was floating about a foot above the floor of a long gray corridor. At the far end of the corridor stood a lone door. The door bore the image of a black dragon, which Anne recognized immediately as the Sign of Zarala, the image on the medallions from all her quests. A plaque on the wall next to the door read DR. ZARALA COLE.

Anne thought about going to the door and found herself drifting slowly forward. When she reached the end of the corridor, she stretched out a hand for the doorknob. As soon as she touched it, a deep metallic voice spoke from nowhere in particular.

"This is your scheduled dream sequence, as per Item 777 of your official quest itinerary," said the voice. "Be advised this dream may be monitored for quality-control purposes. Your dream guide will be with you momentarily. Please refrain from pinching yourself while download is in progress."

"Um, what?" asked Anne.

A cloud of color formed next to her. Wisps of smoke curled and chased one another, taking shape, becoming more and more substantial with each passing moment. Soon the mass resolved into a recognizable shape.

"Jocelyn!" shouted Anne.

Anne floated forward and threw her arms out to give Jocelyn a big hug, but she passed completely through Jocelyn's body and crashed into the wall.

Anne turned around, which was a tricky thing to do while floating in the air.

"Why can't I touch you?" she asked.

"Because technically we're ghosts," said Jocelyn.

"Who's *we*?" asked Anne.

Jocelyn pointed behind her. Several more shapes appeared, and now Princess Whiskers, Rokk, Captain Copperhelm, and Sassafras were all standing in the corridor as well.

Anne gasped. "You're all dead?!"

Jocelyn shook her head. "Of course not, dear. It's just an effect of the dice. Our bodies have been placed in temporary stasis, but our spirits are free to wander about. We've actually been watching your progress this morning."

"And keeping notes?" Anne asked hesitantly.

"But of course," said Jocelyn. "You'll have my full evaluation once this pirate kidnapping business is all over. Keep in mind you'll be graded on both the effectiveness as well as the creativity of your plan to rescue everyone."

Apparently not even becoming a temporary ghost could keep Jocelyn from grading her students.

Anne looked around. "So, where are we? A weird voice said something a moment ago about this being a dream."

"Yes, precisely. And we're your guides. The dream probably chose us because we were the closest available spirits."

"If you're my guides, should someone wake Sassafras?"

Sassafras had fallen asleep on his feet and was quietly snoring. The platypus, on the other hand, was alert and seemed quite intrigued by everything that was going on. Copperhelm grabbed Sassafras by the shoulders and gave him a good shake, but he didn't stir in the slightest.

Copperhelm grunted. "He's probably the only person capable of taking a nap in the middle of a dream."

"So, what am I supposed to do?" asked Anne.

"Whatever you wish," said Jocelyn. "It's your dream. You flutter about, and we'll help you figure out what everything means."

Anne pointed to the door. "I was about to go through here. I think I recognize it from another dream I had back when we were on our second quest."

Jocelyn clapped her hands together. "Oh, a recurring dream. How dramatic!" She brought out a small book. The title on the cover read *The Dream Guide's Guide to Guiding Dreams*. Jocelyn flipped it open and started scanning the pages. "Hmmm, it says here that a recurring dream could suggest you're preoccupied with something. Or that you were born under a blue moon. Or that you've been eating too many red onions."

"Or it could simply indicate a lack of imagination," said Copperhelm.

"Perhaps your program is stuck in an infinite loop because it lacks a functioning exit routine," offered Rokk.

"Thanks, I'll keep all of that in mind," said Anne, more confused than ever.

She turned the knob and opened the door. The room in front of her looked exactly as she had expected. There were several long counters with a variety of instruments. A tall, thin young man with pale white skin stood at the farthest counter. He had dark hair and wore a lab coat and brown leather shoes.

"Good morning, Dr. Cole," he said.

"Good morning, Dr. Grey," Anne replied. She didn't know why she said this. The words simply spilled out of her mouth.

"Oh, do you know this person?" asked Jocelyn.

"Not really. I mean, he was in my dream the last time, too, and for some reason I know his name, but that's about it."

"Should I hit him with my ax?" asked Copperhelm.

"No!" said Anne.

Jocelyn flipped to a different part of the guidebook. "He could represent a possible love interest."

"In that case, maybe Anne should hit him with my ax," suggested Copperhelm.

"No one is hitting anyone with an ax," said Anne.

Jocelyn looked up from the guide. "Oh, maybe he represents that dragon boy from your last quest—"

"Let's keep things moving along, shall we?" said Anne, not wishing to pursue that particular line of speculation. "Where are we exactly?" she asked the young man.

He looked surprised by the question. "Why, your laboratory, of course."

"*My* laboratory? But I've never worked in a laboratory." Anne floated over to the first counter and ran a hand over the nearest instrument. The word *microscope* leapt to mind. "Although I do feel like I know this place."

"Why, these are Old World instruments!" said Jocelyn with a note of excitement. "I recognize some of them from the Museum of Science and Mythology. Oh, this is all very exciting!"

"Would you like this morning's test results?" asked the young man.

"Um, sure," said Anne, not feeling sure about anything.

The young man picked up a thin book with a blue cover and started toward Anne. Halfway across the room, however, he froze midstep.

"Is everything okay?" asked Anne.

The young man didn't move or respond. Anne drifted over and waved her hand in front of his face.

"Uh, hello?" she said.

Jocelyn joined her, still flipping through her guidebook. "Hmmm, his refusal to interact might suggest some sort of inner conflict on your part. Perhaps you fear your love is unrequited?"

"You can still try the ax if you want," said Copperhelm.

"Perhaps your dream is in need of a repair technician," said Rokk.

"I don't know what's going on," said Anne. "This didn't happen before."

The deep metallic voice spoke again. "Our apologies. This dream has been interrupted prematurely by an external stimulus. Please secure your subconscious while reentering reality."

Jocelyn put down the guidebook. "Well, that's disappointing. I was just starting to get the hang of this."

"Wait!" said Anne, and she stretched out a hand, but it was too late. Jocelyn and the others disappeared in a puff of smoke.

Somewhere in the distance a crow cawed.

Anne awoke with a start. She was lying on her back on the deck of the *Blue Daisy*. Someone was kneeling next to her and pinching her arm.

"Ow! Stop that!" said Anne.

Penelope's face appeared directly over hers. "I told them that would do the trick. Are you okay?"

Anne moved each limb one by one. She ached all over, and her right shoulder was especially tender from where she had slammed into the railing, but overall she appeared to be unharmed.

"I'll live," she responded.

Penelope helped Anne to her feet. Marri and Hiro were nearby, along with several members of the pirate crew.

"How long was I out?" asked Anne.

"Only a few minutes," said Hiro. "But that was long enough for Jeffery to compose a eulogy for you."

"Well, only eighty-six stanzas so far," said Jeffery. "I'm especially proud of how I managed to work in the Great Clown Invasion from the last century, but I'm having trouble finding a word to rhyme with *kaleidoscope*."

"Try *shaleidoscope*," said one of the pirates.

"Oh, that works!"

"I'm just glad I'm not the one who got knocked out for once," said Penelope.

Anne quickly filled everyone in on her dream, describing the room and her conversation with Jocelyn and the others.

"It didn't make a whole lot of sense," she said. "But it reminded me of the dream I had during our second quest, when Emmanuelle's dragon stone knocked me unconscious for two days."

"I wouldn't put too much stock in dreams," said Marri. "Your time will be better spent focusing on the quest."

"I suppose," said Anne. "Speaking of the quest, did we reach our destination?"

"Not yet," said Hiro. "The engines gave out."

Marri's expression darkened. "Someone forgot to refuel the dragon-fire tanks during our last stop. We managed to evade the council ships, but it's going to take us a few hours to reach our destination." She turned to the crew. "Well? What are you all standing around for?" she snapped. "Everyone get back to work!"

The crew scurried off.

The ship sailed for the rest of the morning. Shortly after noon, activity on the airship increased as Marri began shouting out various instructions. Every time she gave an order, one of the crew rushed to complete the task. There was a noticeable tension, and the pirates seemed to go out of their way to avoid the upper deck unless absolutely necessary.

For most of the voyage, the ship had weaved its way between the tiers, staying in the shadows to keep out of sight of any patrolling council ships. But they soon broke through a cluster of small tiers into a more open area and headed toward a very large tier floating by itself. It was covered in mountains and forests, but there were no towns or villages. In fact, as far as Anne could tell, there were no manmade structures whatsoever.

"Why are we headed there?" asked Penelope. "It looks uninhabited."

"Looks can be deceiving" was all Marri said.

The airship dropped lower and headed directly for a

point about halfway down the side of the tier. The *Blue Daisy* wasn't slowing, and Anne's pulse increased. The sheer rock was growing ever closer.

Marri raised her hand, and Locke leaned over the railing with a hooded lantern. He opened and shut the hood in a pattern involving short and long flashes. After a brief pause, an answering flash came from the tier. Anne covered her eyes but couldn't resist peeking between her fingers. Just as the ship reached the side of the tier, the rock wall directly in front of them peeled aside like a curtain to reveal a great crack.

The *Blue Daisy* sailed into the opening. Locke barked orders at a furious rate, and the crew worked feverishly to keep up. The sails were furled and various ropes were tied down and hatches made secure. The deck was cleared of any loose equipment, and five crew members spread out on each side of the airship. They called out numbers indicating how far the ship was from the walls looming all around them. Locke listened to this constant stream of information and conveyed the necessary instructions to the helmsman, who made the required course corrections. The ship slipped past the rocks, sometimes by only a few feet.

As they exited the tunnel and immediately banked to starboard, Anne didn't know which way to look first. They were in an enormous cavern, at least a mile across. There was a sizable city surrounding a large lake at the bottom, but even more surprising were the buildings that covered every vertical surface. Some buildings even hung from the ceiling like stalactites. The entire cavern was lit by some sort of glowing moss that dotted the walls and ceiling, and the sight of everything took Anne's breath away.

"Welcome to the Haven," said Marri, sounding grim, and Anne got the impression that the pirate captain wasn't happy to be back here so soon.

Several ships were waiting to exit the tier, but they couldn't enter the great crack until the *Blue Daisy* was out of the way. As they glided along the interior wall, they passed an anchored airship that was easily twice as big as theirs.

"Ahoy, the *Blue Daisy*," shouted the captain of the larger vessel. He was a heavyset man with a thick brown beard and a bright red overcoat. He tipped his tricorn hat to them.

"Ahoy, the *Ticklish Duckfoot*," Marri called back.

"I don't suppose you could spare an old man a bottle of your finest goat's milk?"

Marri crossed her arms. "I believe you already owe me for two bottles."

"Ah, now don't be like that, Marri. Your goats give the finest milk. Take pity on an old pirate's stomach."

"Maybe an old pirate should stop eating hot peppers with every meal."

The other captain grinned. "We all have our vices."

For the first time that morning, Marri cracked a smile. She gestured to Locke, and he grabbed a bottle from a nearby crate and tossed it across. The old captain snatched it out of the air with ease.

"Bless your heart, girl," he said. "I owe you one."

"No, you owe me three," she called back. This elicited a hearty laugh from the other captain, and he raised the bottle in thanks.

That brief moment of levity gave Anne hope. Perhaps Marri's gruff exterior was all an act. But if so, why did she keep such a tight lid on her emotions? What was she hiding from? The other pirates? Octo-Horse Pirate? Something else?

They left the other vessel behind and continued into

the heart of the Haven, passing ships and boats of various sizes and configurations. Anne studied the names as they passed: *Leaping Hedgehog, Prancing Tulip, Snow Weasel.*

Penelope grabbed Anne's arm and pointed across the cavern to a large airship with green and white stripes. "Ooh, there's the *Flying Watermelon*. It was in one of the stories we borrowed from the Saint Lupin's library, remember?"

"It's a hard name to forget," said Anne.

The helmsman weaved the ship through the busy throng to one of the smaller docks halfway up the side of the cavern. They slowed steadily as they approached and came to rest against the dock with only the slightest bump. Crew members threw ropes to waiting dockhands, who tied them securely. Several crew members removed a section of railing and pushed through a ramp that extended from the ship to the dock.

"Mr. Locke, I intend to make our time here as brief as possible," said Marri. "I'll trust you to see to the engines and also conduct a brief inspection. Resupply only what we absolutely need."

"Aye, Captain," Locke replied crisply.

Marri turned to Anne and the others. "Follow me."

A pirate stepped in front of the ramp and blocked their way. It was Pirate Fifty-Three, the one who had taken all the medallions from the main office at Saint Lupin's. "A word, Captain?"

"We don't have a lot of time," said Marri. "It will have to wait."

"I'm afraid this can't wait, Captain. Mr. Locke ordered me to return those medallions."

"I fail to see the problem."

"By contract we get to keep whatever loot we can carry away. Those medallions are my rightful treasure."

"I have an arrangement with these three, and the medallions are part of it," said Marri.

The pirate glared at Anne. "And that's another thing. Since when did we start working with adventurers?"

"Since I said so," said Marri. "Now get back to your duties."

Marri started forward again, but the pirate continued blocking their path. "You're either our captain or you're a member of their adventuring group. You can't be both."

Marri scowled. "Step aside, sailor."

"If you insist on this course of action, then I see no

recourse but to challenge you for leadership of the *Blue Daisy*."

All activity on the deck ceased. Marri stared at the pirate for so long that Anne began to wonder if she was going to respond at all.

Locke stepped forward. "He's new, Captain. Came aboard with the last group of hires back in the winter. If you'll permit me a few minutes to speak with him, I'm sure we can get this all straightened out."

Pirate Fifty-Three shook his head. "No. I might not have been here as long as some of the others, but I know my rights. Where I come from, pirates keep their loot, and they don't join with adventurers. They attack them."

Anne scanned the rest of the crew. Everyone seemed tense, and many of the pirates had not-so-casually placed their hands on their sword hilts.

"I accept your challenge," said Marri in a measured tone. "As the one who has been challenged, I get to choose the weapons. The duel will be conducted with swords. But I see no reason for anyone to die, so we will fight to first blood only. The winner will be the undisputed leader of this crew. The loser will be forever banished from serving aboard this ship. Agreed?"

Pirate Fifty-Three spat on the deck. "Agreed."

"Mr. Locke oversees all duels, and his decisions are final," said Marri.

"That's fine," said Pirate Fifty-Three. "Let's get on with it."

The other pirates quickly fanned out in a circle, leaving the center of the deck clear. Marri pulled out her sword and casually checked the blade.

Anne walked over to her and spoke in a low voice. "I take it back. Let him keep the medallions."

"It's too late. I can't ignore a valid challenge," said Marri. "The pirate laws are clear: If I won't fight, I automatically concede victory to my opponent. Besides, if I refused now, I would lose the respect of the crew."

"But what if you lose the duel?" asked Anne.

Marri shrugged. "Then I don't deserve to be captain of this airship. A crew needs a strong leader."

"There are lots of ways to show strength. Fighting doesn't solve everything. As a member of my adventuring group—"

"This is pirate business," growled Marri. "It has nothing to do with your group or the quest, so you have no authority in this matter. Now stand back!"

Anne reluctantly joined the others at the edge of the circle.

Pirate Fifty-Three stood opposite Marri. He twirled his sword around in several sweeping arcs, switching hands and even passing it behind his back in an intricate display of martial ability. Soon the sword was moving so fast that the blade was practically a blur. Marri simply gave her sword a few subtle practice swings to loosen her arm and wrist.

Penelope leaned over and whispered in Anne's ear. "Do you want to place a bet? One of the crew is offering three-to-one odds on the captain."

"That's terrible!" said Anne.

"Actually, it's pretty good under the circumstances. They've all seen the captain in action, but this Fifty-Three character is a bit of an unknown."

Anne crossed her arms. "I am not betting on the outcome of this fight."

Penelope shrugged. "Suit yourself. Hiro and I each bet a copper piece."

Anne gasped. "Hiro!"

Hiro blushed. "I did it for scientific purposes."

Locke stepped into the center of the circle. He pointed at each combatant, and they nodded at him to indicate their readiness. Pirate Fifty-Three paced like a caged tiger ready to pounce. He was an imposing figure to begin with, but he looked all the more formidable when compared to Marri sitting in her chair. Marri's face was unreadable. After a quick survey of the deck to make sure it was clear of any equipment that might interfere with the fight, Locke raised his arm, then quickly dropped it and backed away. The duel had begun.

Pirate Fifty-Three wasted no time. He charged at Marri, his sword whirling back and forth, the blade singing as it cut through the air. Although Fifty-Three was almost upon her, Marri had made no move, either offensive or defensive. Anne resisted the urge to shout a warning. The blade of Fifty-Three's sword came whistling down—

—only to be deflected by Marri's blade.

Anne couldn't believe it. She hadn't even seen Marri move her arm. There were various grunts of approval from the pirates, as though they had been expecting no less from their captain.

"That was amazing!" Penelope exclaimed, keeping her voice low so as not to cause a distraction. "He's two and a half times her size. Captain Copperhelm says a smart fighter should always look for ways to redirect the strength of a larger opponent rather than meet them head-on." Penelope was mimicking the moves of the fighters, even without a sword in her hand.

Pirate Fifty-Three spun away but immediately launched an attack from another angle. He brought his sword around in a powerful arc—only to be deflected again. And once again, Anne barely saw Marri move. Marri had a look of grim determination.

Penelope continued her commentary. "See how she moves her chair in small, tight arcs each time he charges in? That allows her to control the center and forces her opponent to come to her. It's great economy of energy, but you have to really know what you're doing."

Pirate Fifty-Three came at Marri with three quick thrusts, and she deflected each with ease. The crowd was tense, and cries and shouts rang out with each successful parry.

Frustration was showing on Pirate Fifty-Three's face. He bellowed and leapt straight at Marri, his sword moving so fast that Anne couldn't see the blade. At the last instant, Marri deftly swiveled her chair out of his path, deflecting his blade yet again with a swift block and countering with an impossible riposte.

Pirate Fifty-Three stumbled into the circle of onlookers. They jumped aside, and he crashed into the railing. When he regained his feet, he was clutching his arm. A line of red trickled from between his fingers.

"First blood," said Marri.

Her opponent clutched his sword even tighter and looked ready to charge again, but this time the air rang with the sound of a dozen swords being drawn and pointed at him.

Locke stepped forward, sword in hand. "The duel is over. You lost. It's time to go."

Pirate Fifty-Three hesitated only a moment. Seeing that he was clearly outnumbered, not to mention outmatched by the captain, he sheathed his sword and stormed off toward the crew cabin.

Marri approached Locke and spoke in a low voice, although Anne could still hear every word.

"Let him gather his belongings before leaving the ship," said Marri. "Everything except the medallions."

"According to pirate law, everything he has belongs to you now," said Locke.

"And I'm letting him keep it," said Marri. "Make sure no one harasses him about it, either. Also, I see no need to put a black mark on his record. When word of the duel gets around, he'll have a difficult enough time signing on with another ship."

"He deserves a black mark."

"Nevertheless, those are my orders."

Locke nodded and strode after the departing pirate.

Anne walked over. "That was very kind of you."

Marri looked startled. She clearly hadn't meant anyone else to hear the conversation. Ignoring Anne's remark, she sheathed her sword. "That cost us precious time. We must get going."

Anne, Penelope, and Hiro followed her down the ramp and into the city.

THE INTRODUCTION TO *A TOURIST'S GUIDE TO THE PYRATE MUSEUM* READS AS FOLLOWS:

The Pyrate Museum contains over five hundred thousand exhibits, housed on twenty-one levels. This includes the popular peg leg exhibit, the gold teeth exhibit, and a vast collection of famous swords used as bottle openers. It also includes hundreds of famous treasure maps, such as the well-known Triple Cheese Map (technically a replica, since the original was eaten), Lady Bentley's Map of Curious Places That Explode (charred beyond legibility), and the much-pondered Invisible Map of Captain Suspicious (which has never been put on public display because, you know, why bother?).

The Cylinder Seal

The streets of the city were steep and winding, but Marri didn't head up the hill. Instead, she led them to where several pirates were waiting in line to use a series of moving platforms. Anne watched as an old pirate hobbled onto one of the platforms. Once aboard, he pulled a small chain that released a stream of water. The water hit a waterwheel and the platform lurched into motion, carrying the pirate upward.

"There are platforms like this all over the Haven," said Marri. "Pirating isn't the safest of professions, as

I'm sure you can imagine, and there are plenty of pirates who find it difficult getting around a place like this. These and other devices make it much easier."

"Is that what happened to your legs?" asked Penelope. "Were you injured in some battle?"

Anne gasped. "Penelope! That's none of our business."

"It's okay," said Marri. "I don't mind. And the answer to the question is no, I wasn't injured in my career as a pirate. My legs have been like this since birth. I do find it somewhat ironic, though, given the reputation pirates generally have, that a pirate haven would provide the best accessibility in all the Hierarchy. It's hard to hunt for treasure in places where there are only stairs."

Anne was perplexed. Away from the demands of the pirate ship, Marri seemed less on edge and more relaxed and conversational. It was a welcome change. Anne was curious how someone so young had even become the captain of a pirate ship, but now wasn't the time to inquire.

When their turn came, they took the next empty platform. Marri activated the waterwheel, and the platform carried them up. They passed several levels until they reached the one labeled PYRATE MUSEUM. Marri deactivated the waterwheel, and the platform came to a halt.

"It's just at the end of this street," she said.

The museum was an architectural wonder, although less in the that's-the-most-beautiful-building-I've-ever-seen sort of way, and more in the I-wonder-why-it-hasn't-yet-collapsed-under-its-own-weight sort of way. It was an eclectic mix of crumbling stone buildings, dilapidated wooden shacks, and broken towers. It extended haphazardly in all directions, with no sense of design or even common sense. One section even stretched toward the center of the cavern on a loose (and continuously bobbing) series of anchored airships.

"That's...interesting," said Penelope.

"I could stand guard outside," offered Hiro. "You know, in case the Wizards' Council shows up."

Anne shook her head. "Everyone's going in. We're staying together."

Marri handed Anne a strip of material. "You'd better wrap this around your gauntlet. It's bad enough we're returning to the scene of the crime, but we're carrying the stolen medallion with us."

Anne wound the cloth around her gauntlet until it was fully covered. Hopefully no one would question why she was wearing it.

The front doors of the museum opened into a

spacious lobby. A mosaic of small black and white tiles formed a skull and crossbones on the floor. The skeleton of what Anne assumed to be a massive whale hung from the ceiling, and the air smelled of dried seaweed, pipe tobacco, and musty old ship's logs. They proceeded to a long counter. A wizened clerk had his back to them filing papers. Marri cleared her throat loudly, and the clerk jumped.

"Goodness me," he said. He adjusted his spectacles and studied her face. "Ah, Captain Blackwood. Back again so soon?"

Marri nodded. "I'm afraid so. I need to get back into the special medallion exhibit."

"Oh, dear," croaked the clerk. He lowered his voice as though he didn't want anyone to overhear, even though there was no one else in the lobby. "I'm very sorry, Captain, but I'm afraid we've had a robbery. Not long after you left yesterday, in fact. It's just terrible. One of our most valuable pieces. The special medallion collection is closed while the investigators gather evidence."

"We promise we won't disturb anything. I just need to double-check the information I copied down when I was in there."

The clerk wrung his hands. "They said they don't want

anyone going in while they're looking for clues. They were quite specific about that. Everyone's very upset."

Marri leaned closer. "I'm embarrassed to have to confess this, but I messed up. I was supposed to get some information about an old quest, but I looked at the wrong medallion. Any other time I would be happy to wait, but let's just say Octo-Horse Pirate isn't very pleased with me right now."

The clerk let out a squeak at the mention of Octo-Horse Pirate, and Anne wondered again what it was about him that put everyone on edge.

"You're on a mission for the supreme leader?" the clerk asked after he had regained his composure.

Marri glanced to her left and right before answering, as though she too were concerned about being overheard. "A top-secret mission," she said in a low voice. "And now I'm in big trouble. There's no telling what he'll do if I don't get the right information to him soon."

The expression on the clerk's face suggested that he knew exactly the types of things Octo-Horse Pirate might do and that he had no interest in any of them happening here.

"I heard that once, while in a terrible rage, he pulled the arms off an entire coop of chickens," said the clerk.

"Um, chickens don't have arms," said Hiro.

"Not after he finished with them, they didn't. That's for certain."

With a wink to Anne, Penelope leaned an elbow on the counter. "I heard about that one," she said in a conspiratorial whisper. "And rumor has it he did the exact same thing to a pit full of snakes."

The clerk shuddered. "You don't say?"

"Can I just point out—" Hiro started to say, but Anne clamped her hand over his mouth.

"Please, can you help us out?" said Marri.

Despite their efforts, Anne feared the clerk wasn't going to let them in. His expression kept changing, as though a great internal debate were raging inside him. Finally, he seemed to come to a decision.

"Very well, very well," he said while wiping his brow with a handkerchief. "Exceptions must sometimes be made for extenuating circumstances. Come with me."

"Thank you so much," said Marri.

They followed the clerk across the lobby to a large archway that led to the east wing of the museum. A sign over the archway read MEDALLION COLLECTION. Two guards were blocking the archway, but with a wave from the clerk they stepped aside and let the group pass. The first room was huge, with hundreds of medallions on display in large glass cases. This part of the museum was built out of stone and appeared marginally less likely to fall apart, although Anne did note that one wall was currently being propped up with oars from a rowboat.

"Oh, wow, that's Countess von Cheesecake's Emerald Medallion," said Hiro as they passed the first row of display cases. "And there's the Double Medallion of the Wizard of Krackleberry. And the thirteen-pointed Starfish Medallion!"

Anne couldn't help but notice the half dozen guards stationed around the room. Her gauntlet-hand felt abnormally heavy all of a sudden, and beads of sweat began to trickle down her back. She kept her eyes forward and hoped no one was studying them too closely.

Penelope pointed to a display case. "Why does that medallion look like a shriveled avocado?"

"Because it is a shriveled avocado," said the clerk. "Surely you've heard the story of Captain Avery's Avocado?"

"Um, I don't think so."

"Captain Avery was a cunning pirate, but unfortunately he became convinced that the avocado in that display case was a quest medallion. Wouldn't hear a word to the contrary. He claimed it spoke to him in a dream one night and told him to go on a quest to make himself king of the dragons. The dragons killed him, of course. They tend not to mess around. But the avocado was preserved in his memory."

"Why?"

The clerk shrugged. "As a warning not to believe everything an avocado tells you in a dream, I suppose."

Several archways led to other exhibits. The clerk guided them to one on the far wall labeled SPECIAL COLLECTIONS. The next room was considerably smaller and contained a number of alcoves. One of the alcoves had been cordoned off with a lattice of branches. The lattice had small purple flowers and was growing from a small plant pot. Anne felt confident it was an everlasting branch similar to the one Sassafras had shown them that morning.

The clerk pointed to two men standing next to the blocked alcove, one younger and one considerably older. The older one was writing something on a notepad.

"I have to return to the front counter," said the clerk. "Those are the gentlemen you'll need to speak to for permission to check out any of the exhibits in here. Best of luck!"

The clerk left.

The plan was for Anne, Penelope, and Hiro to distract any guards while Marri obtained the cylinder seal. The four approached the two men. Through the latticework, Anne could make out half a dozen display cases in the alcove. The first two stood empty with their glass doors open. Presumably they had held the medallion and the map. Other cases held jewels or outfits, and one at the end contained a small green object on a pedestal—the cylinder seal they were after.

Anne cleared her throat.

"This section has been sealed off," said the older man without looking up.

He and his partner wore identical dark overcoats over identical dark suits with identical crisp white shirts. In fact, the only discernible difference between them, besides their age, was the younger man's bright pink shoes. Although there was no way for Anne to be certain, she got the sense from the way the older man was scribbling on his notepad that he greatly disapproved of those shoes.

"We'd like to request access to one of the exhibits," said Anne.

The older man glanced at her and went back to writing. "It will have to wait."

"It's very important."

"It will still have to wait."

"You'll have to forgive him," said the younger man. "He gets like this whenever we're on a case."

The older man grunted.

"Still, I'm afraid you really do need to leave," the younger man continued. "We're investigating yesterday's robbery, so unless you have some valuable piece of information that could help us—"

"Our friend was here yesterday," Penelope blurted out. "Just before the robbery happened."

The older man lowered his notebook.

"I'm Special Agent Bleakroot," he said. He jabbed his thumb at the younger man. "This is Special Agent Evans."

The younger man smiled and waved. "Hi there."

Bleakroot gave the distinct impression that he wished Evans wouldn't wave like that when he introduced him to people.

"Are you with the Wizards' Council?" asked Hiro.

Bleakroot shook his head. "Different jurisdiction. We're FDA."

Anne frowned. "FDA?"

"The Faerie and Dragon Administration. Originally founded to deal with magickal creatures, but now also charged with enforcing the various laws and regulations pertaining to the use of magickal objects and public safety." Bleakroot surveyed the group. "So, you were here yesterday, were you?"

Marri cleared her throat. "Just me, actually. For several hours. I was studying one of the other medallions."

"Did you see anyone else enter the room?"

"I saw several people," she said brightly, clearly trying to get their interest.

"Mind if I get a statement?"

"Okay."

The agents led her across the room. As she went, Marri pointed to the display case beyond the lattice and made a shooing motion.

Penelope nudged Anne. "I think she means you."

"Why me?" said Anne.

"Because I'm way too loud and Hiro would probably pass out just thinking about it. This is our one chance to get that seal, and Marri obviously can't do it now. Hiro and I will do our best to block their view."

"But that's an everlasting branch across the front of the alcove," said Anne. "Someone is going to have to make it create a door or something. I was the only one who couldn't make it work in class."

"Well, now you get a second chance. And be quick about it, too, because the clock is ticking." Penelope gave Anne a push. Anne stumbled but quickly recovered. Neither of the agents seemed to notice.

Penelope was right. They didn't have the luxury of time. Anne wandered about the room as though she were merely there to do some sightseeing. When she returned to the lattice, she glanced back to see whether anyone was looking in her direction. Penelope had dragged Hiro to a spot where they would at least partially shield Anne from view. The two agents seemed focused on Marri, who was gesturing wildly and seemed to be saying something about an ogre. If Anne was going to do this, it had to be now.

Anne gripped one of the branches in her hand and willed it to make an opening. She squeezed her eyes shut and pictured an elegant archway. Nothing happened. She squeezed her eyes even tighter and imagined a grand oak door. Still nothing.

"This is going to take forever," she muttered to herself.

She dug in her cloak for her pocketknife, figuring if nothing else she might be able to cut her way through.

Suddenly the branches began to move, and a small circle formed in the center of the lattice.

Anne rolled her eyes. "Great, a plant that only responds to threats."

The circle would be a tight fit, but Anne was certain she could make it. She put one leg through and then shoved her body after it. Tight didn't begin to describe it. Her body became momentarily trapped, but after a couple of pushes her torso popped out like a cork. She fell on the floor. A quick glance back told her she was still in the clear. Penelope and Hiro had joined Marri and the two agents, and for some reason Penelope was pounding Hiro on the back as though to demonstrate something.

Anne's palms were sweaty, and she wiped them on her pants. She made her way to the first display case. A description on the side of the case read: "Herein lies the Darkflame Medallion, originally owned by Hieronymus Darkflame. A gift to him from the Lady of Glass. Acquired following his death in the Battle of the Great Rift."

Anne gasped when she read the part about the Lady of Glass. That was the person the dragon queen had told Anne to seek out, the one person who could tell her everything. Anne read the description twice more before moving on, just to make sure she would remember all the details. The next display case said much the same, except instead of "Darkflame Medallion" it read "a map of unknown tiers."

She knew her time was running short, so she made her way to the display case at the end. The description here read as the others did except it referred to the cylinder seal. Hands shaking, Anne pulled on the glass door. Much to her surprise, it opened easily. So much for museum security. She reached in and snatched the jade cylinder seal off its pedestal. Hardly believing her luck, she hurried back to the barrier and launched herself through in one go. The circle closed on her foot, momentarily trapping it, but she gave a deft twist and her foot popped out.

Once safely out of the alcove, Anne risked a quick peek at the seal. It was barely two inches long. From a distance it had appeared to be uniform in color, but up close, she could see it was slightly marbled. Unfortunately, she couldn't decipher any of the markings.

"Hey, what are you doing there?" said Bleakroot.

Anne jammed the seal into her pocket and hoped he

hadn't seen. If one of the agents noticed the cylinder seal was missing from the case, they would know for sure she had taken it.

"Me? I was just admiring the exhibits," said Anne as she tried to step casually over to one of the display cases in the middle of the room.

Bleakroot scanned the lattice and the display cases for any obvious signs of tampering. Anne squeezed her eyes shut and waited for the inevitable accusation, but none came. The everlasting branch had completely closed, but surely he had spotted the missing seal.

"That's fine," said Bleakroot. "Just make sure you don't touch anything. Wait a minute, though."

Anne had started to walk away but froze in place.

He peered at her curiously. "I've never seen anyone with yellow eyes before."

"Really?" said Anne. "Because where I come from, everyone has them."

He grunted. "Interesting."

Then he resumed writing in his notebook.

Anne was bewildered.

How in the world had she not just been caught?

She looked back at the display case. Much to her surprise, the cylinder seal was once again sitting on its pedestal. How could that be when she could still feel it in her pocket?

"Attention, all museum patrons," said a voice that sounded suspiciously sparrowlike. "Please proceed to the main lobby at this time for your free gift of—of—erm—maple-dipped bananas. And dried seaweed."

"You'd better hurry," said Evans. "I hear those bananas go quickly."

"I'd steer clear of the seaweed, though," said Bleakroot, rubbing his stomach.

"Uh, right," said Anne, and she and the others left the special collections room. When they reached the archway that led to the lobby, Marri stopped them.

"We can't leave without that cylinder seal," she said.

"I have it," said Anne, and she dug the tiny jade seal out of her pocket and held it for everyone to see.

"But it's still in the display case," said Hiro. "I noticed it as we left."

Jeffery appeared beside them in a flash of light. "That's because I replaced it."

"Replaced it with what?" Anne asked suspiciously. "It's not like there are a lot of extra jade cylinder seals lying around."

"Don't worry. Someone left a moldy avocado in one

of the other displays. I used that. Once you peel it, you can hardly tell the difference from a distance."

"How could you possibly peel it? That thing is practically petrified."

"I have a sharp beak."

Anne put her hands on her hips. "That wasn't just any moldy old avocado, you know. It was one of the exhibits."

"Oh," said Jeffery. "Well, it's not like anyone's going to miss a crusty old piece of fruit, is it?"

A shout came from the other room. "Hey, there's been another theft! Someone stole Captain Avery's Avocado!"

"Or maybe they will," he continued.

Marri grimaced. "So much for getting in and out without a hitch." She pointed to the door. "Everybody run!"

Run, pirate, run!

—Lyrics from "The Walking Pirate" by the infamous pirate
bard Two-Eyed Jimmy the Cyclops

Flint, Parchment, Knife

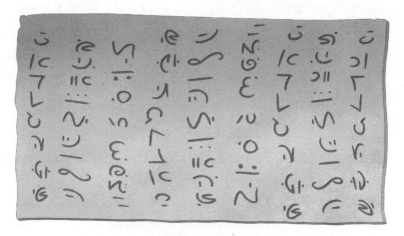

They burst out of the front doors at full speed, the jade cylinder seal tucked safely in Anne's pocket. Jeffery shot into the air and soared overhead. There was a chorus of shouts behind them. Anne risked a backward glance and saw several dozen guards pouring out of the museum in hot pursuit.

Instead of heading back to the platforms, Marri steered her chair into the first available alleyway. They sprinted the full length, swerving around piles of garbage and dodging hanging laundry. The thump of the guards' heavy boots on the uneven cobblestones reverberated off the walls of the buildings. The adventurers bolted across the next street and down another alleyway. Then they took a third and a fourth. Luckily, the streets back to the dock were all downhill. At one point, Jeffery peeled off down another alley to coax some of their pursuers in the wrong direction. The shouts of the guards receded as they widened the gap, and after twenty minutes of zigzagging through the back alleys of the city, the guards were nowhere to be seen or heard. The four adventurers ducked into the entryway of a large wooden building and took a moment to catch their breath.

"Phew," said Penelope, leaning against the wall. "I didn't think we'd ever give those guards the slip."

"This is bad," said Hiro. "They're going to put our faces on posters now, aren't they? We're going to be wanted criminals. We could do hard time for this. Not to mention, my mother's going to kill me!" His breathing became quick and shallow.

"Don't hyperventilate," said Anne.

"Or at least wait until we're back aboard the ship," Penelope added.

Marri pointed down the street. "We're nearly there. The dock is just at the bottom of this last alley."

The door directly across from them opened, and a man in a long red robe stepped out. He looked familiar, but Anne couldn't place him. The sign hanging beside the door read: WIZARDS' COUNCIL PIRATE LIAISON OFFICE REAR ENTRANCE. The man's eyes went wide as Anne realized who he was: Lieutenant Formaldehyde, the wizard who had let them leave Saint Lupin's.

"Time to get moving," she said. They took off.

"They're here!" the lieutenant shouted.

At least ten guards in Wizards' Council robes came out of the building at a dead run.

"Talk about out of the frying pan and into the fire," said Penelope.

Marri headed straight down the steep slope toward the dock. Anne's legs and arms were pumping so fast that she worried she would trip over her own feet and tumble the rest of the way. Her heart pounded in her chest, and her lungs burned from the effort. From the looks of it, neither Penelope nor Hiro were faring any better.

Just as they reached the bottom of the hill, a dozen museum guards sprang from various hiding places and blocked their path. Anne and the others were forced to stop short of the dock.

"Ah-ha! We have you now," said one of the guards. The badge on his chest read CHIEF OF SECURITY.

The wizards from the Wizards' Council came running up behind them.

"You don't have anything," said the lieutenant. "We've been chasing them since this morning. They're our prisoners." The other council wizards nodded their heads vigorously in agreement.

The chief pointed to Marri. "Oh yeah? Well, we've been after this thief since last night. She robbed the museum."

Marri's face remained as unreadable as ever.

"The news reports said the identity of the thief was unknown," said the lieutenant.

"True. But then she returned today and stole an avocado."

"Ah, but see now, that's a separate incident. Doesn't count as far as determining chronological priority goes."

The chief grabbed the handle of his sword. "There are other ways of determining priority." The rest of the museum guards also drew their swords, and the wizards from the council whipped out their spell books.

Marri tapped Anne's leg and pointed at the docks. Anne nodded and poked both Penelope and Hiro. They casually stepped off to the side.

The lieutenant held up a hand. "Look, there's no need for violence here. I'm sure we can come up with a way to settle this like civilized people who are only trying to capture these alleged criminals and subject them to some mildly uncomfortable interrogation techniques."

Both sides relaxed slightly, although there was still definite tension in the air.

"Flint, Parchment, Knife?" suggested the chief.

The lieutenant nodded. "Agreed. Best two out of three?"

"How about three out of five? It always takes me a couple of rounds to get warmed up."

"Fine."

The chief of the museum guards and the lieutenant from the Wizards' Council faced off. The rest formed a circle around them and began shouting out suggestions. The two combatants each tapped a fist against the palm of the other hand, and on the third tap showed a specific form. A cheer went up from the council wizards as the lieutenant showed knife and the chief showed parchment in the first round.

With the guards fully engaged, Anne and the others made their way down the dock toward the *Blue Daisy*. Another cheer went up from the council guards, along with a chorus of groans from the museum guards, as the lieutenant apparently took the second round as well.

"Don't worry," Anne heard the chief say. "I told you, it takes me a couple of rounds to get going."

Upon reaching the ramp, the four of them dashed aboard. Jeffery was already there waiting for them, perched on the rail.

"What took you so long?" he asked.

"We ran into more trouble," said Anne.

"Get us out of here, Mr. Locke," said Marri. "Quietly."

"Aye, Captain."

Locke issued instructions in subdued tones. There were no shouted orders nor raucous laughter from the crew. Everyone moved as silently as possible to avoid alerting the two factions. The crew retracted the ramp and untied the ropes that secured the ship.

Just as the airship began to ease away, a shout came from the guards. "Hey, where did those thieves go?!"

There was a great commotion as the museum guards and council wizards rushed toward them. It didn't matter, though, because by the time they reached the end of the dock, the *Blue Daisy* was well out of reach. Jeffery gave them a little wave, and then disappeared back into the gauntlet.

"To the ships!" yelled the council guards.

They hurried to a nearby dock where two large council warships awaited.

"All haste to the exit," instructed Marri. "Let's hope for a good crosswind."

Locke returned to bellowing his orders, and the crew leapt into action. Several climbed the masts and began unfurling the sails.

"Um, how can we catch a crosswind inside a tier?" asked Hiro.

Marri pointed ahead. Anne watched as a ship in front of them drifted into the very center of the cavern. Its sails suddenly filled, and it shot toward the opening.

"There's a crack on the opposite wall as well," Marri explained. "It's not big enough to sail a ship through, but it provides a decent boost."

The two council ships were now on an intercept course with the *Blue Daisy*. One of them fired a single cannon, but the angle was poor and the shot went wide. Still, they were quickly catching up and could throw out grappling lines if they came close enough. The helmsman maneuvered the *Blue Daisy* into the center of the cavern. When it caught the crosswind, it too leapt forward, and Anne had to place a steadying hand on a rail to keep from falling.

As they approached the exit, Marri called to a ship anchored off to the side. It was the same ship whose captain liked Marri's goat's milk.

"Ahoy, the *Ticklish Duckfoot*," she called out.

"Ahoy, the *Blue Daisy*," came the reply. The captain pointed to the two council ships. "Looks like someone's taken an interest in you."

"A simple misunderstanding," said Marri. "Nothing we can't handle."

The captain smiled. "I'm sure. Still, if there's anything I can do to help..."

Marri tapped her chin. "Well, I suppose if you were to block the exit for a few minutes after we leave—completely by accident, of course—I might consider it a favor."

"I think I could see my way to doing that, if only to keep my supply of goat's milk safe."

"A crate of my very best to you the next time we meet if you can give us a five-minute head start."

"Done!" cried the captain, and he began issuing orders at a furious rate.

The sailors aboard his ship worked with incredible speed, and the ship was soon moving. The council ships were picking up speed as well, but as the *Blue Daisy* entered the tunnel, the bow of the *Ticklish Duckfoot* drifted into their path. They were forced to veer away. The crews of the three airships exchanged insults, but the damage had been done. It would take several minutes for the *Ticklish Duckfoot* to clear the path and for the council ships to realign themselves with the exit.

Aboard the *Blue Daisy*, crew members once again called out the distances between the hull and the sides of the tunnel. Locke issued swift course corrections to the helmsman, even faster than during their entrance. As soon as the *Blue Daisy* was clear of the tier, Marri ordered them to engage the dragon-fire engines, and the ship sped off.

Thirty minutes later, the *Blue Daisy* was anchored beneath a jungle tier over a hundred miles away from the Haven. Jungle vines hung down from the edge of the tier, creating a curtain that made the ship difficult to spot but still allowed the crew to keep a lookout. Every once in a while, a Wizards' Council airship could be seen patrolling in the distance, but none came close to finding the pirate ship in its hiding place.

While they kept watch, Anne shared with them what she'd read on the display cases. Unfortunately, neither

Marri nor any of her crew had ever heard of the Lady of Glass or the Battle of the Great Rift.

Once Marri felt certain the danger had passed, she invited Anne, Penelope, and Hiro into the captain's quarters. A low bunk was built into one wall, and a desk and bookshelf were bolted to the opposite wall. A small table occupied the center of the room. A bowl of dried flower petals sat on the shelf, and the cabin smelled like a mix of lavender and jasmine.

Hiro held the cylinder seal in his hand. "I can't believe this belonged to my great-great-great-great-grandfather."

"Really though, how great can one person possibly be?" asked Penelope.

Hiro placed the cylinder seal on the table. Marri retrieved a jar from the shelf labeled DOCTOR MUD'S FAST-DRYING CLAY. The jar contained a lump of pliable reddish-brown clay, and she worked it into a flat rectangle on the top of the table. Anne carefully pressed the cylinder seal into one end of the clay, rolled it across the surface, and lifted the seal away.

Everyone leaned in to study the impression.

"The writing is so tiny I can barely read it," said Penelope.

"The words are all gibberish," said Anne. "I thought

reversing it would make it easier to figure out, but I still can't decipher a single word."

"It might be some sort of code," suggested Marri. "For example, pirate maps always use a cipher so no one else can read them. Maybe the owner of this map didn't want anyone to read it, either. But there's almost always a clue to help you figure it out. You just have to know where to look."

Everyone studied the clay tablet for several minutes as it hardened, but no one found anything that remotely looked like a clue on how to decipher the legend to the map.

"What about your GPS?" asked Marri.

"What about her GPS?" asked Jeffery as he appeared in a flash of light.

Marri pointed to the bookshelf. "You can eat written material to absorb the contents, correct?"

Jeffery nodded enthusiastically. "Absolutely! I always say the best way to read a book is to serve it for dinner. Why, do you have something for me?"

"Maybe," said Anne. "Are you able to decipher coded texts?"

"Sure. Some of them leave a weird aftertaste, though."

Hiro pointed to the cylinder impression on the clay tablet. "Can you decipher this?"

Jeffery hopped onto the table and sniffed the clay.

"Gah! You want me to eat *this*?" He held a wing over his beak and started staggering around the table.

"It's really important," said Anne.

"This map contains the directions to the High Castle," said Marri. "If we don't decipher it, we'll never complete the quest."

"Can't we just ask someone for directions?" asked Jeffery.

"No," said Anne. "I know this isn't exactly ideal, but we really need you to do this. We've already used up several hours just getting the cylinder, and the clock is ticking. If there was any other way, I would try it, but you're our only hope."

Jeffery sighed. "The things I do for this group."

"What, like insult us?" asked Penelope.

"Exactly. Do you have any idea how exhausting it is to keep coming up with zingers?"

Anne broke off a corner of the clay tablet and held it out to Jeffery. He sniffed it again, gagged slightly, and then plucked it out of her hand with his beak. He started to swallow, but then paused.

"Is something wrong?" asked Anne.

"Just how old is this?" asked Jeffery, his beak full of clay.

"You mean the clay?" asked Marri. "I just bought it a few weeks ago."

Jeffery swallowed. "No, I mean the map legend. It tastes like some pirate's stinky old socks. Blech!"

Anne tore off another piece and fed it to him. He tipped his head back and swallowed it whole.

"It's like someone took the bandages off an ancient mummy, wiped their feet on them, invited their neighbors to wipe their feet on them just for good measure, and then turned the bandages into this code."

He choked down several more pieces, making gagging noises with each swallow.

Halfway through, Jeffery held out his wings and examined them. "My color isn't looking so good."

"You're a rainbow-colored sparrow," said Hiro. "How can you tell?"

"My blues feel muted."

Marri maneuvered her chair over to the bookshelf and removed a small volume. She returned and placed the book on the table.

"What's that?" asked Jeffery, perking up slightly.

"Incentive," said Marri. "It's a book of terrible pirate poetry. I've never particularly liked it, but it was a gift and I never felt quite right throwing it away. If I have to sacrifice it for the sake of the quest, though..." She tore out one of the pages and fed it to Jeffery. He snapped it up and swallowed it quickly.

"Ah! Delicious!" he said. "I mean, yeah, this author couldn't rhyme to save his life, but anything is better than that ancient clay torture meal garbage thing."

Alternating between pieces of clay tablet and pages of terrible pirate poetry, Jeffery eventually managed to eat the entire legend. When he was finished, he lay on the table, slowly rocking back and forth.

"That was awful," he croaked.

Marri spread the map out next to Jeffery.

Jeffery waved her away. "Thanks, but I couldn't possibly eat another bite. Save it for me, though."

"This isn't for you to eat," said Marri. "This is the map of the Hierarchy we need you to decode. Can you show us the location of the High Castle?"

"It's in my belly, sitting there like a cannonball."

Anne placed her hands on her hips. "The whole point of you eating the legend was so you could decipher the map and tell us how to get there!"

Jeffery stopped his rocking. "Before I tell you where it is, I want you to acknowledge that I'm only the messenger. It's not my fault if the castle is someplace you're not going to like, right?"

"Just tell us already," said Penelope.

"Because I'm telling you, you're not going to like it."

"Now you're just stalling," said Hiro.

"Of course I am. How else do you expect me to delay telling you what it says?"

"Is he always like this?" asked Marri.

Jeffery glanced at the shelf. "Any chance I can wash the map down with a nice short story? Preferably a light comedy?"

"Jeffery!" the four of them yelled in unison.

"Fine, but don't say I didn't warn you."

He crawled over to the map, studied it for a moment, and then pointed at an area in the right-hand corner.

Anne could tell by the expression on Marri's face that the answer wasn't good.

"What's the problem?" asked Anne.

"That's the Dead Zone," said Marri, her voice barely above a whisper. "Everyone avoids it. No one even ventures near it."

"So, you're saying if we go there we have to be very careful?" asked Penelope.

"No, I'm saying if we go there we might never return."

THE PICKLED LEMON'S GUIDE TO BEING STEALTHY RECOMMENDS THE FOLLOWING RESOURCES:

When it comes to the art of tiptoeing around, there are several volumes every sneak should have on the shelf. *The Stealthy Person's Guide to Being Stealthy* is an obvious choice and has twenty-four chapters filled with step-by-step instructions (accompanied by color illustrations) on how to make yourself stealthier. It also has one chapter on how to make the perfect baked potato, because, hey, even stealthy people sometimes crave complex carbohydrates. The second book on the list is *Spies, Lies, and Flies*, a book about spying and lying and common house flies. The final book is *What to Do After You've Gotten Yourself Caught Because You're Not Nearly as Stealthy as You Thought You Were.* That one should be self-explanatory.

9

The Castle High

The trip to the Dead Zone took several hours. The crew spent that time readying the ship for possible battle. Penelope practiced her swordplay, and Hiro flipped back and forth through his spell catalog, which he had taped back together. Anne stood at the bow pondering the quest riddle for any clues they might have missed. Who might be waiting for them at the castle? Could it be the Lady of Glass? What gift of power did Anne have to give her? And how would any of that free the world?

In the late afternoon, Hiro and Penelope joined Anne.

"So, what do you think?" asked Penelope, keeping her voice low.

"About what?" asked Anne.

"About any of this. It can't be a coincidence that some long-forgotten quest medallion owned by an ancestor of the Darkflame family gets brought to Saint Lupin's, where his great-great-whatever-grandson just happens to be attending school. Not to mention it's the third medallion we've encountered that bears the Sign of Zarala."

Hiro nodded. "I agree. I've studied my family history, but all I remember about Hieronymus Darkflame is that he died before he turned thirty. There's no mention in any of the books about a quest medallion or a notable part he played in any battle, and believe me, if there was, my family would be the first to make a big deal of it."

"Or maybe they wouldn't," said Anne. "Maybe it was supposed to be a secret. The plaque on the display case said the medallion and the other artifacts were acquired after his death in the Battle of the Great Rift, whatever that is. That means he must have had those items in his possession when he died, which at the very least would suggest there were pirates at the battle."

"What makes you think pirates took the medallion?" asked Penelope.

"How else did they end up in a pirate museum?" said Anne. "So, what we know so far is this: One hundred and fifty years ago, Hiro's ancestor took part in some great battle involving pirates. He was carrying several items that were gifts from someone known as the Lady of Glass. Either just before the battle or during it, he presumably activated the gold medallion. And not long after that he was killed."

"You're leaving out one important detail," said Hiro.

Anne frowned. "What detail?"

"The gold medallion was activated by your gauntlet. How was it that my ancestor had your gauntlet in his possession, and how did it end up at Saint Lupin's and not at the museum along with everything else?"

Anne nodded. "That's a good point. And the answer is we don't know yet. Jocelyn was the one who brought it to Saint Lupin's, but she didn't say where it was before that. Only that her parents gave it to her so she could then give it to me. One thing I do know, though: There's more going on here than a simple treasure hunt."

"You think Marri is lying?" asked Penelope.

Anne checked to make sure no one else was listening. "I honestly don't know what to think. I believe that she didn't expect the quest to reactivate, but she's not telling us the whole story, that's for sure. For one, who exactly is Octo-Horse Pirate, and why did he send her to steal the medallion in the first place?"

Before Penelope or Hiro could respond, a call came from the crow's nest. Everyone who wasn't busy with a specific task rushed to the bow of the airship, so they had to cut their conversation short.

Anne had been so focused on their discussion that she hadn't noticed the sky getting unnaturally darker. She turned her attention to the direction they were heading. Miles of dark gray tiers stretched ahead of them, fading into the late-afternoon mist and blocking out the sunlight. The tiers appeared devoid of all life. Not so much as a mosquito buzzed.

"Welcome to the Dead Zone," said Locke.

Anne surveyed the scene before them. "Are those dead tiers?"

"Yes."

"How did they get here?" asked Penelope.

"No one has been able to explain it," said Marri. "For some reason dead tiers tend to drift into this area all on their own. They come here from all over the Hierarchy. Some of them take years, even decades, to reach here. Pretty much everyone avoids this place, including pirates. I certainly don't relish the idea of taking the *Blue Daisy* in there."

"Wouldn't at least some of the tiers be filled with treasure, though?" asked Penelope.

"Probably. But the Dead Zone tends to attract all manner of strange creatures and monsters, and it isn't worth risking my ship and my crew for only the possibility of treasure. There's plenty to be had elsewhere."

"D-did you say monsters?" stammered Hiro.

Marri's expression turned grim. "Airship killers."

As the ship entered the zone, the air filled with a dark gray dust, and the crew members pulled out handkerchiefs and strips of cloth to tie around their mouths and noses. Anne, Penelope, and Hiro ripped strips from their cloaks and covered their faces as well. Marri ordered the crew to furl half the sails to slow the ship down. Even with the clock on the quest ticking, she was obviously going to proceed cautiously, and Anne couldn't blame her.

As they glided between the shadowy chunks of floating rock, no one said a word. The lack of any noise from the tiers whatsoever, either animal or otherwise, was eerie. Anne kept scanning the horizon, hoping to see something to indicate where they should be headed.

"Movement to port," said one of the crew in a low tone, breaking the silence. "Three flying squids. Ten to twelve feet long."

"Have they spotted us?" asked Marri.

"No, Captain."

Anne looked off the port side and strained to see where the sailor was pointing. In the distance, she could just barely make out three dots gliding on the air currents. She never would have spotted them had someone else not pointed them out first.

"Adjust course five degrees to starboard," said Marri.

"Aye, Captain," said Locke. He muttered something to the helmsman that Anne couldn't hear, and a moment later the airship altered course.

Another crew member called down from the crow's nest. "Two groups to starboard. A group of three is moving away from us, and a group of four is flying on a parallel course."

"Adjust course back two degrees to port, and keep an eye on that group of four," said Marri. "If it changes course in the slightest, I want to know immediately."

They continued like that for well over an hour, spotting groups of flying squids and making course corrections, or sometimes even coming to a complete stop to avoid making contact.

The air was oppressive. Anne didn't know if it was a trick of this place or if the gray dust was having an effect on them. Everyone's mood darkened, and even the sunlight seemed dimmer and farther away. Anne understood why people avoided this place; she had no desire to stay any longer than necessary.

Eventually the mist cleared a little, and the ship approached a thick cluster of tiers.

"Full stop," said Marri.

"Full stop," repeated Locke.

The *Blue Daisy* came to a rest between two relatively small tiers. They sat there for five minutes in total silence, straining to hear even the slightest sound or hint as to what lay ahead. Anne looked over the railing, but the mist below was still thick, and she could barely make out the dim glow of the BGFM.

"Thoughts, Captain?" inquired Locke.

"I don't like it," said Marri. "It's too quiet, especially considering we're almost at our destination. I would have expected there to be *more* squid patrols, not fewer."

"Unless something else is keeping them away?"

"Exactly."

They waited a few more minutes, until it became clear they were going to have to proceed without any more information than they currently had.

"Orders, Captain?" asked Locke.

Marri frowned. "Ahead slow, but tell everyone to keep a sharp eye out."

That order was probably unnecessary. The tension among the crew was palpable. Everyone had been on high alert since they had entered the Dead Zone, and Anne couldn't imagine anyone letting their attention drift.

The airship eased forward, even more slowly than before. They left the shelter of the two tiers and moved into an open area ahead of the tier cluster. This was the most exposed the ship had been since leaving Saint Lupin's. If anything was lurking in the shadows waiting to attack, now would be the perfect time.

"Hey, there's the castle!" cried Penelope.

"I see it, too!" said Hiro.

They were pointing in different directions. Anne studied the two tiers. Both contained castles. Moreover, both castles looked exactly the same. In fact, even the tiers themselves looked the same. Anne blinked several times. Was it some trick of the light? As the ship moved closer to the cluster of tiers, it soon became apparent that all the tiers looked identical and contained identical castles. There were dozens of tiers, maybe even hundreds.

"But—but which one is the correct castle?" asked Anne.

"This is definitely going to make it harder," said Marri. "Jeffery, did the legend say anything about—"

"Giant squid!" a voice shouted. "Giant squid! Giant squid! Giant *urk*—"

The shouts abruptly cut off.

Anne looked up and saw a huge tentacle curling over the ship. It had snatched a pirate out of the crow's nest and was thrashing him about. As the tentacle whipped back and forth, Anne could see that it was segmented. Its skin had a metallic sheen. That was all they needed: to be attacked by a giant metal squid. Anne flashed back to her fight with a giant metal dragon queen several months earlier. That had been a harrowing experience, but at least she had had her own suit of armor, one of the Old World power suits. She sorely wished she had it now.

"To arms! To arms!" shouted Marri. "Archers on deck! Blades into the rigging!" Her voice was raised but not panicked. Her tone was firm as she issued commands. The crew, as always, obeyed instantly.

Another large tentacle appeared and wrapped itself around the bow, and then the body of the giant squid peeked above the railing. Its two bulging eyes were as large as doors, and its body nearly the length of the *Blue Daisy* itself. Its other shorter arms flailed about, grasping at whatever came near.

Several crew members quickly strung bows and began pelting the monster with arrows. The shafts bounced off the metal plating of the tentacles without leaving so much as a scratch. The archers fired volley after volley, to no avail. There was a brief moment of hope when one of the arrows lodged itself between two of the armored plates, but the tentacle twisted and shattered the arrow into pieces with ease.

More than a dozen of the crew headed up the rigging, blades held firmly between their teeth. As soon as they could reach any part of the monster, they began hacking away. One pirate leapt from the rigging onto the tentacle. The tentacle snapped back and forth, and the pirate lost her grip. She tumbled away, down through the mist and into the BGFM far below.

As the giant squid continued to squeeze the ship, the

planks of the deck began to creak and groan in protest. The ship would not be able to withstand such an assault for very long. Marri urged the pirate crew to redouble their efforts and even threw herself into fray, thrusting her sword at any part of the squid's legs she could reach. Penelope leapt into the middle of the throng as well, swinging wildly. Hiro tried an ice spell, but all he managed to do was freeze his own arm to the starboard railing.

The airship bucked and rocked, and Anne was about to summon the Three-Handed Sword when suddenly a deep booming voice sounded above the din of the battle.

"Hold!"

The tone was so commanding that everyone paused, including the giant metal squid. Anne looked around for the source of the voice. A creature descended out of the sky, bright orange flames shooting from two circular objects on its back. The creature landed on the *Blue Daisy* with a heavy thud. The flames cut out but left two smoldering scorch marks on the deck. It took Anne a moment to figure out what exactly it was she was looking at.

The creature appeared to be made entirely of metal, not unlike the giant squid. The creature's body, though—if it could be called a body—was not at all squid-shaped. It had the torso of a man, with two arms. The helmet it wore, however, was shaped like a horse's head, and instead of two human-looking legs there were eight octopus-like tentacles. Also, there was a brightly colored parrot sitting on his shoulder.

"That must be Octo-Horse Pirate," whispered Penelope.

Anne had to agree. Who else could it possibly be? But the real question was, how had he found them?

An awed murmur rippled through the crew. As much as they seemed to fear Octo-Horse Pirate, they seemed to have a great deal of respect for him as well. Many of the crew had even lowered their weapons in his presence.

Octo-Horse Pirate held up an arm in greeting. "Welcome to the High Castle," he said in a voice that echoed strangely inside his helmet, giving it an eerie metallic quality. "I've been expecting you."

He walked over and stood in front of Marri.

"Hello, Marri," he said.

Marri sighed and sheathed her sword.

"Hello, Father," she replied.

THE COMPLETELY TRUE ORIGINS
OF OCTO-HORSE PIRATE

Born as a foal on the first full moon in the year of the Exploding Rubber Pineapple, raised by a family of superintelligent beavers, nourished on the sap of the deadly purple cactus, this promising young hero first made a name for himself when, as a member of a trapeze group known as the Flying Equestrians, he rescued twenty-three audience members from a burning circus tent. His career nearly came to an early end, however, when a stunt involving a windmill, a humpback whale, and a giant slingshot went tragically wrong.

To treat the foal's grievous wounds, a doctor used an experimental serum made from an extract of octopus venom. The serum cured him, but as a side effect it caused eight tentacles to grow where his legs used to be. Deciding to put circus life behind him, he went in search of a greater meaning for his life. The search only took five minutes because he was right around the corner from a quest academy. The instructors promised to train him in the ancient fighting arts, teach him to commune with nature, and instill within him a respect for all life.

That sounded like way too much work, so instead he renamed himself Octo-Horse Pirate and became a bandit of the high seas.

10

The Rose That Never Bloomed

He's your dad?!" shouted Penelope.

"Pen, calm down," said Anne.

"No, I will not calm down! What is it with this group? Does every quest have to involve a new student with a secret identity and a weird family trying to kill us all?"

"My parents aren't trying to kill us," said Hiro.

"Your parents are assassins!" yelled Penelope.

"No, they're not. They're secret agents."

"Who sometimes assassinate people!"

"Only the really bad ones," mumbled Hiro.

Octo-Horse Pirate slithered over to them, his eight tentacles carrying him swiftly across the deck. Anne wondered how such a creature came to be: the head of a horse, the body of a man, and the legs (or rather, tentacles) of an octopus. As he approached, she realized that her first impression had been wrong. He wasn't *made* of metal, but rather he was wearing a metal suit of armor. It somewhat resembled the iron knights. There was even a crystal in the center of the chest plate. Was it a dragon stone? Could this be a different type of Old World power suit?

"Polly want a kraken?" said the parrot on his shoulder.

"If everyone is finished with their little outbursts, perhaps we could move on to more pressing matters," said Octo-Horse Pirate. He turned to Marri. "Captain Blackwood, surrender your vessel and tell your crew to stand down."

Marri took a deep breath. "Father, I can explai—"

"Silence!" Octo-Horse Pirate scuttled sideways until he stood directly in front of her. "You're in quite enough trouble as it is, young lady. I instructed Marvin to go easy on your crew, but he could crush this ship and everyone on it, so I strongly suggest you obey my orders. Also, I am the supreme leader of the pirates, and when we are conducting pirate-related business, you will address me as such."

A look of shock passed over Marri's face, but she quickly recovered. "As you wish...Supreme Leader."

She nodded to Locke, who shouted orders, and the crew put away their weapons. They formed into ranks and stood silently at attention.

Octo-Horse Pirate gave the crew a cursory glance and turned his attention back to his daughter. "Marvin will tow you in. We'll talk further once you've docked and joined me in the castle."

Marri opened her mouth to speak, but before she could get even a single word out, two jets of flame shot out of the cylinders on Octo-Horse Pirate's back and he rocketed into the sky. If it was indeed a power suit he was wearing, it was a step up from the ones Anne had encountered.

The giant squid—or Marvin, as Octo-Horse Pirate had called him—dragged the *Blue Daisy* to the cluster of tiers and through a narrow passage. The path was tight and had many twists and turns, but Marvin didn't seem overly concerned about either their comfort or safety. The airship crashed into one tier after another, its planks groaning in protest. Most of the crew ended up either sprawling on the deck or hanging from any piece of equipment within arm's reach. With each sharp turn, bodies slammed against railings, masts, and even one another. After ten harrowing minutes, they entered a small clearing and headed for a tier near the bottom of the cluster. The tier in question was identical to all the others, and how the giant squid could distinguish it Anne had no idea.

They had dropped beneath the mist. The BGFM lay far below, with its waves of magick crashing together and sending up geysers of colorful energy.

Marvin dragged the *Blue Daisy* to a dock. Several crew members leapt across the gap and tied the ship to the pilings. Once everything was secured, the giant squid released his hold and disappeared back among the tiers. Anne somehow doubted he would go far.

The airship was heavily damaged. Several long gashes ran along the hull, and one of the masts had a large crack in it, not to mention the busted railings, broken equipment, torn rigging, and injured or missing sailors. It would be a while before the *Blue Daisy* was ready to sail again, if ever. Marri looked crestfallen at the damage, but she soon masked her expression.

"Have the crew disembark and form up in ranks of two on the dock," Marri instructed Locke in a commanding tone. "Tell them to leave their swords, but make sure everyone is carrying a concealed weapon," she added.

Locke conveyed her orders to the crew. Once they had secured all the equipment on deck, Anne and Marri led the crew off the airship, along the dock, and up a path that led to the main castle gate. Fortunately, the paving stones were smooth enough that Marri didn't have too much difficulty in her chair. They were followed immediately by Penelope and Hiro. Locke and the helmsman came next, and then the rest of the crew in twos. They walked in silence, but Anne could feel the tension in the air. They were all hardy sailors, and none had shied away from the fight with the giant squid, but now they seemed ill at ease.

The main gate into the castle towered over them. They entered through two massive oak doors and marched into the wide circular courtyard beyond. Some of the courtyard stones were darker than the rest and formed a large X, except each arm of the X consisted of a long, narrow diamond that was half black, half white. The overall shape looked familiar, but Anne couldn't quite place it.

Octo-Horse Pirate was standing in the center of the courtyard with the parrot still perched on his shoulder.

"Have your crew line up in ranks," he said.

The crew moved into formation, ten sailors to a row, without further instruction from either Marri or Locke.

Octo-Horse Pirate clasped his hands behind his back and began pacing in front of them. "In consideration of the time constraints under which we are currently operating, I'm going to get straight to the point." He stopped in front of Marri. "Did you recover the gold medallion as I requested?"

Marri shifted uneasily. "Yes, but—"

"And what did I instruct you to do with the medallion once you had it in your possession? Did I instruct you to experiment with it?"

"No, I just thought if I could—"

"Did I instruct you to activate it?"

"That—that was an accident. I was only trying to—"

He leaned in menacingly. "What did I instruct you to do?"

Marri met his stare with one of her own. "To bring the medallion directly to you, O Great and Wise Supreme Leader."

Octo-Horse Pirate ignored her sarcasm and resumed his pacing. "And yet despite those very clear orders, you elected to access the medallion on your own." He stopped again, this time in front of Anne. "And how did that turn out?"

Anne glared at him. "It could have gone better."

He laughed. "Indeed, I can well imagine. You'll notice I haven't even asked about the vial of black liquid missing from my supplies. You're lucky you didn't blow yourselves up, and half the Hierarchy with you."

Octo-Horse Pirate returned to the center of the court-yard and faced them. "Well, I fully admit this isn't how I planned to do this, but sometimes you have to work with what you've got. So, to the quest riddle, then."

"We're not telling you anything about the riddle," said Penelope.

"And why would I need you to?" he replied. "How do you think I found my way here?"

"You already knew the riddle," said Anne with dawning realization. "But how? We thought Hierony-mus Darkflame originally activated the quest."

"He did, but he didn't follow through with it, did he? He left it to someone else to do his dirty work. So, here we are, ready to finish what dear old great-grandfather started."

"It's great-great-great-great," said Hiro.

"Whatever." Octo-Horse Pirate gestured to the castle walls. "We're at the castle high, that much is obvious, but what could the rose that never bloomed possibly refer to? Any thoughts?"

No one said a word.

"Anyone? No? Well, I have one." He pointed to the shape on the ground. "Being sailors, I presume you're all familiar with this symbol."

Anne studied the shape again, and this time she remembered: It was a compass rose. They were used to indicate north, south, east, and west. You could find one on any map.

"A compass rose, of course, doesn't bloom," he continued. "But how does one wake it?"

Octo-Horse Pirate stepped to one side so that he was no longer standing on the round stone in the exact center of the rose. Then he reached out with one of his tentacles and tapped the stone three times. The stone slid aside, and a pillar rose out of the ground. When it stopped, it was just shorter than Anne. It was an Old World computer terminal, if she wasn't mistaken, albeit cylindrical instead of square like the ones they had previously encountered.

Octo-Horse Pirate waved Anne over. "Come here, please."

Marri wheeled herself forward. "It was my fault! Anne and her friends are only here because I gave them no other choice. We didn't know the medallion would activate."

"I'm well aware of the things you don't know."

Marri hung her head, but Anne grew angry. That was no way to treat a subordinate officer, definitely not in public, and especially not when she was your own daughter. Even if Marri was a kidnapping pirate captain, in that moment Anne wanted nothing more than to give her a big hug and reassure her everything was going to be okay. The crew remained stone-faced, although Locke's hand twitched at his side several times.

"I'll do as you ask," said Anne. "Just leave her alone."

Anne joined Octo-Horse Pirate at the computer terminal. As she approached, a circular hole opened in the side. The hole was large enough for someone to place an arm inside. She had encountered a similar device on their first quest.

"I don't know if anyone has told you or not, but that's a very special gauntlet you're wearing," said Octo-Horse Pirate. "One might even call it legendary, if you take my meaning." He pointed to the terminal. "I believe you know what to do next."

Anne assumed that by "legendary" he was referring to the line in the riddle about a legend's power, and since they'd already found the castle and the rose, she guessed she was about to fulfill the third line of the quest. She steeled herself and inserted her gauntlet-hand into the hole. The gauntlet clicked into place, and the hole closed around her forearm. She gave a subtle tug, just to test it, but her arm was stuck fast. As she had anticipated, something pricked the end of her index finger through the gauntlet and the computer terminal emitted a high-pitched whirring sound.

"Do you know what it's doing?" asked Octo-Horse Pirate.

"I assume it's taking a sample of my blood."

"Would you like to know why?"

Anne let out a huff. "I'm not interested in playing your games."

"Oh, it's not a game, I assure you. You see, the real power of a gauntlet comes from the person who wears it."

Octo-Horse Pirate leaned down until he was face-to-face with Anne (or rather helmet-to-face). Anne swallowed, but with her arm trapped in the computer terminal it wasn't like she could go anywhere. As she stared defiantly at him, he reached up and tapped the side of his horse-shaped helmet, and the visor slid open. It didn't show his full face, but it did reveal his eyes.

His bright yellow eyes.

Anne gasped. "Your eyes! They're—they're—"

He closed the visor and stepped back. "I thought that might interest you."

The last thing Anne had expected to encounter out here in the middle of nowhere was someone like her, someone who might know who she really was and where she came from. All her hopes for a home and a family came flooding into her, and it was difficult to keep them from overwhelming her. Why? Why here? Why now? Why him?

The terminal clicked again and brought Anne back to the present moment. The hole in the computer terminal reopened, and she removed her arm. She remained standing where she was, however, too stunned to move.

"Let me tell you a little story," said Octo-Horse Pirate. "It might not seem immediately relevant, but I assure you it is. In fact, I expect you're already familiar with parts of it. Once upon a time, near the end of the age we refer to as the Old World, a young scientist named Dr. Zarala Cole decided to experiment with power far beyond her knowledge to comprehend and her skill to control. She attempted to create a world but failed time and again."

"Zarala didn't fail," said Anne, finally finding her voice. "She created this world."

"Or so you've been led to believe."

"The Construct told us she created it," said Penelope.

The Construct was the holographic interface for Zarala's computer. Anne and her group had met the Construct on both of their previous quests. Zarala looked exactly like Anne, like a twin sister, except for her brown eyes.

Octo-Horse Pirate shook his head. "The Construct says whatever the Construct has been programmed to say. And that is exactly the problem with computer programs: They can be altered."

"You're saying the Construct lied?" asked Hiro.

"I'm questioning whether she is aware of the full

truth herself. For example, did you know there was another scientist? One whose name has been maliciously stricken from the history books, a brilliant young man by the name of Dr. Oswald Grey? Did you know he was the real genius behind the work Zarala so eagerly claimed as her own?"

"No one's ever heard of an Oswald Grey," said Penelope. "You're just making this up."

Anne recalled her dream. "No, he isn't," she said with dawning realization. "When I was unconscious in the Never-Ending Maze, after touching Emmanuelle's dragon stone, I had a dream or a vision or something. Zarala was there, and so was Oswald. He was also in the dream I had this morning."

"That doesn't prove anything," said Penelope.

"No, but this does," said Octo-Horse Pirate, and he took a thin blue book from his pocket. "This was Oswald's journal. It confirms that he was the one who built the computer and used it to create this world, achieving what Zarala had been unable to. Unfortunately, in her jealousy, Zarala tried to seize control. Oswald resisted, and a terrible war was fought that shattered the world and introduced an error into the matrix, a corruption. In an act of self-preservation, the computer erected a barrier to contain this evil, thus dividing the world into two parts."

"What barrier?" said Penelope.

"Isn't it obvious?" said Octo-Horse Pirate. "Walk to the edge of any tier and look down."

"He means the Big Glowing Field of Magick," said Hiro.

"Correct. Unfortunately for Oswald, he found himself trapped on the wrong side of the barrier, the one containing the corruption, while Zarala remained safely on this side."

"What does any of this have to do with my blood?" asked Anne.

Octo-Horse Pirate rested a tentacle on the top of the computer terminal. "Why, everything, of course. In the Old World, a person's blood was used to prove identity. It contains something called DNA, a unique blueprint that describes how each person is put together. It wasn't enough for Zarala that she had won. She was intent on destroying her opponent. With total disregard for every other living creature in the Hierarchy, she tried everything she could think of to bring down the barrier. Unbeknownst to her, however, and lucky for everyone else, the computer had put a safeguard in place. Only a blood sample from both Zarala *and* Oswald would work, thus ensuring their cooperation to eradicate the corruption before the barrier could ever come down."

"And let me guess, the gold medallion brings down the barrier," said Anne.

"Correct again."

"But if it will release this corruption, why would you want the barrier to come down?"

"That is for me to know," said Octo-Horse Pirate. "Suffice it to say, there is something on the other side I very much desire."

Penelope snorted. "You're doing all this for some lame treasure?"

Anne sensed it was more than treasure he was after.

"How do you expect to get any blood samples?" Hiro interjected. "Both Zarala and Oswald have been dead for thousands of years."

Octo-Horse Pirate chuckled. "Have they? Let's find out, shall we?" He turned and spoke to the terminal. "Do you have the results from the blood sample provided?"

"Yes," said a metallic voice. "The genetic sample belongs to Dr. Zarala Cole."

Anne couldn't believe what she was hearing. How could her blood possibly be a match for Zarala's?

"That's ridiculous!" shouted Hiro, clearly exasperated. "She's only thirteen!"

"DNA doesn't lie," said Octo-Horse Pirate.

"You said the program needed the blood of both Zarala *and* Oswald," said Anne.

"That's true," said Octo-Horse Pirate.

He reached into his pack and brought out an object made of brown leather overlaid with strips of gray metal. It was a gauntlet that looked identical to Anne's. There was even a circular inset on the underside of the wide extended cuff. Octo-Horse Pirate pulled the gauntlet onto his hand—his *right* hand.

He seemed to register the shock on Anne's face. "Oh, I'm sorry. Did you not know your gauntlet had a sibling?" he asked. "No, I don't suppose anyone mentioned that to you. Or perhaps they simply didn't know. No matter. I'm happy to acquaint you with some of the features of twin gauntlets, the most important being this."

He stretched his gauntlet-hand toward Anne. "Transfer medallion!"

Anne's gauntlet snapped forward of its own accord, nearly pulling her off her feet. There was a blast of light as the gold medallion leapt out of the inset on her gauntlet—

—and flew straight into the inset on the gauntlet worn by Octo-Horse Pirate.

"Hey, give that back!" Anne shouted.

"Thief!" cried Penelope.

"Activate stasis field," said Octo-Horse Pirate with his gauntlet-hand still outstretched.

A green dome sprung over the courtyard. Anne found herself frozen in place, unable to move or even speak. Only Octo-Horse Pirate and his parrot seemed unaffected.

"My apologies," he said. "The quest is at a delicate stage, and I can't afford to take any chances."

With everyone stuck in place, he shoved his gauntlet-hand into the hole in the computer terminal. There was a distinct click as the gauntlet locked into place, and the hole closed over his forearm. The whirring sound came again, and then there was another click and the hole reopened.

"Do you have the results from the second blood sample?" Octo-Horse Pirate asked the terminal.

"Yes," said the voice. "The genetic sample belongs to Dr. Oswald Grey."

Anne's head was spinning: gauntlets, blood, Zarala, Oswald, the medallion. She willed her limbs to move, even just a little, but she was stuck fast, just like everyone else.

There was a loud rumble, and the ground shook beneath their feet, although the stasis field continued to keep them frozen in place. The tier had started moving. Moreover, all the tiers within view were leaving as well, fanning out in all directions.

Octo-Horse Pirate faced them again. "For the quest to finish, this castle has to connect to the BGFM at a specific location. The castle was originally aligned directly over this spot, but when the world fractured, the castle was flung far away. It will take some time for it to realign itself—roughly fourteen hours from now, if I'm not mistaken—and when it does, the barrier will fall. And now we must deal with the loose ends, namely, what to do with all of you." He looked to the parrot. "Thoughts?"

"Polly want an execution?" said the parrot.

Anne tried to protest, but she still couldn't move a muscle. Was this truly the end of everything? Had they finally met their match? Everything they had worked so hard to build gone in a flash? And on top of it all, she couldn't even move her eyes to signal some sort of goodbye to her friends.

"Oh, I think we can do better than that," said

Octo-Horse Pirate. He walked over to Marri again. "I would like to be able to trust you, but given all that has transpired, that's simply not a risk I can take. Also, I have always tried to impress upon you that actions have consequences, so if it helps, you may consider what is coming as discipline for your poor choices today.

"Also, I need to borrow this," he added, removing her leather pack from her chair.

The pack containing the bag with the dice!

Anne struggled again to move, but it was no use.

Octo-Horse Pirate proceeded to remove each pirate's weapon and drop it in the pack. He even took Penelope's wooden sword and Hiro's letter opener. When he was done, Octo-Horse Pirate shouldered the pack and walked back to the center of the compass rose. He tapped the top of the computer terminal and moved to the edge of the courtyard. Anne's heart thumped loudly as she watched the gray cylinder sink back into the ground.

"This will be…unpleasant," said Octo-Horse Pirate, holding up his gauntlet-hand. "Deactivate stasis field."

"Say hello to the lady," squawked the parrot.

The stasis field disappeared, and the stones of the courtyard vanished beneath them. They dropped down a vertical shaft, straight through the heart of the tier and out the bottom. Several pirates cried out as they fell, and even Anne let out a gasp before the wind stole it away. Bodies tumbled and flailed and crashed into one another. Anne spotted Penelope and reached for her, but before they could lock hands, one of the pirates careened into them and they went spinning off in opposite directions, completely out of control. There was no sign of Hiro.

They plummeted toward the BGFM at a terrifying speed, and the vast ocean of magick seemed to rise to meet them. First one pirate struck the surface, then another and another, like raindrops on a lake. Anne watched in horror as the BGFM swallowed them up one by one.

Finally, Anne herself hit the barrier. Jagged lines of energy arced over her body, as though she had been struck by lightning, and then the whole world turned white.

Interlude

In a blatant attempt to artificially heighten the dramatic tension, this brief interlude has been inserted to give the reader time to imagine what horrible fate has befallen our heroes. In that spirit, please enjoy these two selections of truly terrible pirate poetry.

ODE TO A MISSING SHOE

Sunlight is yellow,

Wow, do my feet smell-o,

Other things are also yellow (except for non-yellow things),

Hey, look, an ant!

SWORDS AND FLOWERS

Swords are like flowers,

Except when they stab you,

And then you realize

They aren't really like flowers at all.

THE BEGINNING OF THE WORLD

Once upon a time the world did not exist, and since the world not existing also included there not being any chocolate to eat, everyone agreed that the situation was completely unacceptable (except for the few cranky people who thought existence in general was overrated and made it a point to never get along with anyone). So a young wizard decided to create the world using magick. The wizard cast a powerful spell, and the world came into being (much to the annoyance of the cranky people, which is fine because they were going to be annoyed no matter what happened).

Another wizard, however, tried to steal this magick to create a different world.

This turned out to be a bad idea.

A very, very bad idea indeed.

11

The Other Side

I t took a moment for Anne to get her bearings. At least she was no longer falling, which was a good thing. She recalled entering the BGFM, but her memory became a bit fuzzy at that point. It felt as though she had passed directly through the magickal barrier into currents of pure energy. And then suddenly she was here—wherever here was.

She looked around.

A long gray corridor stretched out before her. There was a single door at the far end bearing the image of a black dragon. A plaque on the wall beside the door read: DR. ZARALA COLE. She'd already been here earlier that day.

Anne was back in the dream.

As before, Anne found herself hovering several inches off the floor. She floated down the hallway toward the door, and as soon as she touched the doorknob a deep metallic voice spoke from nowhere in particular.

"This is your second scheduled dream sequence, as per Item 779 of your official quest itinerary," said the voice. "Please be advised that any personal information you divulge could be used in embarrassing ways as part of our advertising campaign."

"This place again?" said a voice beside her.

Anne jumped (as much as one can jump while floating several inches above the floor).

Captain Copperhelm appeared next to her.

"Don't you dream of anything besides long boring corridors?" he asked.

"Don't mind him," said a voice from her other side, startling her again.

Jocelyn had appeared as well, along with Rokk, Sassafras, and Princess Whiskers.

"He's just grumpy that our status as dream guides

doesn't grant him the power to command an army of the undead," said Jocelyn.

Copperhelm harrumphed. "One little skirmish. That's all I'm asking."

He produced a small card that read:

GHOST GENERAL

In the event of an untimely death, this card grants the user the power to control any and all undead creatures, including zombies, skeletons, ghosts, and vampires.

NOTE: USER MUST TRULY BE DEAD. BEING IN A STATE OF SUSPENDED ANIMATION DOESN'T COUNT.

Jocelyn placed a semitransparent arm around Anne's shoulders. "How are you faring, my dear? We watched that nasty business with Octo-Horse Pirate from the netherworld. I couldn't believe it when he stole your medallion. You have our deepest sympathies."

"Deep enough that you're not going to mark me down for it?" Anne asked hopefully.

Jocelyn patted her shoulder. "I'm afraid not. But at least we can help you with your second dream."

"Wonderful," said Anne, feeling anything but.

Anne knew she should be elated, especially with the arrival of her mentors, but all she felt was a knot of anger burning deep within. Strangely, this particular knot didn't seem directed at Marri or her father or anything else that had happened that day. Anne was angry at Marri for dragging her into all this, no question, but she was also sympathetic. It was obvious Marri had a lot to deal with. And although Anne was definitely furious with Octo-Horse Pirate and vowed to make him pay for every bit of harm he'd caused, right now he wasn't her primary concern. No, the anger she felt was about something else entirely. In truth, it had been growing for a while, even before this quest had started, and she decided it was finally time to deal with it.

Anne yanked open the door to the lab and marched inside. As before, the room was filled with several long counters, and the young man in the white coat and brown loafers was standing at the far counter.

"Good morning, Dr. Cole," he said.

Anne stared at him but said nothing.

"Aren't you going to respond?" asked Jocelyn, following her into the room. "This might be your chance to finally get some answers."

"What's the point?" said Anne. "He thinks I'm Zarala Cole, and for all I know, maybe I am. The computer at the High Castle certainly seemed to think so. But it also thinks Octo-Horse Pirate is Oswald, so maybe it's just gone bonkers." She rounded on Jocelyn. "But you're right, this might just be my chance to get some answers. Finally. From you."

Jocelyn looked taken aback. "I beg your pardon?"

"Why did you give me the gauntlet?"

"What do you mean?"

"Back when Saint Lupin's was still an orphanage and your sister was running it. You arrived one morning and handed the gauntlet to me. Why?"

Jocelyn frowned. "I told you already: Our family was entrusted with the gauntlet as well as the silver medallion from your first quest. My mother had instructed me to return to Saint Lupin's on a specific day and give the gauntlet to you. Activating the medallion was an unfortunate accident, and if I could go back and prevent—"

"Your mother mentioned me by name?" asked Anne, perplexed.

"No, she gave me your orphan identification number. 6-5-5-3-5."

Anne felt her frustration growing. "But why? Why that number, and why on that specific day?"

"I honestly don't know. But really, Anne, how is any of this relevant? As your dream guide, I really do feel you should be focusing your attention on your current quest. Why, just have a look here." She pointed to a book on the counter—a thin book with a familiar red cover. The title read *The Adventurer's Guide to Crystal Formations and Quantum Computing*. "It's your guidebook. Perhaps it has some pertinent information."

Anne ignored the book. "I don't want the guide. I want answers to my questions. What exactly does your family know about me? Why did Hiro's great-great-whatever-grandfather have another one of Zarala's medallions? Who is the Lady of Glass? And what was the Battle of the Great Rift?"

"The Battle of the Great Rift? Oh, well, that is actually quite an interesting tale. You see—"

The metallic voice from nowhere interrupted. "We're sorry, but we have determined that your current line of questioning has an eighty-three percent chance of revealing information that is above your current security level. This dream will therefore be terminated."

Anne waved her arms at the ceiling. "No, wait! She was just about to—"

But it was too late.

Jocelyn and the others disappeared in a puff of smoke.

And somewhere a crow cawed once again.

At first it simply seemed to Anne as though all the lights had gone out. But then something blue pulsed nearby, and she realized she was no longer in the dream—or at least she was no longer in the laboratory. She was lying in a clearing in the middle of a forest. The ground felt rough beneath her and was littered with branches, dried leaves, and long twisted vines. The air was cool but stale. There were no sounds of tiny animals scurrying about in the night, or any sounds at all, for that matter. It resembled a dead tier, although it was difficult to tell in the dark.

"Activate GPS," she whispered.

Jeffery didn't appear.

She lifted her gauntlet-hand, and only then realized that the blue light was coming from her. Every second or so her gauntlet emitted a pulse. It gave the impression that the vines on the ground were moving—until one brushed against her leg and she discovered they really were moving. She jumped to her feet and danced out of the way. Looking closely, she clearly saw several of the vines writhing on the ground. They had been inching toward her, but as soon as the light touched them they recoiled as if the light were somehow causing them pain.

A long crystal pod was lying on the other side of the clearing, near the edge of the trees. The moving vines all seemed to be attached to it, and they slithered beneath it, away from the pulsing blue light, as she approached. From the end of the crystal pod, a single thicker vine stretched into the forest. Not daring to get too close, Anne peered into the pod and was able to make out a dark form at the center. It looked like a person, but with no distinct features.

A twig snapped to her left, and Anne dropped into a crouch, holding the gauntlet in front of her. Someone stepped from between the trees, an arm raised against the light.

"Anne?" said Penelope. "Is that you?"

"Pen!" Anne exclaimed.

Anne ran over and gave her friend a big hug.

"Where have you been?" asked Penelope. "I've been searching everywhere for you."

"I had another dream and only woke up a few minutes ago. How long have you been awake? Who else have you found?"

"A few of the pirates. They've spread out to look for the rest of their crew, but I came looking for you and Hiro."

Anne gripped Penelope's arm. "You don't know where Hiro is?"

"Not yet, but I'm sure we'll find him. I found you, didn't I?"

Anne studied their surroundings. "Do you have any idea where this is?"

Penelope shrugged. "Someplace weird."

"That's an understatement. I think those vines were trying to grab me." Anne looked around the clearing nervously. "If we fell into the BGFM, and we're not inside it, then maybe we're on the other side."

"What other side?"

"Remember? Octo-Horse Pirate said the BGFM was a barrier between the two parts of the world. This might be the other part, the one that contains the corruption."

If that was true, it disturbed Anne even more that this place reminded her so much of the dead tiers. Was there some connection? And if there was, who could possibly live in such a place?

"So what now?" asked Penelope.

"There's something very familiar about these pods," said Anne. "I say we follow that big vine and see where it leads."

"Are you sure that's a good idea? Maybe we should just wait here for the others."

Anne arranged several branches on the ground into a big arrow.

"There," she said. "Now anyone who passes through here will know which direction we went."

"Only if they have a light," said Penelope.

Anne headed into the forest, and Penelope followed, albeit somewhat reluctantly. They picked their way carefully through the trees, and Anne kept her gauntlet-hand out, both for light and to keep any stray vines at bay. They passed dozens of other clearings, all with crystal pods and slithering vines.

Anne shuddered. "Those things give me the creeps."

"They're not so bad," said Penelope. "They're just different from what you're used to."

"Different in a kill-me-and-eat-me kind of way, sure."

Some of the vines were gathered together in big clumps, as though they had caught something. Like the crystal in the first clearing, each pod had a single thicker vine that extended into the forest.

"Those thicker vines are all going in the same direction," said Anne.

"Is that supposed to be a good thing or a bad thing?" asked Penelope.

They continued onward. Eventually the forest gave way to a much larger clearing. The vines led to a giant crystal at the far side. Dozens of pods were here, all attached to the weave of vines.

The giant crystal looked all too familiar.

It very much resembled a Heartstone.

During their previous quest, Anne, Penelope, and Hiro had been summoned to appear before the queen of dragons in her throne room. The throne itself was actually a giant crystal known as a Heartstone. When dragons from the royal family were placed on the Heartstone as infants, it created a small stone inside them called a dragon stone. This granted them the ability to access the Old World archway network. Later, the Heartstone had been used to power a giant metal dragon, and a second Heartstone had powered a giant metal knight that Anne herself had operated.

But if this truly was a Heartstone, something was wrong with it. It was dark and cloudy and seemed to suck all the heat from the clearing.

"Are you sure we should be here?" asked Penelope, shivering.

"You're starting to sound like Hiro," said Anne, and she wondered at her usually fearless friend's sudden trepidation.

Anne approached the Heartstone cautiously. She walked around it, studying it from every angle but being careful not to get too near. Only a few yards beyond the stone was the edge of a deep black chasm. Anne shuddered as she peered down, trying not to imagine what it would be like to fall endlessly in the dark.

She turned her attention back to the Heartstone. It was definitely different from the others she had seen. In addition to its murky appearance, there appeared to be something inside. Not a person, but a shorter cylindrical object that very much resembled the computer terminal at the High Castle. It was almost as though the Heartstone had grown around the terminal.

A voice shouted from somewhere nearby.

"Quick," said Anne. "Over here."

They ducked behind a pod near the edge of the clearing, and Anne removed her cloak and wrapped it around her gauntlet-hand to hide the glow.

From the trees emerged two figures carrying a third

who appeared to be unconscious. It was difficult to be certain, but Anne thought she recognized the one being carried as a pirate from Marri's crew.

"Do you see an empty one?" asked the first carrier.

"Over there," said the second.

They put the pirate down beside a pod. Anne watched in horror as the vines slowly wrapped themselves around him. When the vines stopped moving, the crystal pod emitted a single green pulse. The green light traveled along the vine all the way to the Heartstone. In reply, the Heartstone emitted a steady red pulse that ran back along the vine. As soon as it reached the crystal, the dark form inside it began to writhe. The vine became transparent, and a thin line of black liquid flowed through it, all the way from the terminal inside the Heartstone into the pod. It looked just like the black liquid Marri had used to modify the gauntlet.

Anne placed her hands over her mouth to suppress the urge to cry out. The body inside the crystal pod thrashed back and forth, changing from a featureless blank into the form of an actual person. Finally, the black liquid stopped, and the body became still once again.

A seam appeared around the top of the pod, creating a lid. The two carriers pushed this off.

"Arise, brother," said the first carrier, and he helped

the person inside climb out. The blank body had completely transformed itself and now looked identical to the pirate wrapped in the vines. Around this new pirate's neck was a gold chain with a small crystal hanging from it.

The second carrier pointed to the tangle of vines. "What about this one?"

"Leave him," said the first. "We'll deal with the body later, once the vines are done with him."

The two carriers escorted the newly created double out of the clearing. As soon as they were gone, Anne leapt from her hiding place and ran over to the pirate. She pulled at the vines with her right hand, but they were too strong. Then she unwrapped her gauntlet-hand. As soon as the light hit the vines, they withdrew.

Anne placed her ear on his chest.

"He's still breathing," she said, greatly relieved.

She looked at the other pods in the clearing. Most seemed to have someone wrapped up in their vines. Anne hurried to the next clump.

"Anne, wait," said Penelope.

But Anne kept at it. Who knew how much time they had? She pressed her gauntlet-hand into the mass of vines, and the vines wiggled away. It was another of Marri's crew. Once the vines were completely gone, she moved to a third body and did the same. And then a fourth. In a matter of minutes, she managed to uncover all the bodies in the clearing, which amounted to nearly half the pirates. When Anne reached the final body, however, she recoiled in horror.

The face staring back at her was none other than Penelope.

"Pen?!" she cried.

Anne knelt down and shook her friend's shoulders.

This Penelope opened her eyes and screamed. "Anne, behind you!"

A pair of rough hands grabbed Anne by the shoulders and pulled her up. It was the first carrier. He had returned. She struggled to get away, but his grip was too strong. Someone else tried to grab her gauntlet-hand. Anne swung it and was rewarded with a satisfying thud accompanied by a cry of pain. Her would-be captors didn't give up, though, and grabbed for the gauntlet again, this time managing to wrap something around it. Finally she got a look at her other assailant.

It was Penelope.

The other Penelope.

A duplicate Penelope.

The gauntlet had made a shallow cut on her cheek,

and a thin stream of oily black smoke was seeping from it.

Anne gasped. "You're one of them. One of the doubles."

The Penelope Double smiled at her with a ghoulish grin. "I told you we should have stayed put."

"Do you want me to take her back to the other clearing?" asked the man holding Anne.

The Penelope Double tapped her chin. "Oh, I think we can find a place for her right here."

She strode over to one of the few empty pods. Anne struggled to break free from her captor, but he was too strong. He picked her up and followed.

"Place her here on the ground," said the Penelope Double. "Soon we'll have an Anne of our very own."

The man dropped Anne roughly to the ground, but just as the vines began to encircle her legs, a voice shouted from the forest. "Wait!"

Hiro burst into the clearing, gasping for breath. Anne's heart leapt for joy, which quickly turned to fear. Did Hiro have any idea what he'd just walked into? Before she could cry out a warning, he spoke.

"Some of the pirates escaped into the woods," he said between gulps of air. "The others need your help to capture them."

"Why aren't you helping them?" asked the carrier.

"I was, but this body isn't exactly built for endurance. I need a break. I can keep an eye on the prisoners here for you."

The Penelope Double looked at him suspiciously. "I didn't think the Darkflame boy had been captured yet."

"Well—well, I was. I mean *he* was."

The Penelope Double took a step toward him. "Prove it."

Anne's stomach muscles clenched. If this was the real Hiro, how in the world was he going to convince the other doubles that he was one of them?

"Fine. You want proof?" said Hiro. He rolled back the sleeve of his cloak, revealing the bandage Penelope had wrapped around his arm that morning. He undid the knot and began unwrapping the bandage. The last strip of cloth fell away, exposing his injury. Instead of blood, though, a thin stream of black smoke seeped from the wound.

"Satisfied?" he said.

"How did you get that cut?" asked the Penelope Double.

Hiro pointed to her cheek. "How did you get yours?"

The Penelope Double snarled at him but didn't argue

further. She checked on the still unconscious pirates to ensure the vines had reestablished their hold. Then she waved to her partner, and they headed out of the clearing. As soon as they were gone, Hiro ran over to Anne and unwrapped her gauntlet. Once exposed to the light, the vines that had been creeping around her quickly recoiled.

"Leave her alone!" yelled Penelope from the ground— the real Penelope.

"It's okay," said Hiro. "It's me."

Once Anne was free, Hiro moved to help Penelope, but she jerked away as far as the vines would allow her to move. "Don't you touch me! I saw what came out of your arm. Where's the real Hiro?"

"I *am* the real Hiro. I promise."

Penelope picked up a nearby branch and wielded it like a club.

Hiro sighed and retreated several paces, and Anne went over instead. She chased away several vines that had been making their way back toward Penelope and helped her to her feet.

"Stay back!" said Penelope, not taking her eyes off Hiro.

Hiro remained where he was. Penelope seemed

clearly convinced that he was a double, but Anne wasn't so sure.

Anne took a tentative step forward. "Hiro, is it really you?"

Hiro nodded.

She looked at his bandaged arm. "How did you do that thing with the black smoke? Was it magick?"

"No," he said.

"But you're not—surely you can't be a—a ..."

"The word you're looking for is *doppelganger*," said Hiro. "And yes, I am one. I always have been."

Question: How many doppelgangers does it take to screw in a light bulb?

Answer: What's a light bulb?

12

Construct and Chaos

Anne stumbled back, a hand over her mouth as if to stop the questions from flooding out. Had Hiro really just said what she thought he said? Had he really claimed to be one of those creatures? She flashed back over the months they had spent together, all that time getting Saint Lupin's ready, not to mention the two quests they had gone on. It didn't make any sense.

"But—but how can you be a—one of them?" asked Anne. She was afraid to use the word, as though not speaking it aloud could somehow make it not real.

Doppelganger. The word felt slippery and perilous on her tongue, and Anne desperately wanted Hiro to take it back, to say it wasn't true. They'd all have a good laugh at his joke and then figure out what to do next.

Hiro shifted nervously on his feet. "I guess I owe you both an explanation."

"Gee, you think?" stormed Penelope. Her fists were squeezed tight around the branch and her cheeks were flushed with anger. "Let's start with this: When you cut yourself this morning, you bled real blood. Red blood. Why is there black smoke now?"

Hiro pointed to the back of his neck. "My tattoo. It has magickal properties. My parents put it there to disguise my blood in case I ever got injured."

"Why did it stop working?" asked Anne.

Hiro shrugged. "I don't know for certain. I think maybe it doesn't work on this side of the barrier. I could always feel it there on my neck, like having a cold cloth pressed against my skin. As soon as we arrived here, though, the feeling disappeared. I immediately checked my wound, and sure enough, black smoke instead of blood."

Anne stepped closer and looked at his neck. "The tattoo is gone."

Hiro placed his hand over the back of his neck. "I guess that would explain why I don't feel it anymore."

"Could passing through the BGFM have removed it?"

Hiro shrugged. "Maybe."

"Why are you chatting with him like we even believe what he's saying?" demanded Penelope. "Don't you see? The missing tattoo proves he's one of those...those copies. The real Hiro, our Hiro, could be wrapped up in those vines somewhere, just like I was a moment ago. This could all be some trick."

"I'm telling you, it's really me," said Hiro. "I'm the same Hiro that's been with you all these months going on adventures and repairing the school."

"Prove it. Tell us something only we would know."

"Um, okay. I joined your adventuring group at the Death Mountain Quest Academy."

Penelope frowned. "Yeah, just before you blew it up. And anyone could access those records. How exactly is that supposed to make us trust you?"

Hiro nodded. "Right. Not the best example. How about this: You saved my life at the top of the Infinite Tower."

"By cutting the arm off one of your doppelganger friends. How much time did you have to plan out that little scenario while Anne and I were off looking for clues? Hmmm? Or did you and Mr. Shard discuss it before we even entered the tower?"

"I'd never even met him before that!"

"Sorry, not buying it. Try again."

Hiro looked desperate. "Fine. Back in the Never-Ending Maze, while Anne was unconscious those two days, you shared something with me you said you had never told anyone, not even Anne. You said your biggest dream was to become the most renowned sword fighter in all the Hierarchy, that it was more important to you than anything else, and that you would even leave our adventuring group if that's what it took to achieve your goal."

The revelation rattled Anne. Had Penelope really said that? After all their talks over the years of staying together, of planning wild adventures, she would really consider leaving?

Penelope glowered at Hiro, and it was clear she felt betrayed by this disclosure of their private conversation. She took a half step forward and raised the branch as though she intended to strike but then stopped.

"Satisfied now?" asked Hiro, sounding somewhat defiant.

"Not even close," growled Penelope.

She turned and ran into the forest.

"Penelope! Wait!" shouted Anne, but it was no use. Penelope had already disappeared among the trees.

Hiro wrung his hands. "I'm so sorry, Anne. My parents made me swear never to tell anyone."

"We can discuss it later. Come on!" yelled Anne, and she sprinted after Penelope.

The path Penelope had taken led along the chasm. Thankfully they didn't have to travel far. After just a few minutes of running, they entered another clearing. Penelope was there, kneeling in front of five pale stones the size of cannonballs. Anne motioned for Hiro to wait near the edge of the clearing while she continued forward. She approached slowly until she was just behind her friend.

"Penelope?" she asked hesitantly.

Penelope wiped tears from her eyes. "It's them."

"Who's them?"

Penelope pointed at the stones. There were inscriptions on them. Five names. One name per stone. HIERONYMUS. SIRI. RACHAEL. CONSTANTINE. It was the inscription on the fifth stone, however, that caught Anne's attention.

EVELYN.

"Jocelyn's sister," whispered Anne.

Penelope nodded. "Evelyn Daisywheel. That's what I guessed, too. And the one on that end must be Hieronymus Darkflame, Hiro's great-great-great-great-grandfather." The stone bearing the name Hieronymus sat somewhat separate from the other four and appeared much more weathered, as though it had been sitting there many years longer—perhaps even decades longer.

"Is that who you were referring to just now?" asked Anne. "When you said, 'It's them'?"

Penelope shook her head. "No. I meant Rachael and Constantine. Those were my parents' names. These are their graves. I tripped over a root and landed right in front of them." She reached a hand toward the stones but pulled back as though afraid they might disappear at her touch. "No one ever found—no one recovered their bodies. After their quest was reported failed, they were simply listed as dead. No one went looking for them."

Hiro walked over. "I'm sorry about your parents," he said in a subdued tone.

Penelope stiffened at the sound of his voice, but she kept staring straight ahead. "I don't know how my parents ended up buried here next to your ancestor, lost in some doppelganger-infested land, but I promise you this, Hiro Darkflame: I will never, ever forgive you, not for all eternity." She spoke the words softly, without a hint of anger, devoid of all emotion, and they were all the more heartbreaking because of it.

Hiro seemed about to respond, but Anne placed a gentle hand on his shoulder and shook her head and he held his peace. They had learned an astounding amount of information in a very short time, much of it disturbing, and even though Anne knew it wasn't fair to blame Hiro for what had happened to Penelope's parents, she also knew Penelope was going to need time to absorb everything. They all were.

A light appeared off to their right, not far inside the tree line.

"Someone else is here," said Anne.

"Or something," muttered Hiro.

Penelope rose to her feet and clutched her branch.

Anne took several cautious steps toward the trees. "Hello? Is someone there?"

The light moved closer.

"I'll deal with them," growled Penelope, and she started forward.

"No, wait!" said Anne. She couldn't explain why, but she didn't sense any danger from whoever or whatever this was. "It's okay," she called. "You can come out."

A young woman emerged timidly from the shadows. Her black hair was sticking out in all directions. She wore a sleeveless tunic that might once have been considered white but was now dark with dirt and grime. Her light brown pants were equally filthy and also torn at the knees. Her right arm ended just below the elbow, and strips of dirty white cloth had been wrapped around the stump and were being held in place by a tarnished silver belt.

The source of the light became apparent as soon as she stepped into the clearing. It was coming from her. She was surrounded by a soft glow.

Even more surprising than that, however, was her face. She looked exactly like Anne, except she had brown eyes, not yellow.

"Anne, they copied you, too!" said Penelope.

"No, it's not a doppelganger," said Anne. "It's the Construct!"

The young woman flinched at the sound of their shouts.

Penelope looked unconvinced. "How can you be sure?"

"Because I saw how they make the copies. They use those crystal pods, but I was never captured by one. Also, she's standing in the middle of a stump."

It was true. The Construct was currently standing half inside a rotten tree stump, as though it wasn't even there. She seemed oblivious.

Hiro leaned closer and whispered in Anne's ear. "I agree it's the Construct, but I think there's something wrong with her."

"You mean that she's lost her ability to become solid?"

"That, too. But I meant more than that. She seems frightened."

The Construct had a wild look in her eye.

Anne held out her hands in what she hoped would be taken as a gesture of peace. "We're not going to hurt you."

The Construct's eyes darted from side to side, constantly scanning the clearing for signs of danger. She kept her hand pressed close to her waistband, as though she were hiding something under her tunic.

"D-do I know you?" asked the Construct.

"Don't you recognize us?" asked Anne. "We've met before. Twice. You helped us defeat the Matron, and you fought with us against the dragon queen."

The Construct shook her head. "I have no recollection of such events. I have...difficulty...remembering things."

"Do you know how you got here?" asked Anne.

"I do not."

She remained well back, watching them guardedly and jumping at the smallest of noises

Anne turned to Hiro. "What do you think?"

"I don't know," he said. "Maybe this place is having a bad effect on her."

Anne looked back the way they had come. "The other times she appeared to us, there was always a computer terminal present. The only terminal we've seen around here is the one back inside that Heartstone, and it didn't look too healthy."

"It could have been affected by the corruption," suggested Hiro. "If that's the terminal she's projecting herself from, it might explain what's wrong with her."

Anne nodded.

There was a commotion from the other side of the clearing, and a moment later Marri and the other half of her pirate crew came bursting out of the forest. Marri had managed to hang on to her chair, although one of the pirates was helping her over the rough terrain.

"We heard someone shouting a minute ago and followed the voices," said Marri. "Is everyone okay?"

Anne wasn't quite sure how to answer that question.

"We're all in one piece," she said.

Marri approached and stopped in front of Anne. "I owe you and your group a sincere apology. First, for robbing your school. Second, for dragging you into this quest business. I was so focused on treasure that I couldn't see anything else. I had no idea my father would do something like this. I assumed he was after the treasure, too, and I wanted to impress him by finding it all by myself. But there's obviously something much bigger going on here. I've never seen him like this before. I certainly never thought he would send his own daughter into exile."

"What about the thing with his blood?" asked Anne. "Is he really Oswald?"

Marri shrugged. "I don't know anything about that."

"Don't worry. I'm sure we can figure all of this out," said Anne. "First, though, we need to escape from this place. If you haven't run into them already, there are creatures called doppelgangers. They can take on the appearance of a person."

"Oh, we've met them all right." Marri pointed at the Construct. "I see you even managed to capture one. We encountered several as well, but they got away. I'd be careful if I were you. They carry weapons."

"How did you figure out who is who?" asked Penelope.

Marri held up her hand. There was a strip of cloth wrapped around it with a tiny red spot in the center of the palm. "We bleed red. They don't."

Anne could see that the other pirates were all wearing bandages on their hands as well. They had obviously tested everyone to make sure no copies were hiding among their ranks. It was quick thinking on their part.

Marri held up a sharp stick. "Do you want us to test your group, too?"

"Everyone here is fine!" cried Anne a little too loudly. "I mean, we've already tested ourselves. We're all good. And for the record, this isn't my doppelganger. She's a hologram known as the Construct. We encountered her on our previous quests. She was created to act as an interface with the computer that created the world."

This seemed to pique Marri's interest. "Can she help us get back through the barrier?"

"I'm not sure. She seems to be having some trouble with—"

"Did someone say *barrier*?" asked the Construct.

"Why?" said Anne. "Do you remember something?"

The Construct rocked back and forth and pulled at

her hair. "It is difficult...to think....I remember the barrier....A rift opened...many years ago....We tried to prevent it....There was an explosion...and pain... and then darkness."

The Construct was panting from the effort, but there was no way for Anne to comfort her if she couldn't even touch her.

"Do you know how to stop the barrier from coming down?" asked Anne.

The Construct closed her eyes and nodded. "The... medallions."

"What medallions?"

"Zarala's medallions. Copper, silver, gold. Return them to the Lady of Glass. She will know what to do."

Before Anne could question her further, there was a sudden burst of light, and Jeffery appeared in the air above their heads.

"Finally," said Jeffery. "Can you believe—"

"Demon!" screamed the Construct, and she pulled a dagger out of her waistband.

"Where did she get a weapon?" cried Hiro.

Anne tried to block the Construct, but she passed right through Anne's body, dagger and all. She lunged at Jeffery. He swooped away, but only just in time. A thin slice from one of his feathers floated in the air for a split second and then dissipated into nothing. Apparently, even when holograms weren't solid they could still interact with other holograms.

The pirates surrounded Marri and adopted defensive postures.

"Whoa! Whoa! Whoa!" said Jeffery, hovering well above everyone. "What's the big idea?"

The Construct shook the dagger at him. "Return to the ground, you fiend, so that I might administer justice."

Anne jumped in front of the Construct and waved her arms. "It's okay! He's not a demon! He's with us!"

The Construct clenched her jaw. "He's the one who sent me here. He's the one who exiled me in this... this... desolate place. Come down and face me, wretch!"

"So, look, I'm just going to leave now and never return," said Jeffery. "Best of luck with everything."

"Jeffery, stay right there," said Anne. Even though she couldn't physically stop the Construct, Anne remained between them and held up her hands. "Please, whoever was responsible for sending you to this place, I promise it wasn't Jeffery."

The Construct eyed Jeffery with loathing. "And you are willing to vouch for this... this... vermin?"

"I am," said Anne.

"Fine," said the Construct, and she put away the dagger.

The pirates relaxed.

"Is everything all right?" asked Marri.

"I think it's just a matter of mistaken identity," said Anne.

Jeffery swooped down and landed on Anne's shoulder. "Or someone needs a lot less caffeine in their diet."

The Construct scowled. "Do not push me, bird."

"Where have you been?" Anne asked Jeffery.

"Trying to get through the barrier," he said. "When Octo-Horse Pirate sent you here, the BGFM blocked me, and I was forced to take a detour. The security program tried very hard to keep me out, and it took a while to break through the firewall—which uses real fire, by the way. I think I might have gotten a little singed." He ruffled his feathers. "But eventually I found my way through."

"Security program? Firewall?" asked Anne. "What are you talking about?"

"The computer. Ever since your pirate friends messed around with the gauntlet, my connection to the world computer has been growing. And there's a massive amount of information in there, let me tell you. I've barely put a dent in it."

Anne wasn't entirely sure how she felt about Jeffery being connected to the computer.

A chorus of shouts sounded in the distance.

"Now who is it?" asked Hiro.

"Oh, right," said Marri. "We might have run into a small group of doppelgangers. And by small group I mean massive army. I thought we gave them the slip, but it's entirely possible they've picked up our trail again. We need a way back through the barrier now."

Anne turned to Jeffery. "You broke in here. Is there a way out?"

Jeffery hesitated. "There is, but this is another of those things you're not going to like."

More shouts echoed in the distance. This time they sounded even closer and came from multiple directions.

"At this point, I don't think *liking* it matters," said Anne.

Jeffery pointed his wing in the direction of the chasm. "You have to jump."

Hiro groaned.

"That sounds like a bad idea," said Anne. "What's at the bottom?"

"Nothing."

"Then it really sounds like a bad idea," said Hiro.

"Don't worry, it's just how the BGFM looks from this side," explained Jeffery. "If we jump as a group, I can even control where we come out."

Marri pointed to the Construct. "What about her?"

"We need to bring her with us," said Anne. "Somewhere in her memory is the way to stop the barrier from coming down."

"And if she can't remember?"

"Then we'll cross that bridge when we come to it. For now, we need a way to bring her with us."

"She could travel inside the gauntlet," said Jeffery.

"Really?"

"Sure. I'm a hologram; she's a hologram. And there's plenty of space in here. Hold out your arm."

"Are you sure?"

"With my new connection to the computer? I can transfer her over no problem."

Anne felt uneasy, but they didn't have time for a lengthy debate. She raised her gauntlet-hand as instructed. Jeffery hopped onto it and closed his eyes. The gauntlet grew warm, but it was nothing like the heat from when she inserted a medallion. A moment later, a pulsing beam of pure white light shot out from the inset slot in the cuff and struck the Construct. She disappeared.

"Woo-hoo!" said Jeffery. "I have a houseguest!"

"Where did she go?" Anne said in a panic.

Jeffery inspected the gauntlet. "Don't worry. It will take her program a few minutes to sort itself out, but she's definitely in there."

"Fine," said Anne. "Let's get going, then."

Jeffery disappeared in a flash of light.

Everyone hurried back to the clearing with the Heartstone. They roused the rest of the pirate crew and positioned themselves along the chasm. The cold, dark void stretched away in front of them.

The shouts from the doppelgangers were close now. Very close.

Anne knew this was the right decision—the only decision, in fact. She just really wished at least one of their quests wouldn't involve falling off a ledge.

They all joined hands, took a collective breath, and leapt into the void.

HONEST EHD'S USED AIRSHIPS

"Gather close and feast your eyes on this one-of-a-kind airship. Forget those modern, ultrasleek vessels. This is a craft with real personality. Those holes in the hull? Ventilation to keep your crew nice and cool on those hot summer days. That crack in the mast? It adds character. The fire damage to the deck? As the saying goes, what doesn't kill you makes you stronger. Pardon me, ma'am? Er, yes, I'm afraid it did kill the previous owners. Which is why you won't beat our low, low price!"

The *Leaky Mermaid*

Anne's feet hit the ground hard. She stumbled but managed to remain upright. When she lifted her head, though, she nearly fell over in shock. It was still dark, but now there were stars and a full moon providing enough light for her to see the massive airship directly in front of her—or rather, providing enough light for her to see that she was directly in front of it.

She raised her arms, but the airship missed her completely. This wasn't surprising considering it wasn't actually moving. Nor were any of the dozens of airships around it. They were all resting on the ground, propped up on wooden beams. The airships were of various sizes and configurations, from tiny one-person rowboats to bulky trawlers and streamlined yachts, but they all had two things in common: One, all of them appeared to be empty, and two, all of them were in a serious state of disrepair.

While Anne tried to figure out exactly where she had landed, the gauntlet crackled with lines of blue energy. Seconds later the Construct appeared beside her in a flash of light. She looked somewhat transparent, and Anne could almost make out the shape of the airship behind her.

"Are you okay?" asked Anne.

"I think so," the Construct said shakily. "But that was...disturbing. It felt like I was being ripped into pieces, and then the gauntlet kicked me out here."

Jeffery appeared next to them in his own burst of light. "Yeah, it looks like space actually *is* going to be an issue. It's not that the gauntlet is small, but her program is megahuge. The gauntlet simply can't contain her."

Intermittent streaks of energy continued to snake around the gauntlet.

"Will she be okay?" asked Anne.

Jeffery landed on Anne's arm and examined the

energy bursts. "Her program is already leaking out. The longer she's in here, the more unstable she'll become. Which means the sooner we can upload her into a proper computer terminal, the better."

"Do not concern yourself with my well-being," said the Construct. "Proceed with your mission."

"Is there any chance this could affect you, too?" Anne asked Jeffery. She hadn't even considered that possibility before agreeing to the transfer.

Jeffery saluted Anne with a tiny wing. "No worries, ma'am. I'm good to go."

Penelope, Hiro, Marri, and the rest of her crew ran out from between two airships.

"There you are!" said Marri. "I thought we'd lost you."

Neither Penelope nor Hiro said anything. Hiro's cheeks looked paler than usual, and Penelope had her arms crossed and was making a point of not looking in his direction.

"What is this place?" Anne asked Jeffery.

"You said we needed transportation," said Jeffery.

"I don't recall saying that."

"Isn't your plan to prevent the barrier from going down?"

"Yes."

"Well, in order to do that you need to return to the High Castle, right? With the *Blue Daisy* no longer available, how exactly were you planning to do that?"

"So why didn't you just take us directly there?" asked Anne. "You said you could control where we came out."

"I tried, but something blocked me from taking us there. It's the one place we couldn't go. It might have to do with the fact that the castle has already been activated. Maybe it's a security feature, to prevent people from simply dropping in and turning it off again."

They made their way among the airships until they came to a clearing with a small shack. Most of the windows were boarded up, and the one window that wasn't had been smashed at some point and never replaced. The front door wasn't in the doorframe but instead was being used to prop up one end of the porch roof.

"This looks promising," said Marri.

Anne stepped onto the front porch and pulled a thin chain hanging by the door. Inside the shack a little bell rang. A series of grunts, thumps, and curses emanated from the interior. There was the sound of footsteps approaching, and a thin man with greasy black hair and wearing a ragged coat and carrying a rusty lantern came to the doorway.

"Can't you read?" he said in a gruff voice. "The sign says 'Keep Out.' Not to mention it's nearly midnight."

Anne cleared her throat. "We'd like to purchase an airship."

The man's expression darkened. "If you've only come here to make fun of me, you can be on your way. I have better things to do with my time, thank you very much. Like watch the mold grow on my walls."

He started back inside.

"Wait!" said Anne. "We're not making fun of you. We really do need an airship."

The man stopped. "I'm not in the used-airship business anymore. The council revoked my license."

"You mean the Wizards' Council?" asked Hiro.

"Is there another council? Accused me of selling substandard airships. The nerve of them, right?"

"Er, *were* they substandard?"

"Of course not!" the man roared, clearly offended by the mere suggestion. "Best used airships on the market. I mean, sure, some of them had probably seen better days. But that's the whole beauty of buying used. You get something that's stood the test of time."

"So what happened after the council took away your license?" asked Anne.

He shrugged. "I turned the place into a junkyard."

Marri pointed to the rows of airships visible in the moonlight. "Okay, so sell us a piece of junk, then. Is there anything here that can still fly?"

The man leaned against the doorframe and studied them. "Do you have any money?"

"Um," said Anne.

"That's what I thought. I might not be in the business anymore, but I can smell a bunch of deadbeats a mile away"

"Hey, we're not deadbeats," said Jeffery. "We just happen to be financially challenged at the moment."

"Look, I wish we had time to explain," said Anne, "but we have something very important that needs doing and we need a ship. Please, won't you help us?"

He crossed his arms. "Why should I?"

"Because we're on the run from the Wizards' Council, and helping us would really annoy them," said Marri.

The man brightened considerably at this. "You don't say? Well, in that case, my junkyard is your junkyard. What do you need?"

"An airship that flies," Anne said hopefully.

He scratched his chin. "Most of them have been sitting here for years. I sell the parts whenever I can. I doubt there's a working ship on the lot." He clapped his hands together. "But for a chance to stick it to those wizards, I'm willing to put in a little overtime." He stuck out his hand for Anne to shake. "I'm Honest Ehd, by the way."

"I'm Anne," she said, and shook his hand.

Anne introduced the rest of the group.

Honest Ehd smiled. "Pirates, eh? Even better."

He led them along the rows of airships to a ship near the back of the lot. It was a three-masted galleon with fore- and aftercastles, metal plates along the sides of the hull, and two great propellers jutting from the stern. At some point in its history it might have been a formidable warship, but those days were long past. The sails needed mending, there was only one working cannon, and many of the deck planks were either rotten or missing altogether.

"The *Leaky Mermaid*?" said Hiro, reading the name painted on the side of the ship.

"It's the best ship on the lot."

"It looks like the sort of death trap even Death itself might be afraid of," said Penelope.

"Don't worry," said Honest Ehd. "It'll fly, or my name isn't Honest Ehd."

"Is that your real name?" asked Hiro.

"No, it's actually Morally Ambiguous Patrick. But the ship will still fly, guaranteed."

Honest Ehd's enthusiasm couldn't be rivaled. For the next several hours they stripped any parts they needed from the surrounding ships. When they couldn't find a necessary part, Ehd fashioned a workable substitute from other pieces of junk lying about. While the crew worked with Honest Ehd to get the ship ready, Anne, Penelope, Hiro, Marri, Jeffery, and the Construct met in Ehd's shack to devise a plan. They lit several warped candles and gathered around a small table. Penelope made a point of not standing next to Hiro.

"So which medallion do we go after first?" asked Marri.

"The gold medallion is still with Octo-Horse Pirate at the High Castle," said Jeffery.

"How do you know that?" asked Anne.

"I can locate my current quest medallion anywhere in the Hierarchy."

"Even though it's in the other gauntlet?"

"Yep," said Jeffery. "And if he takes it somewhere else, I'll still be able to find it."

"Okay, that's good to know," said Anne. "In that case, I guess it makes sense to concentrate on the other two first."

"They should still be in the cargo hold of the *Blue Daisy* along with the rest of your medallions," said Marri. "I had Mr. Locke put them there after he confiscated them from Pirate Fifty-Three."

"No, the silver medallion is at Saint Lupin's," said Anne. "The gauntlet released it after I finished the first quest. It's in a laboratory at the bottom of the tier. I ended our first quest inside a chamber labeled PROJECT A.N.V.I.L., and it took the medallion. Your crew wouldn't have found it."

"But someone else might have," said Hiro. "I did a full inventory while we were completing the renovations, including the laboratory. The Wizards' Council conducted a thorough investigation after the quest and all the equipment was removed."

Anne was shocked by this news. "What?! But that's my stuff!"

"I don't suppose anyone knows where the council might keep such objects?" asked Marri.

Hiro nodded. "I do. There's a secret warehouse tier where they store all major quest-related items."

Penelope sneered. "And you just happen to know that?"

"It's also where the council day care is located. My parents used to drop me off there all the time."

Anne pressed her fingers against the sides of her head. Stopping the barrier was becoming more and more complicated by the minute, and time was running out. If they didn't gather the medallions and find the Lady of Glass by early morning, it would be too late.

"Since the other two medallions are already at the High Castle, I suggest we focus our efforts on acquiring the silver medallion first," said Marri. She turned to Hiro. "I assume you can lead us to the secret facility you mentioned?"

"I can," said Hiro. "But they have heavy security. There are checkpoints at each warehouse and guards patrolling everywhere. The perimeter is guarded by hidden traps. There are lots of wizards, too. It would be pretty much impossible to sneak in, and attacking it would be inadvisable, to say the least."

"I could easily sneak past the guards and locate the medallion for you," offered the Construct.

"And pick it up how?" said Penelope.

"Ah, yes, there is that."

"Well, we can't just walk in the front door and ask for the medallion," said Marri. "How would we explain a bunch of students popping in for a visit?"

"Hiro's letter!" shouted Anne.

"What?" said Hiro.

"Don't you remember? Your mother invited you to Take Your Student to Work Day. We can go to the facility under the guise of being visiting students, and then search for the medallion."

"In the middle of the night?" Hiro sputtered.

"Honest Ehd figured the repairs to the *Leaky Mermaid* would take close to six hours," said Anne. "By the time they finish, it'll be closer to morning. We can just say we were eager to get an early start."

"An early start? It'll be five o'clock in the morning!"

"Trust us," said Penelope. "Coming from you it will be totally believable."

Marri smiled. "That sounds like the perfect plan, and we apparently have the perfect candidate to lead the way."

Hiro looked stunned. "M-me? But I can't—I couldn't possibly."

Anne rested a hand on his shoulder. "You've been there. You're already familiar with the layout. That makes you the best person for the job."

"But I'm no good at this stuff," Hiro protested. "I'm terrible at lying. My tongue gets all twisted up, and I start rambling."

"Oh, I don't know," said Penelope. "I'd say you're a pretty convincing liar myself."

"Hiro, if we had another option we'd take it, but we don't," said Anne. "We need to get into that warehouse, and you're going to have to lead us. That's final."

"But—but why do you still get to decide what's final?"

"Because I'm the protagonist."

"Er, that's not quite true," said Jeffery.

"What do you mean?" asked Anne.

"Well, Octo-Horse guy has the gold medallion now, which technically makes him the Official Protagonist."

"Then what does that make me?"

"Why, the villain, of course."

"The what?!"

Jeffery hopped back several steps. "Or the Official Antagonist, if you prefer. Whatever floats your boat."

"But that's terrible!" cried Anne, flabbergasted. "I don't want to be the bad guy."

Jeffery flapped his wings. "You? What about me? Being the GPS for some scoundrel isn't exactly going to be a glowing entry on my résumé."

"But what does that mean? What do I do?"

"Well, typically the antagonist tries to sabotage the quest," said Penelope.

"That's terrible!"

"What's the big deal? It's what we're already trying to do, isn't it?"

"Yeah, but it's the principle of the thing," said Anne.

"Perhaps we should worry about crossing the antagonist bridge when we come to it," suggested Marri. "First we need to get into that warehouse."

Despite his protests to the contrary, Hiro turned out to be an excellent planner. He drew a rough layout of the secret warehouse facility from memory, and Locke crafted four very convincing fake IDs, for Anne, Penelope, Marri, and the Construct. Hiro would use his real ID, since he was playing himself.

"That should be enough," said Marri. "The rest of the crew will remain aboard in case something goes wrong and we have to leave in a hurry."

Just under six hours later, a newly painted *Leaky Mermaid* sailed out of Honest Ehd's lot. The sails even sported the seven-pointed black star of the Wizards' Council. Ehd had also managed to scrounge up some knives and swords for the crew, although most of them were rusty and bent.

"Give those wizards a swift kick in the rump for me!" Honest Ehd shouted from his porch.

Beyond acquiring a means of transportation, there was also the issue of how they were going to reach their destination. Despite scouring the junkyard from top to bottom, they had been unable to locate working dragon-fire engines to install on the airship. Using regular sails under normal conditions would take them several weeks to reach the warehouse tier from their current location—maybe even months, Marri estimated. They had discussed the problem at length and had finally arrived at a solution: They needed a real dragon.

There was only one problem.

"So let me see if I understand correctly," grumbled Nana after they had released her from the metal sphere in which she had been imprisoned. "You can't change me back to my normal size, but you still want me to fireball an entire airship halfway across the Hierarchy—"

"Using a premium fireball," added Anne.

"—yes, using a premium fireball no less, thank you— which is something I wouldn't attempt even on my best day. And that's overlooking the fact that I've been imprisoned in a hollow metal sphere, in the dark, hanging from some pirate's belt for the past twenty-one hours."

"Nana, we're so sorry," said Anne. "So much has been happening, and we completely forgot you weren't with the others trapped in the dice."

"Will I at least get paid this time?"

"Er," said Anne.

Nana harrumphed.

"Don't mind her," Jeffery said to Marri. "Her personality dial is permanently stuck on cantankerous."

"Please, Nana," Anne begged. "This is really important."

"Oh, well, if it's *really* important, then I guess I'd better do it."

Anne could tell that more than anything, they had hurt Nana's feelings.

"Whatever you want, as soon as we stop the barrier we'll do it. We'll buy you a whole herd of cattle. We'll send you on a lavish vacation to a dragon spa. We'll let you sleep in the office corner again."

"In Dog's basket?"

Dog's sleeping basket was a point of contention between the fire lizard and Nana. Prior to their first quest, Nana had disguised herself as Dog and gotten used to sleeping in the basket in the main office.

Nana smiled. "I'm just joking. Of course I'll help. I just like to see people grovel every once in a while." She flew to the stern of the airship. "Normally I would follow directly behind, but given my current size I don't know how long it will take me to catch up with you. It certainly won't be instantly."

"Just try your best," said Anne. "I'm sure it will take us a little while to find the medallion anyway."

Despite her diminutive size, Nana sucked in an impressive amount of air. After a brief pause, she shot out a green fireball. It was tiny at first, but it quickly expanded until it engulfed the *Leaky Mermaid*. The fireball shot off at an incredible speed. Green energy burst all around, causing Penelope's teeth to chatter and Anne's hair to stand on end. The hull of the *Leaky Mermaid* creaked and groaned, but it held together.

When the fireball dissipated, it dropped the airship smoothly back into normal flight.

A single tier glowed in the moonlight in the distance. It was perfectly flat, as though someone had razed the hills and filled the valleys. There were dozens of rows of long narrow buildings, no doubt the warehouses in which the council stored any quest-related items it had confiscated. As Anne took everything in, she wondered how in the world they were going to find one tiny silver medallion.

"That's it," said Hiro. "Nana was exactly on target."

As they glided toward the tier, the pirates were unusually subdued. Everyone knew that any irregularities whatsoever could spell disaster and get them all arrested—or worse. They had all taken Hiro's warnings about the security very seriously.

The docks were mostly empty. Only two airships were currently tied up. One was under repair, and the other was having its cargo unloaded. The *Leaky Mermaid* eased into a berth. The crew secured the ship and extended the ramp, and Anne, Penelope, Hiro, Marri, and the Construct disembarked.

A robed figure approached, no doubt one of the wizards from the council. The wizard was flanked by two iron knights. They were easily as tall as the ones at Saint Lupin's, and even more heavily armored. Anne experienced the momentary impulse to run back up the ramp and sail away, but she resisted.

Penelope leaned over to the Construct and whispered, "You're standing in my foot."

Indeed, the Construct's foot was currently inside Penelope's.

"Sorry," said the Construct, and she took a step to the right. They could only hope the wizard hadn't noticed.

The wizard marched up to them and lowered her hood.

"This is a top-secret facility," she said. "And it's not even dawn yet."

Hiro stepped forward to present himself as the leader of their group. "Yes, we know. We're here for—"

"No one is permitted on these premises without proper authorization."

Hiro held out the forms. "Well, actually, we do have—"

"In fact, no one is permitted to know these premises even exist without proper authorization."

"If you look at these forms, I think you'll see—"

"And even if you do get proper authorization, this facility is so top secret we would ignore it and arrest you anyway."

Hiro faltered. "I, uh..."

The wizard crossed her arms. "Also, the penalty for trespassing is immediate execution."

"E-execution?"

The wizard snapped her fingers.

And the iron knights drew their swords.

———◄•►———

*THE ADVENTURER'S GUIDE TO
SUCCESSFULLY INFILTRATING A TOP-SECRET
FACILITY* OFFERS THE FOLLOWING TIPS:

1) Use a disguise.

2) Always have a backup plan.

3) Always have a backup plan for your backup plan.

———◄•►———

Secrets of the Wizards' Council

Hiro stumbled back and reached for his spell catalog. Marri and Penelope drew their swords and fanned out to either side, ready to throw themselves into the fray. The Construct also drew her dagger, even though having a non-solid hologram in a fight wouldn't really help much. Anne raised her gauntlet-hand to summon the Three-Handed Sword. Then the council wizard started laughing and everyone paused. In fact, the wizard was laughing so hard that she nearly fell over.

"What's so funny?" demanded Penelope.

"The looks on your faces," said the wizard between wheezes. "I'm telling you, this never gets old." She wiped a tear from her eye. "Sorry, that's just a prank we like to play on visiting students. I assume you're here for Take Your Student to Work Day. Bit early, though, aren't we?"

"We didn't want to miss out on anything," said Hiro.

Anne looked again at the looming hulks of the iron knights and the sharp edges of their sword blades.

"Oh, don't mind them," said the wizard. She held out her hand; in her palm sat a glass cube with a dragon stone suspended inside. "They can't do anything unless I order them to."

"You have iron knights here?" asked Anne.

The wizard nodded. "Only recently. They're extremely helpful to have around."

"So, just to be clear, we're not being executed?" asked Marri.

"Of course not," said the wizard, still chuckling. "But your reactions were priceless. Wait until I tell the others." She extended a hand. "Kelley Stampfoot. Pleased to make your acquaintance."

Hiro quickly regained his composure and shook her hand. "Hiro Darkflame."

Stampfoot clapped her hands together. "Oh, you'd be Tora and Raiden's boy, yes? I haven't seen them in months. How are they doing?"

"They're fine," said Hiro. "And in case it seems in any way unusual or strange that we've arrived here without them, they said to tell you they would be along later, after they finish secret agenting...people...and stuff. Because that's what they do. For their jobs. Because they're agents. Secret ones."

Anne elbowed Hiro in the ribs to get him to stop talking.

"Wonderful!" said Stampfoot, seeming not to notice anything unusual. "So, what would you like to see first?"

Hiro passed her their student forms with trembling hands. "We completely at random heard about a silver quest medallion. It was removed from a place called Saint Lupin's, although in using the word *removed*, I don't mean to insinuate any wrongdoing on the part of the Wizards' Council. I'm sure they have perfectly legitimate reasons for confiscating objects with no legal basis for doing so, however questionable that might appear to the general public. Anyway, we thought seeing the medallion might be interesting, though not to steal it or anything. And not all of us thought it would be interesting, because uniformity of opinion among students our age might present undue cause for suspicion. So we took a vote, and some of us won and the rest of us are having a bad attitude about it."

Marri kept motioning for Anne to give Hiro a swift kick to make him stop, but again the wizard didn't seem to notice anything odd. Penelope's surly demeanor at least lent a certain credibility to his last comment about some of them having bad attitudes.

Stampfoot scratched her chin. "Saint Lupin's, hmmm? Name sounds familiar, but I can't quite place it. No matter. Come with me, and I'm sure we can get you looked after."

She put an arm around Hiro's shoulders and led them along the dock into a two-story building, still chuckling to herself as they went. Stampfoot regaled the several wizards inside with the little joke she had played on the students. The other wizards laughed out loud, and one even shook Stampfoot's hand. Anne kept a tight smile on her face and simply nodded along, hoping to show a good sense of humor.

Stampfoot told them to wait and went into another room. When she returned, she was holding a long piece of parchment. "Warehouse Thirteen. We should be able to find what you're looking for in there. I'll take you over so you don't get lost. The layout here can be a little confusing at first. You don't want to step in any of the bear traps."

Anne wondered if the wizard was serious about bear traps or whether it was another joke, but she was too nervous to ask.

With the iron knights still accompanying them, they zigzagged their way across the grounds, down small streets and between enormous warehouses. Any guards they met along the way seemed to take Stampfoot's presence as conveying an unspoken stamp of approval upon their entire group. At each checkpoint, the guards simply waved them through until finally they arrived at a building with THIRTEEN painted on the side. Stampfoot ushered them inside.

"Here we go," she said. She pointed down the center aisle. "According to the manifest, the items you're looking for are in the third section, about halfway down on the left. Feel free to make your way there, and I'll join you after I fill out some paperwork."

The first section of the warehouse was filled with long rows of shelves and stacks of crates. They walked down the center aisle to the far end and proceeded through the doors there. Everyone came to a halt. Row upon row of iron knights filled the second section. Their armor had been polished until it shone like new, and every one of them had a sword strapped to its side. Each also had a dragon stone in its helmet. The stones were what powered the knights.

"Erm, that's a lot of iron knights," said Anne nervously.

Hiro looked ready to pass out. "I—I didn't realize there were that many knights in the whole Hierarchy."

"What could the Wizards' Council want with them?" asked Marri.

"World domination," said the Construct.

"I'm not sure," said Anne uneasily. "But we might be able to make use of one. Jeffery, can you tune the dragon stone on one of those knights to the gauntlet?"

Jeffery appeared in a flash of light. "No problem."

The little sparrow flitted up and landed on the helmet of the nearest iron knight, just above the dragon stone. He concentrated for a few seconds, and there was a brief flash from the stone. Anne gestured toward the knight, and it took a step forward.

"Are you sure this is a good idea?" asked Marri. "Someone might notice a missing knight."

"I've learned it's always good to have a backup plan," said Anne. "If something goes wrong, we can use the extra muscle. And if anyone asks, we'll simply tell them we don't know what happened. They're not going to suspect that a group of students moved one of their knights."

They continued between the rows of knights and proceeded through the doors at the far end.

The third section was much like the first: long rows of shelves with crates of all shapes and sizes. Halfway down the center aisle sat a stack of crates belonging to their school, just as Stampfoot had indicated. Oddly, though, they were all labeled SAINT LUFFIN'S.

"Is all this stuff from Saint Lupin's?" asked Marri.

Anne stared in disbelief. "They told me everything was destroyed in the fire."

"It looks like a few things weren't," said Hiro.

Anne couldn't believe how much the council had removed without her knowledge or permission. It infuriated her, but she willed her fists to unclench. There would be plenty of time for outrage later. Hopefully. Right now they needed to focus on the task at hand.

Marri picked up a crowbar that was lying atop one of the crates. "We'd better get to work. There's no telling when that wizard will be back."

She shoved the crowbar under the lid of the nearest crate and pried the lid off. It fell to the floor with a clatter. Anne peered inside and immediately stepped back. The smell of smoke and charred wood was overpowering.

"I'm guessing there's not too much of value in that one," said Hiro, holding his nose.

The contents of the next several crates were much the same.

"Why would they want all this junk?" asked Anne.

"It's Old World technology," said Hiro. "Even burned to a crisp like this, it could prove to be of value someday."

Penelope leaned against one of the crates. "Maybe the council stored anything of real value someplace else. You'd think our 'leader' would have known that."

Hiro looked hurt but said nothing.

Anne wandered over to the next row. There were five large cylindrical chambers clustered together in the aisle—or what was left of them, anyway. Seven chambers had formed a semicircle in the middle of the laboratory, but they were all at least partially destroyed from the fire, and two of them completely so.

"Over here," said Anne.

The others joined her.

"What does 'Project C.R.O.W.N.' mean?" asked Marri, pointing to an inscription barely visible near the bottom of the least damaged chamber.

Anne shrugged. "I don't know. I was never able to—"

"It's an acronym," said Jeffery. "It stands for Cryostasis Recovery Operation World Network."

Anne blinked. "How do you know that?"

"I'm telling you, this upgrade has given me access to everything."

"What's cryostasis?" asked Marri.

"It's kind of like freezing," Hiro explained. "In the Old World, it was used to preserve things for a really long time. Chambers like these were designed to hold people in stasis."

"There was an eighth cylinder, or cryochamber, or whatever," said Anne.

Everyone spread out and searched up and down the rows.

"Here," said Penelope a minute later.

She was standing next to a stack of crates, but another cylinder could be seen peeking over the top. Even with everyone working together, the crates proved too heavy to move. Anne brought over the iron knight. It easily pushed the crates out of the way until they had a clear path. Anne examined the chamber. Scorch marks on the surface showed it had clearly been damaged by fire as well. Anne could just barely make out the words engraved at the bottom: PROJECT A.N.V.I.L.

"This was the pillar I used to complete the quest," said Anne.

"And what does *that* inscription stand for?" asked Marri.

Everyone looked to Jeffery, but he shook his head. "Beats me. For that one all I'm getting from the computer is 'File not found.'"

"Where's the silver medallion?"

"It should be inside," said Anne.

She searched the interior of the chamber and found the slot where she had inserted her gauntlet. The medallion wasn't in the slot, although there was a small button at the bottom. Anne reached down and pressed it. A small hatch opened, and the silver medallion was lying inside. Anne picked it up and jumped out of the chamber.

Holding the medallion brought back a lot of memories: jumping from the Matron's office window, leaping off the drawbridge, climbing the Infinite Tower, fighting off a swarm of mechanical dragonflies.

"Did you find what you're looking for?" asked a voice behind them.

Stampfoot had arrived along with her two iron knights.

Everyone jumped at the sound of her voice, and Anne bumped into one of the crates so hard that she knocked it over.

"Uh, sorry about that," said Anne, rubbing a throbbing shoulder. She bent down and tried to shove some of the items back into the crate.

"Not to worry," said Stampfoot. "Happens all the time. Let me help you with that. Hold this for a moment, would you?" she said to Penelope, and she handed her the glass cube with the dragon stone.

They quickly gathered up the contents of the crate and resealed it. Still crouched on the floor, Stampfoot tapped her finger on the label on the side of the crate.

"Ah, Saint Luffin's! Now I remember it," she said. "Didn't some famous quest happen there recently? It was in all the news."

"I'm not sure," said Anne.

"We wouldn't know anything about those events or have participated in any way, despite our likenesses to the individuals involved," added Hiro.

Stampfoot rose to her feet. "Curious. And speaking of quests, that's a very interesting gauntlet you have there."

Anne could have kicked herself. She should have wrapped it again.

"It's, uh, part of a school project," said Anne. "We had to build a replica of our favorite gauntlet. I chose the gauntlet that won the award this year for Best Illegal Quest That Nearly Destroyed the Entire World."

Stampfoot snapped her fingers. "But that's the one. That's the same quest I was just talking about. It's where we got the idea to create these control cubes for the knights. Surely you must know of it, then, yes?"

Stampfoot bumped into the iron knight Anne had used to move the crates and looked up. "Say, who left this here?"

"It wasn't us," said the Construct, and it was only then that Anne realized the Construct was standing half inside one of the crates.

Stampfoot stared at the Construct for a moment, and then looked at Anne, and then at her gauntlet again. Her eyes widened as realization struck her.

"But if you're...and that medallion is...then that would mean...but how did you—"

A metal hand clamped onto the wizard's shoulder

from behind and lifted her into the air. It wasn't the iron knight Anne had been controlling. It was one of the wizard's own knights. Her other iron knight turned and opened its back, and the first one stuffed the wizard into it. Her shouts were cut off as soon as the back of the second knight closed.

"It worked!" said Penelope incredulously. She was still holding the glass cube in her hand. "I thought about stuffing her in there, and the knights actually did it."

"Will she be okay?" asked Marri, pointing to the iron knight with the wizard trapped inside.

Penelope nodded. "I ordered the knight to place her in stasis."

"She should be fine, then," said Anne. "But *we* won't be if we stay here any longer."

They headed back out of the warehouse, resisting the urge to run as fast as possible. Anne decided it was best to bring all three iron knights with them, just in case. As they exited the warehouse, the guard on duty stopped them.

"Where's Stampfoot?" asked the guard.

"She, uh, said she had some business to take care of," said Anne. "But we finished the tour, and she ordered her iron knights to escort us back to the docks."

"Very well," said the guard. "You may proceed."

He waved them on, and they passed through the other checkpoints just as easily.

Anne left the three iron knights at the end of the dock, assuming someone would check on them eventually. She was tempted to take one of them with her but couldn't risk the wizards catching her doing it.

There was a commotion on the deck of the ship when they got there. Nana had finally arrived, out of breath, but that wasn't it. The pirates were gathered in a circle around two people dressed all in black. One was a small woman with tan skin and shoulder-length, gray-black hair, and the other was a tall man with a very large stomach. Anne recognized them immediately. They were Hiro's parents, and if they were aware of what she and the others had been up to, it could mean big trouble.

Hiro pushed past her. "Mother? Father? What are you doing here?"

Mrs. Darkflame walked over and placed a hand on his shoulder. "We've come to take you home."

They crowded into the captain's cabin once again. This time it was Anne, Penelope, Hiro, his parents, and the

Construct. Marri and her crew had been kind enough to give them some privacy, but Hiro had insisted that Anne and Penelope be allowed to come with him. The Construct was only present because she was tied to Anne's gauntlet.

"What are you doing here?" Hiro asked his parents as soon as the door was closed.

Mrs. Darkflame raised an eyebrow. "We work here, young man. The real question is, what are you doing here at a top-secret council facility? And why is the council issuing warrants for your arrest?"

"I—I—that is, we—we..."

Mrs. Darkflame tutted at him. "If you can't lie faster than that, don't bother."

"But how did you even know I was here?" Hiro protested.

"We didn't," said Mr. Darkflame. "We placed a security alert on the materials taken from the laboratory beneath Saint Lupin's. We didn't agree with the council removing them from the premises and thought it best for someone to keep an extra eye on them. The guards were to notify us in the event anyone came to investigate the contents, which they did less than an hour ago. We had no idea it was you until we arrived here. And then, of course, we were informed that you were here for Take Your Student to Work Day. Imagine our surprise, since we never received a response from you."

"You didn't tell them anything, did you?" asked Anne.

Mr. Darkflame's eyes flared. "Tell them what? That our son is obviously involved in some ridiculous school prank? Honestly, I thought Jocelyn had a better handle on things than that. You're just lucky the guards here haven't received the news reports yet. We brought the reports with us but held them back once we heard you were on-site."

Mrs. Darkflame noticed the bandage on Hiro's arm and her demeanor changed. "Is everything okay?"

"If you're asking whether we know your son is a doppelganger, the answer is yes," spat Penelope.

Mrs. Darkflame's expression became very grim. "Hiro, what have you done?"

"He saved us," said Anne. "We were trapped on the other side of the barrier, and the doppelgangers, the bad ones, would have taken us prisoner and made copies of us. It was quick thinking on Hiro's part, but to convince them, he had to reveal who he really was. Lucky for us, the barrier removed his tattoo."

Hiro's parents were momentarily thunderstruck.

"The tattoo is gone?" said Mrs. Darkflame.

Mr. Darkflame tapped his fingers on the table. "Hiro, we must insist that you come with us right now!"

"I'm not going anywhere with you," said Hiro. "At least, not until we've finished."

Mr. Darkflame snorted. "Now see here—"

"Please," said Hiro. "We don't have a lot of time. This is important, and I won't abandon my group. Can't you just restore the tattoo?"

"Certainly we can, but the spell takes days to perform, so you'll have to return home."

Hiro shook his head stubbornly. "We don't have days. I'll make do without it."

Mrs. Darkflame placed her hands on her hips. "What is so important that you would risk real prison time, and possibly even worse, if anyone else finds out about your condition?"

"What can you tell us about Hieronymus Darkflame and the gold medallion?" Anne interjected, hoping to steer the conversation in a more useful direction.

Mr. Darkflame fell into a coughing fit, and Mrs. Darkflame turned pale.

"We found his grave on the other side of the barrier. We're trying to figure out how he ended up there."

Mr. Darkflame recovered and nodded. "Very well, then. But understand that what we are about to tell you involves a secret held by our family for many years. Long ago, the Darkflames were entrusted with a gold medallion bearing the image of a dragon."

"The Sign of Zarala," said Anne, Penelope, and Hiro in unison.

"Er, yes, that's correct. Well, roughly a hundred and fifty years ago, Hieronymus was approached by a strange woman in need of help."

"The Lady of Glass," the three of them said in unison again.

"Look, who's telling this story, me or the three of you?"

"Sorry," said Anne. "Please continue."

Mr. Darkflame adjusted his collar. "Hieronymus went with her immediately. For some unknown reason, a rift had opened in the Big Glowing Field of Magick, and the only solution was to activate the gold medallion."

"Why would they want to activate it?" asked Anne. "I thought the quest was designed to bring down the barrier."

"Not exactly. The quest was designed to *control* the

barrier. It could raise or lower it, depending on the wishes of the person in charge of the quest. And it could be activated as many times as needed. Hieronymus and the lady thought they might be able to use it to seal the rift."

"What went wrong?" asked Hiro.

"No one is certain. They successfully activated the quest, that much is known, but something happened, and there was an explosion. Neither Hieronymus nor the lady was seen again after that. They were presumed dead."

"Was it pirates?" asked Penelope, clearly not mad enough to ignore a good story.

"A pirate ship did show up eventually, but they didn't cause the explosion. They simply watched everything unfold from a distance and sifted through the debris afterward for anything of value."

"So why is it called the Battle of the Great Rift?"

"Marketing, mostly. It sounds more impressive than the Unknown Incident at the Small Rift Where No One Really Knows What Happened."

"Did it work?" asked Anne. "Did they seal the rift?"

"They did. And it remained sealed until a little over thirteen years and six months ago."

Anne did the math. That would have been right around the time of her birth—and that of Penelope's and Hiro's as well, for that matter. The three of them were close in age, with Penelope being the oldest by a couple of months and Anne being the youngest.

Mrs. Darkflame continued the story. "From that point onward, the Darkflames have always kept tabs on the BGFM. A month before the rift opened the second time, some unusual activity was recorded around the site of the original incident. I was nine months pregnant with Hiro at the time, but we went to investigate anyway. While we were there, a small rupture appeared, releasing a burst of black magick. I got caught in the cloud and fell immediately ill. Although I eventually recovered, the damage had been done. Whatever substance had invaded my body had transformed Hiro into a doppelganger."

Hiro hung his head. Anne couldn't begin to imagine what he must be feeling, and she felt bad for ever doubting his loyalty to the group. Penelope remained silent.

"Unable to close it this time, two years later the council formed an expedition into the rift," said Mr. Darkflame. "Unfortunately, it ended in disaster, and only one member of the group made it back."

"Was that the quest led by my parents?" asked Penelope.

Mrs. Darkflame gave her a sympathetic look. "I'm afraid so. It was a terrible proposal that should never have been authorized. Your parents were made the scapegoats, but it wasn't their fault. We've spoken out on their behalf at every opportunity, but the powers that be would rather sweep the whole thing under the rug and forget it ever happened."

"Who made it back?" asked Anne, although she already knew the answer.

"That was Evelyn Daisywheel, the former headmistress of Saint Lupin's. Poor thing, she was never quite the same after that. I'm sorry to say we fell out of touch."

"She was a doppelganger."

"Oh. Well, that would explain it, then."

"Who was Siri?" asked Hiro.

Mrs. Darkflame raised an eyebrow. "Who?"

"We came across their graves. Hieronymus, Penelope's parents, Evelyn, and someone named Siri."

"I'm sorry, but I'm afraid that name doesn't ring any bells. The only other member of the group we're aware of was a young man named Oswald."

"Oswald Grey?!" exclaimed Anne. "He was a part of the expedition to the other side of the barrier?"

"Yes. I take it you've heard of him?"

Anne turned to Hiro. "I think it's time we told your parents the truth. The whole truth."

Hiro sighed. "I suppose you're right."

As succinctly as possible, Hiro recounted for his parents the events of the past day, starting with the pirate attack on Saint Lupin's and culminating with their escape from the other side of the barrier and the Construct's instruction to recover the three medallions. Where necessary, he also included any pertinent details from their previous quests, such as the true nature of Mr. Shard and the Matron. When he finished, his parents looked completely dumbfounded.

"You had the gold medallion in your possession?" asked Mr. Darkflame.

"Yes," said Anne. "But now Octo-Horse Pirate has it."

"And it's active once again?"

"I'm afraid so. And we only have a few hours left before the castle reaches its destination."

Hiro's parents conferred with each other in hushed

tones. Finally, after a heated discussion, they turned back to the group.

"What can we do to help?" asked Mrs. Darkflame.

Anne nodded. "We can't hope to beat Octo-Horse Pirate by ourselves. He's too strong, and he has that squid and who knows what else protecting him. We need you to convince the council to send every airship and dragon they have at their disposal to the High Castle and have him arrested."

Mr. Darkflame tapped his chin. "That won't be easy. The council has been up in arms over your escape, and Lord Greystone has locked himself away in a long series of secret meetings. It's been impossible to reach him, and the council won't lift a finger on any quest-related matters without his express authorization."

"Just tell him I'll be at the castle and he can arrest me again," said Anne. "That should do the trick."

"We'll try our best. Anything else?"

"We need to find the other two medallions. They're both at the High Castle. The copper one is aboard the *Blue Daisy*, and Octo-Horse Pirate has the gold one."

"Actually, that might not be entirely correct," said Mrs. Darkflame. She reached into her satchel, pulled out a stack of papers, and flipped through them until she found the sheet she was looking for. "This is an alert about the sale of possible stolen property." She handed the paper to Anne.

Anne read the paper. "Listen to this. It says Pirate Fifty-Three was flagged by some council agents for trying to sell them a known quest medallion, namely a copper medallion bearing the image of a dragon." Anne looked up. "It's not on the ship at all. Pirate Fifty-Three has it!"

"The agents set up a meeting with the pirate in question," said Mrs. Darkflame. "The plan was to arrest him, but if we pull a few strings, we can arrange it so you and your group go to that meeting instead. There's only one problem."

"What's that?" asked Hiro.

"The location. The meeting is in a place no adventurer in their right mind would ever willingly set foot."

THE ADVENTURER'S GUIDE TO TAVERNS SAYS THE FOLLOWING:

While any recounting of a heroic journey inevitably mentions a stop at some warm and inviting village tavern, the experienced traveler knows to be wary, as not all taverns are the safe havens the stories claim them to be. Consider the Polka Dot Dragon Tavern, for example, where any nondragon patrons could easily find themselves turned into an appetizer if they're not careful. Or consider the Inn of Pancakes and Death, where they do indeed serve the best pancakes in the Hierarchy, but the cost is steep. Very steep. And don't forget the Small Yappy Dogs Pub. Patrons who stay inside longer than three minutes lose their minds.

Above them all, however, sits an establishment that shall not be named. Its well-worn tabletops and mismatched chairs strike terror into the heart of even the fiercest warrior. Those brave souls who have summoned the courage to set foot inside its unevenly plastered walls speak of it only in hushed tones—when they dare speak of it at all.

If you do go, be on your guard and make sure to comb your beard.

Bob is watching.

15

The Inn of Sensible Names

The inn stood in the center of a small village on the northern slope of a large mountainous tier. The structure was three stories of white plaster framed by thick, dark beams. Double chimneys puffed gray smoke from the rooftop, and the smell of freshly baked bread wafted through the windows. A sign over the front door swung gently in the early-morning breeze. It featured a mounted knight in shiny armor carrying a sword and riding a black stallion. There was a red circle around the knight with a diagonal slash through it.

"Er," said Anne.

"Are we certain this is the right place?" asked Hiro.

"Trust me, this is it," said Marri. "This is the most feared tavern in all the Hierarchy. We must be extremely careful."

They followed Marri up a ramp leading to the front door. As they entered, the heat of the dining room and the noise of the crowd nearly overwhelmed them. Several dozen tables were crammed together, filling every last inch of available space. Anne was surprised to see the inn so full, especially at this early hour and especially after Marri's multiple warnings. There was a stone fireplace on the far wall, and the air smelled of spiced ale and roasted meat.

Anne raised herself up on the tips of her toes to see over the other patrons. "How are we supposed to find anybody in all this?"

"Hiro's parents said to get a table and that Pirate Fifty-Three would find us," said Marri.

"So, what, we ask them if they have a reservation for a Darkflame, a Shatterblade, a Blackwood, and an Anvil?"

"Hey now, that'll be quite enough of that!" said a loud voice.

The shout came from a burly man who was elbowing

his way through the busy room. He was heavyset, had a thick black beard, and wore an apron that hadn't decided whether it was having trouble staying on or had gotten stuck trying to come off. He marched directly over to them, his cheeks red and his expression stern.

"Is there a problem?" asked Anne.

"Can't you read?" said the man. He pointed to a sign on the wall next to the front door. In bold black letters, it read:

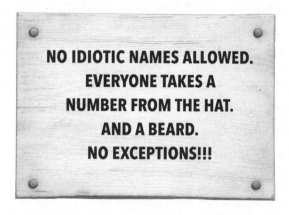

NO IDIOTIC NAMES ALLOWED.
EVERYONE TAKES A
NUMBER FROM THE HAT.
AND A BEARD.
NO EXCEPTIONS!!!

Beneath the sign was a small table. On the table sat an upturned hat with little slips of paper inside. Next to the hat was a pile of fluffy black lumps of cotton.

"The name's Smith," said the man. "Bob Smith. And this here is the Inn of Sensible Names."

Penelope wrinkled her nose. "'Sensible Names'?"

"That's right. I'm the owner, and I run a tight operation. Strictly on the up-and-up. We don't have much tolerance for adventurer types around here, and we especially don't go for any of those fancy-schmancy adventurer names. So mind your manners, or else Ogre One and Ogre Two will escort you back outside." He directed their attention to two large ogres standing to the side. The pair were clearly of the bouncer persuasion.

"I'm sorry," said Anne, "the Inn of what?"

"Sensible. Names." Smith studied them closely, taking in their attire. "Say now, you wouldn't happen to be some of those adventurer types yourselves, would you?"

"Who, us?" said Hiro, laughing nervously. "Certainly not. Just some weary travelers."

"And their holographic sparrow," added Jeffery, appearing in a burst of light. "What did I miss?"

Smith frowned. "And what are your names?"

Anne swallowed. "Mine's Anne."

Smith leaned in closer. "What's the full name on your ID?"

"Anvil."

Smith cringed and asked for the rest of their names.

"Penelope Shatterblade."

"Hiro Darkflame."

"Captain Marri Blackwood."

"Jeffery the Reluctant Map Eater."

"They tell me my name is the Construct, but I have this vague memory it might be Doomslayer the Terrible."

Smith scowled at them. "Everyone take a number," he said, and he handed them each a slip of paper from the hat. Each slip was marked with the same number, 11630, in bold black print.

"Why are they all the same?" asked Hiro.

"Because it's a completely dull and uninteresting number. Plus, it makes everything a lot easier. Except for taking the orders. It's harder to keep those straight."

Smith pointed to the pile of cotton. "Make sure to put those on, too."

They each took one of the black lumps, which turned out to be fake beards. They put them on and looked at each other. The beards were so large that it would have been difficult to tell who was who were it not for their clothing and hair. They waded through a sea of bearded patrons to a table that had just been cleared. It was next to the kitchen, and the sound of clanking pots and shouting drifted through the door, along with the scent of chicken soup.

"So, what are we ordering?" Penelope asked eagerly as they took their seats.

"We're only here long enough to meet with Pirate Fifty-Three," said Anne.

"Well, until we do meet with him, I'm getting something to eat."

"Pen—"

"Yes, I know, we don't have any money. I'll start a tab. Look, we haven't eaten since yesterday morning, and I'm not sitting here in the middle of a tavern and not eating something."

Without waiting to see if Anne agreed with her or not, Penelope flagged down a serving lad and ordered. Minutes later the server returned with a tray full of tankards of apple cider. Another server delivered a large platter of food: sliced roast beef and tender pork chops, mashed potatoes, carrots, green beans, peas, a jar of pickled beets, a jar of mustard pickles, and a bowl of thick gravy.

Hiro surveyed the table. "Is this supposed to be breakfast, lunch, or dinner?"

"It's all of them," said Penelope, stabbing a piece of roast beef with her fork.

At the sight and smell of all the delicious food, Anne had to admit she was hungry. Everyone filled their plates and dug in. The Construct kept trying to pick up her apple cider, but her hand passed through the tankard every time.

"How are we supposed to find anyone in here?" said Anne, scanning the crowd. "It's like looking for a pirate-shaped needle in a bearded haystack."

Hiro tugged at his beard. "Speaking of beards, mine's itchy."

"Pssst, wanna buy a vowel?" whispered a voice beside Anne.

She jumped. A man slid into the empty chair next to her. He wore a red stocking for a cap and the wide-bottomed pants of a sailor and, of course, a thick black beard just like everyone else in the room. His eyes darted back and forth.

"Do I want to what?" said Anne.

"Do you want to buy a vowel?" the man repeated, sounding a little huffy this time.

"I'm sorry, are you trying to sell me something?"

"No. That's my half of the code. Now I'm waiting for you to give the countersign."

"What countersign?"

"Pirate Fifty-Three, is that you?" asked Marri.

It was difficult to tell because of the disguise, but now that Marri said it, the man did indeed resemble Pirate Fifty-Three.

The man looked at her suspiciously and scratched his beard. "Who's asking?"

Marri leaned forward. "It's Captain Blackwood. The Wizards' Council was going to arrest you, but we made a deal with them to let us come here instead. They gave us the message you sent."

He squinted at her. "If that's really true, then why haven't you given the countersign I mentioned in my message yet?"

"Because you never mentioned a countersign in your message."

Marri dug out the letter and handed it to him. He read it over carefully, looking increasingly perplexed as he went. When he finished, he placed the letter on the table.

"Despite your failure to deliver the countersign I never mentioned, I've decided you are indeed the captain," he said.

"Listen, I'm really sorry about what happened," said Marri. "You were right: I broke the rules by asking for the medallions back without offering any kind of compensation. I would be happy to have you rejoin the crew."

Pirate Fifty-Three nodded. "Thank you, Captain. I would like that very much. And for what it's worth, I'm sorry I took the medallion. It was my ancestor who found the gold medallion and donated it to the museum. When I saw the same image on that copper medallion, I got excited. I guess I figured maybe I could do something similar."

"Where is the copper medallion now?" asked Anne.

"I hid it before coming in here," said Pirate Fifty-Three. "Not long after I left the ship, I realized I was being followed. It was some of the guards from the museum. When they learned I had been let go from the crew, they approached me and offered me a job."

"Doing what?" asked Marri.

"Capturing you."

Everyone dropped their utensils and started to back away from the table.

"Wait!" said Pirate Fifty-Three. "I said no, of course. I would never betray a fellow pirate. But I'm pretty sure they kept following me. That's why I chose this place, because at least everyone is in disguise. But I'm pretty sure there are guards from the museum here, just waiting for us to leave."

Hiro glanced around nervously, no doubt suspecting everyone he looked at was a museum guard in disguise. "So how are we going to get out of here?"

"Don't worry, I have a plan for that," said Pirate Fifty-Three, and he stood up.

"What are you doing?" asked Marri.

Pirate Fifty-Three cleared his throat. "My fellow diners!" he shouted. "This is wrong! All wrong! We should have more self-respect. More dignity than to bow in the face of such oppression. Can't you see, my friends, that we're all living a terrible, terrible lie? Don't you understand what this is doing to us? What are we without our names? Where is our pride? This tyranny must end!" He shook a hand in the air for emphasis. Unfortunately, it was the hand holding his mug, and he slopped warm apple cider over the people at the next table.

The two ogre bouncers began shoving tables aside to reach him.

"What are you doing?" said Anne. "Sit down!"

Pirate Fifty-Three's voice became strong and defiant, and he ripped away his beard. "I'm more than just a number. My name is Pirate Fifty-Three, and I'm proud of *urk*—"

A huge ogre fist clamped over his mouth, and another grabbed him by the throat. The bouncer then picked him up, carried him across the room, and, adding insult to injury (and also injury to injury), dropkicked Pirate Fifty-Three out the front door. Silence followed.

Smith cleared his throat. "Now hear this! I run a clean establishment, and I'll tolerate no more outbursts of that sort! I hear one more silly name, and someone's going to pay dearly!" Someone snickered at the back of the room, and Smith whirled in that direction. "Did I just hear an *X* and a *Q* in the same syllable?" And with that, he was gone again. The room gradually settled back to its previous low rumble.

The other ogre ushered the rest of the group toward the door. No one argued. Anne and the others quickly made their way through the throng and back outside, dropping their numbers and beards on the table as they went. As they exited the inn, Pirate Fifty-Three was just picking himself up.

"Are you okay?" asked Marri, looking concerned.

"It was unpleasant, but hopefully we gave them the slip," said Pirate Fifty-Three.

"Er, not to criticize, but how exactly was causing a ruckus and drawing everyone's attention to us supposed to give them the slip?" asked Anne.

"People get thrown out of there all the time. I doubt anyone even noticed."

"Oh, we noticed," said a voice behind them.

A dozen bearded individuals spilled out of the inn. The one who had spoken tore off his beard and revealed himself to be the chief of museum security. The others were obviously more guards from the museum.

"I may have miscalculated," said Pirate Fifty-Three.

"You think?" said Penelope.

The chief pointed at Marri. "You and your avocado-stealing friends are coming with us."

"You don't have any jurisdiction here," said Marri.

The chief pulled out his sword, and the other guards followed suit.

"I'm getting the distinct impression they're not worried about jurisdiction," said Hiro.

"You'll have to catch us first," said Anne. "Where's the medallion?" she asked Pirate Fifty-Three.

"This way!" he yelled.

Pirate Fifty-Three led the group around the corner and down the alleyway beside the inn. The guards chased after them, shouting for them to stop. Rather than providing an escape route, however, the alleyway brought them up short, blocked by a stone wall. At the base of the wall stood a small wooden structure with a single door.

Pirate Fifty-Three pointed at the structure. "In there!"

Everyone squeezed in, including Marri in her chair, and they slammed the door shut and barred it.

"Um, not to point out the obvious, but I think we just locked ourselves in an outhouse," said Hiro.

"That would explain why it obviously wasn't built to hold five people," said Penelope.

"Not to complain," said Pirate Fifty-Three. "But one of the members of your group is standing in me."

The Construct was almost completely inside the pirate. Only her head and shoulders were sticking out. In the cramped space she simply had nowhere to go.

"Just hold your breath," said Penelope.

Anne sighed. None of the heroes in the stories she'd read had ever locked themselves in an outhouse. This was definitely the low point of her adventuring career, and that was saying something, considering the questionable places their adventures had taken her.

Pirate Fifty-Three shrugged. "It was the only place available on short notice." He reached into the rafters, and when he brought his hand back down he was holding the copper medallion. He handed it to Anne.

"Thanks," she said.

A voice came from outside. "Give yourselves up. We have you surrounded."

"You can't have us surrounded," Penelope yelled back. "The outhouse backs against a stone wall."

"Fine. We have you semicircled, then."

Penelope grimaced. "They're using math against us."

"I don't think we have a choice," said Marri. "We're going to have to fight." She attempted to draw her sword, but she had difficulty getting it fully out of its scabbard in the cramped space.

"Wait!" said Anne. She pointed to Hiro. "Do you have any spells that could help?"

Hiro swallowed. "Maybe. I had to tape my spell catalog back together after Marri cut it in half, but there's one spell that might—"

"Cast it."

"Okay, but you should know—"

Anne felt her frustration building. "Look, I don't *want* to know, okay? Whatever it is you're going to tell me, I don't want to know. I also don't want to be the antagonist on this quest anymore; I don't want to collect medallions and stop some doomsday castle; and I don't want to be semicircled in an outhouse. So just cast the spell already and get us out of here."

"Okay," Hiro said meekly.

Everyone shifted position to allow Hiro to stand next to the door. He peeked through the little half moon carved in the door and took out his spell catalog. Then he lowered his head and began chanting.

Anne pressed her face to a crack between the boards so she could see what was happening. The guards seemed to be arguing about something.

"Look, all I'm saying is, semicircles aren't very scary," one of the guards was explaining. "How about we threaten them with a square? At least it has sharp corners."

"I bet if we tried a rhombus, that would get them out of there real quick," suggested another.

"You're both missing the point," said a third. "You're trying to apply four-sided geometry in what is clearly a nonquadrilateral situation."

As Hiro continued chanting, an eerie calm settled over the village. The museum guards ceased their bickering and looked up. The wind gusted. A loose shutter on a nearby building began a slow drumming. Dark clouds gathered overhead, and bursts of lightning flashed within. A deep roll of thunder rattled the walls of the outhouse. Everyone shifted uneasily.

A solitary white object plummeted from the sky and landed on the ground with a splat. A runny yellow substance spilled out.

One of the museum guards crouched down and examined it. "It looks like an egg, sir."

The chief looked up, and Anne followed his gaze as best she could. Several white feathers floated down. One even landed on the chief's bulbous nose.

Then came the chickens.

Not just one chicken or two chickens or even a handful of chickens. It was a deluge, a torrential downpour of poultry.

The museum guards ran for cover, but it didn't matter. Chicken after chicken after chicken hailed down upon them. Several of the guards were instantly knocked senseless. Others received a severe pecking. As if that weren't enough, once the chickens landed they began firing lightning bolts out of their beaks. The few guards who had managed to avoid injury in the initial onslaught were quickly zapped.

A stray bolt of lightning struck the side of the out-house and blew the planks off. It became very clear very quickly that they were no longer safe in their present location.

"Back to the inn!" yelled Anne.

The group burst from the outhouse and sprinted for the cover of the larger building. They dodged and weaved as chickens continued to rain down. One hit the ground behind them with such velocity that it exploded in a burst of charred feathers. Just before they reached the inn's doorway, a plummeting chicken struck Anne and knocked her over. She stumbled to her knees, but Penelope managed to yank her upright. Once safely inside, they fell panting to the floor.

Anne stared through the open doorway, a look of incomprehension on her face. "Hiro, what spell did you cast?"

"I thought it said Chain Lightning," said Hiro.

Penelope yanked the catalog out of his hand and examined it. "Two of the pages are taped together, you ninny. You read the first part of Chain Lightning and the second part of Summon Chicken Swarm." She handed the catalog back to him. "Congratulations, O Master of Magick, you just invented chicken lightning."

Hiro looked horrified, and Anne wanted to comfort him, but she couldn't contain herself. After everything they'd been through in the past day, this was simply too much. She burst into laughter. Chicken lightning. Of all the things to save them, Hiro had to come up with chicken lightning. The others soon joined in, even Hiro himself.

Marri suddenly stopped laughing and pointed at Anne's arm. "Anne, your gauntlet."

Anne held up her gauntlet-hand. Her arm was sore from where the chicken had hit her, but it hadn't occurred to her to check the gauntlet. It sizzled with spurts of erratic energy. Several of the metal strips were bent, and one had even been torn loose and was dangling by a single rivet. The medallion slot was also askew.

"Where are Jeffery and the Construct?" asked Hiro.

Everyone glanced around, but neither Jeffery nor the Construct was anywhere to be seen.

"Activate GPS," said Anne, but Jeffery didn't appear.

"If your gauntlet is broken, will you be able to stop the barrier from coming down?" asked Marri.

"It's worse than that," said Anne. "There were hundreds of identical tiers with castles on them, and they're currently spreading themselves out all over the Hierarchy. Without Jeffery, we have no way to locate the right one and retrieve the gold medallion."

NEZ AND THE ART OF GAUNTLET MAINTENANCE OFFERS THREE PIECES OF SAGE ADVICE:

1) Although gauntlets are designed to withstand considerable wear and tear, the owner of a gauntlet should be careful not to expose it to extreme temperatures for extended periods of time. (Granted, the extreme temperatures that would actually cause damage to a gauntlet would likely kill the wearer long beforehand.)

2) When polishing your gauntlet, always apply the cleaner using your right hand moving in a clockwise direction (wax on), and remove the cleaner using your left hand moving in a counterclockwise direction (wax off).

3) Don't hit your gauntlet with an electric chicken.

16

The Broken Gauntlet

Everyone stood in silence. Anne cradled her damaged gauntlet in her other arm as blue bursts of energy snapped and crackled and popped. For all the trouble the gauntlet had brought her these past months, Anne couldn't imagine life without it. Or without quests. Or without Jeffery.

Her chest tightened in a rising panic. What would happen if they couldn't get Jeffery or the Construct back? Or get the gold medallion from Octo-Horse Pirate?

What would happen if they didn't return to the castle in time to stop the barrier from coming down?

"Could she have simply left?" asked Marri, her voice filled with worry. "The Construct, I mean. She's not exactly thinking straight. Maybe she randomly transferred herself somewhere else."

"I don't think so," said Hiro. "In our experience with the Construct so far, she's only been able to transfer her program when there's a computer terminal nearby. And in any case, that wouldn't explain why Jeffery is missing, too." He turned to Anne. "I'm really, really sorry."

"It's okay," said Anne. "I know it was an accident."

"Why are you always sticking up for him?!" yelled Penelope. "He ruined your gauntlet! He ruined everything! You should be angry!"

"Pen, I don't think—"

Penelope rounded on Hiro and jabbed a finger into his chest. "If we fail to stop the barrier, you and I are going to have serious words, mister, including what role, if any, your origins might have played in this."

Hiro stared at the ground and remained silent.

Penelope started walking away, but Anne followed and grabbed her arm.

"I'm not interested in talking about it, okay?"

snapped Penelope, and she jerked her arm from Anne's grasp.

"That's fine, you can just listen, then," said Anne, not backing off. She had tried to be sympathetic, but enough was enough. She checked to make sure they were out of earshot of the others, and then she spoke again. "Look, I'm sorry you've had all this thrown at you, I really am. It's a lot to deal with. But in case you haven't noticed, you're not the only one having a bad day. What happened to your parents was terrible, but it wasn't Hiro's fault. None of this is. And yes, like you, I'm disappointed he hid such an important part of himself from us. But think about what it cost him to share it. And then remember that he did it to save us. He risked everything for you and me. And from everything that's come out today, he wasn't the only one with a secret."

Penelope shifted uneasily. "Anne, I—"

Anne held up her hand. "Now isn't the time. And in any case, I'm not mad. We all have to live our own lives, and I would never think of standing in the way of your dreams. But right now the group needs you, Pen. And it needs Hiro, too."

Penelope looked stunned. Anne left her standing there and went outside.

The chicken storm was finally abating, with only the occasional baby chick ricocheting off a nearby roof. People were starting to emerge from their homes to begin the day, no doubt curious about the recent storm. Many of them seemed startled to find the street filled with roaming chickens; they were even more shocked each time a chicken zapped them with a bolt of lightning.

Several of the buildings had been badly damaged, and many of the shops had had their signs knocked off. One sign still intact, however, caught Anne's eye. It had a white background with a hammer and anvil painted on it.

Marri joined her in the street. "What are we going to do?"

"We're going to get help," Anne said firmly, and she set off down the street.

At the building with the hammer and anvil, she knocked several times. When no one answered, she knocked again. And again. Finally, there was a click and the door swung open.

A woman with curly brown hair and wearing a heavy wool tunic, looking a little bleary-eyed, stood in the doorway. "I'm afraid I'm not open yet," she said with a yawn.

Anne held up her gauntlet-hand. "My gauntlet is damaged, and I can't access the GPS."

"Well, if you bring it back in a couple of hours, I'd be happy to take a look."

She started to close the door, but Anne jammed her foot in the way.

"Please, it's an emergency," Anne pleaded. "The quest will be over by then, and if I don't get the gauntlet repaired, terrible things will happen. And—and you'd be helping out a fellow blacksmith." Anne dug her blacksmith token out of her pocket and held it up so the blacksmith could see.

Hiro, Marri, and Pirate Fifty-Three came charging down the street. Penelope followed behind.

The blacksmith raised an eyebrow. "An emergency, you say?"

"Yes," said Anne. "Very much so."

"End-of-the-world type stuff, I suppose?"

Anne nodded her head vigorously. "And we have less than two hours."

"Very well. You'd better come in."

The air inside was warm. A fire roared merrily inside a large stone fireplace on one side, and on the other were two long tables: one covered with tools, and one with two stools in front.

The blacksmith pointed to the stools. "Have a seat over there. I'm afraid the rest of your group will have to stand."

Anne sat as instructed and rested the gauntlet on the table. At the other table, the blacksmith put on a leather apron and picked up a leather roll. She sat next to Anne and looked at the gauntlet.

"Well, my first observation is that you're on a quest without a quest medallion," said the blacksmith.

"A half-octopus, half-horse stole the medallion using the twin of this gauntlet," Anne explained. "We need this one repaired so we can take it back."

The blacksmith shrugged. "Fair enough. What caused the damage? Did it happen when the medallion was removed?"

"No, it was zapped by a chicken," said Anne.

The blacksmith stared at her as if to determine whether or not Anne was joking. When Anne didn't add anything else, the blacksmith simply shook her head and opened the leather roll, which was packed with a variety of strange-looking implements. She selected a long probe and began examining the gauntlet, taking special care as she prodded the loose metal strips.

"This gauntlet has been modified," said the blacksmith.

"It was done yesterday," said Anne.

"And before that, too."

"What do you mean?"

"It's been modified twice. Once recently and once a very long time ago. That's part of the reason it's so unstable."

After the blacksmith finished her examination, she put away the probe and leaned back on her stool. "Your gauntlet is in rough shape. It would take several days to do a proper repair job, but since you don't have that kind of time, I'll patch it up as best I can. No guarantees, though."

"Thank you," said Anne.

The blacksmith worked steadily for the next half hour, occasionally directing Anne to hold a certain piece or move the gauntlet a certain way. The blacksmith tightened the rivets and replaced the broken strip with a new one. She then worked on the medallion slot, tapping it gently with her tools to move it back into place. Finally, after a particularly sharp tap with the hammer, there was a distinct click and the slot settled into the cuff. If anything, though, the crackle of blue energy became even worse.

The blacksmith scratched her head. "That should have done it. It might have sustained more damage than I thought."

"What do you mean, more damage than you thought?" asked Jeffery, appearing in a burst of light.

"Jeffery!" exclaimed Anne.

"This isn't just any gauntlet you're talking about, you know," Jeffery continued. "This is my home. What if it's permanently damaged? I'll become an orphan! Do you have any idea what happens to homeless GPSs? Pretty soon I'll be begging for scraps of old cooking recipes on the side of the road."

"Jeffery, calm down," said Anne.

Jeffery began gasping for air. "I—I can't breathe." He fell on the table and began thrashing around. "I think I'm dying."

Anne rolled her eyes. "You're a magickal hologram. I'm pretty sure you don't need air, and I highly doubt you're dying. Also, this isn't helping."

He hopped back on his feet. "Well, if I do die, won't you be sorry?"

Anne studied the gauntlet. "Is the Construct still in there?"

Jeffery pointed to the swirling lines of energy. "Her

matrix has almost completely destabilized. She can no longer appear. We need to transfer her to a computer terminal as soon as possible."

"If I were you, I would place that gauntlet in maintenance mode," said the blacksmith. "That would at least give you a little more time."

"How do I do that?" asked Anne.

"By using your blacksmith token, of course."

Anne brought her token out again. She had always thought it was simply proof of her official role in the group. She didn't realize it could actually be used for something. She handed it to the blacksmith.

The blacksmith looked perplexed when she saw the token up close. "Where did you get this, if you don't mind my asking?"

Anne shrugged. "It's the token I pulled out of the Bag of Chance. Why, is something wrong with it?"

"Nothing's wrong with it," said the blacksmith. "But it isn't a token."

"What? What is it, then?"

The blacksmith turned it over in her hand several times. "Have you ever heard of a skeleton key?"

"That's the same as a master key, isn't it?" said Hiro. "It's a key that fits any lock."

"Well, a specific group of locks, but close enough. What you have here is the medallion equivalent of a master key—a sort of master medallion, if you will."

Anne studied the token with renewed curiosity. "What does that mean?"

"You can use a master medallion in place of any other medallion. It will grant you access to any quest."

"So you're saying that with the master medallion I don't actually need the gold one?"

"That's right. You could simply access the quest using this." The blacksmith gestured to her gauntlet. "May I?"

Anne held out her gauntlet-hand.

The blacksmith pressed the token into the medallion slot on Anne's gauntlet. It was smaller than a medallion, but nevertheless it clicked into place. At first, nothing happened. Soon, however, the token began to warp and change until it became a smooth black medallion that completely filled the slot. Even more curious, the black medallion bore the image of a dragon.

"Hmmm, how interesting," said the blacksmith. "If I'm not mistaken, that's the Sign of Zarala."

Anne's eyes widened. "You know what this is?"

"I've seen it before. It was in a very strange book."

Anne's heart skipped a beat. "What strange book?"

"Well, actually it's just a single page. Curious thing, though, it's constantly changing what it says, although it always manages to be of interest. But it's been stuck on the same thing since yesterday."

"You have it here? Can we see it?"

The blacksmith retrieved a wooden box from the mantel of the fireplace and removed a piece of paper. She handed it to Anne. On the page was a picture of the High Castle, with its three towers showing prominently. There were also three medallions, one next to each tower, and each with a name written beneath it: "Darkflame" beneath the copper, "Shatterblade" beneath the silver, and "Daisywheel" beneath the gold.

Anne nearly cried. "Look at this! It's a page from *The Adventurer's Guide*! And it has information about our quest!"

The others gathered around her.

"But I thought the gold medallion was the Darkflame Medallion," said Marri.

"It's curious you should say that," said the blacksmith. "I've been thinking about it ever since the image appeared two days ago, and I could be wrong, but to my thinking this refers to the tale of the Princess Sara and Uz of the Whold."

"The who and the what?" asked Penelope.

"Legend has it, many thousands of years ago the Princess Sara created three medallions: copper, silver, and gold. Her servant Uz became jealous and coveted the medallions for himself, so she banished him from the kingdom. But she was afraid he would return one day, so she entrusted each of the medallions to three families who had served her well. You can see from the pictures who they were. The copper belonged to the Darkflame family, the silver to the Shatterblade family, and the gold to the Daisywheel family."

"The gold didn't go to the Darkflame family?" asked Hiro.

"See, that's the interesting part. Most people miss it. In addition to containing a quest, each medallion was designed for a specific task to do with this castle, but it could only be activated by a member of the correct family. But the secret was, they traded. Each family kept a medallion for one of the other families. For instance, although the gold medallion could only be activated by a Daisywheel, it was held in safekeeping by the Darkflames. The silver could only be activated by a Shatterblade but was held by the Daisywheels, and the copper could only be activated by the Darkflames but was held by the Shatterblades. That added another layer of security. The picture here shows the proper relationships." She beamed at them. "I'm impressed you're all so knowledgeable on the subject."

Anne handled the page with great care. "Where did you get this?"

"It was payment for some work I did. The client didn't have any money, so she paid me with a single page from her book. I didn't think much of it at the time, but it's turned out to be quite handy."

"Can you describe this woman?"

The blacksmith gave this some thought. "Tall. Thin. Brown skin. Silver hair. Well dressed. She'd recently suffered a terrible accident, though, and lost her hand. She wanted me to attach a metal hand she had in its place. I'd never heard of such a thing. Didn't have the first clue how I'd go about it. But then she had this book that contained all the instructions. Same book that page you're holding came from."

Anne looked to Penelope and Hiro. "That had to be the Evelyn doppelganger. That's how she got her metal hand."

"And she must have had *The Adventurer's Guide* with her," said Hiro.

"That's how it ended up at Saint Lupin's," added Penelope. "The Matron brought it with her when she returned and took the real Evelyn's place."

The blacksmith looked at them curiously. "You speak as if this is all more than just a story."

Anne held up the piece of paper. "Can we borrow this? I promise we'll bring it back."

The blacksmith nodded. "Certainly, if you think it will help. But why do I get the feeling I've missed something very important?"

"Thank you, thank you, thank you!" exclaimed Anne.

They headed out the door, but Anne stopped at the threshold. "I just realized, we don't have anything to pay you with."

"Don't worry about it," said the blacksmith.

"But—"

The blacksmith winked at her. "Consider it a gift, from one blacksmith to another."

"Thank you again," said Anne. "I promise we'll return!"

And with that she was out the door.

Back aboard the *Leaky Mermaid*, the crew worked frantically to prepare the ship for battle, to be ready for Octo-Horse Pirate at the High Castle. The airship had little in the way of weapons or defenses. They pulled the lone cannon into place along the center of the portside railing. The ship had no proper ammunition to speak of, but there was a small pile of baked goods in a basket next to the cannon.

Anne picked one up and gave it a sniff. "Fruitcake?"

"The hardest known substance in all the Hierarchy," said Locke. "I'd rather get hit by a cannonball."

Anne, Penelope, and Hiro helped patch the holes in the deck they hadn't had time to fix back at Honest Ehd's. They also tied ropes to the railing for the pirates to rappel from. As they brought up more rock-hard baked goods from belowdecks, though, Hiro tripped over a rope and collided with one of the pirates. They both tumbled to the deck.

"Sorry about that," said the pirate, but then his eyes went wide.

Hiro's bandage had come loose. He quickly covered his wound with his other hand, but it was too late. The pirate had noticed the thin stream of black oily smoke that came from Hiro's wound.

"Get back!" shouted the pirate. "He's one of those—those things!"

Anne quickly wrapped the bandage around Hiro's arm again.

"Get away from that—that monster!" said the pirate.

"It's not what you think," said Anne hastily. "It's a—a—magickal wound. It does that from time to time."

The pirate backed away from them. "I know what I saw."

By now the other pirates on deck had turned their attention to Hiro. No doubt at least a few of them had seen Hiro's arm as well, and hushed murmurs suggested word was spreading fast. A few of the nearest pirates even placed their hands on the hilts of their swords. There was no way Anne could stop all of them.

Penelope stepped between Hiro and the pirates and drew her sword. The pirates had procured new weapons for themselves, and Penelope now had an honest-to-goodness real sword as a replacement for her wooden one. The polished blade shone in the morning sunlight. "If you want him, you're going to have to go through me first."

"There will be no need for anyone to go through anyone," said Locke as he walked over. "The captain will settle the matter."

Marri exited her cabin and rolled over to where everyone was waiting.

"What seems to be the problem?" she asked.

The pirate who had collided with Hiro pointed at him. "He's one of those creatures, Captain. Bleeds black smoke. I saw it with my own eyes." He pointed at Anne and Penelope. "And they knew about him."

Marri's eyes narrowed. "Is this true?"

"We only just found out ourselves while we were on the other side of the barrier, in the doppelganger world," Anne said defensively.

"So she claims," said another pirate.

Penelope raised her sword. "Are you calling her a liar?"

"Penelope, please put away your sword," said Marri.

Penelope hesitated for a moment, but finally slid her sword back into its sheath.

"I'll just leave," said Hiro.

"No," said Anne. "I know how this must look, and I'm sorry we didn't tell you, but Hiro isn't a danger to you or your crew. And you heard the blacksmith. We can't complete our mission without him."

The crew began muttering, and Marri put her fingers to her lips and gave a loud whistle. "That's enough! Hiro is a part of this crew and has proven himself on more than one occasion. I will deal with the issue of his and his companions' deception, but this is not the time. Anyone who has a problem with that can take it up with me."

A few pirates looked about to speak again, but this time Locke stepped forward and shouted. "You heard the captain. Get back to work!"

The crew dispersed.

"Thank you," said Hiro.

"Yes, thank you," said Anne. "I know that wasn't easy."

"Don't thank me yet," said Marri. "I may have no choice but to kick you off the crew, which will leave you at the mercy of the Wizards' Council."

Anne swallowed. "I understand."

Anne looked at Penelope and Hiro. Neither of them was looking at the other.

"Thanks for sticking up for me," said Hiro.

"Well, I'm still mad at you," said Penelope. "But you're a member of our group, and that means nobody gets to pick on you unless we say so." She gave him a light punch on the shoulder and grinned. Hiro smiled back.

Anne was relieved to see her two friends speaking again.

The *Leaky Mermaid* was soon headed to the High Castle, back to confront Octo-Horse Pirate and with any luck stop the barrier from coming down. Jeffery supplied the helmsman with the castle's current coordinates, and the helmsman brought the ship about until it was aimed in the right direction. They were moving away from any inhabited tiers before having Nana fireball the ship to its final destination. Marri had requested that Nana drop them as close to the castle as possible. She hoped to avoid another encounter with Marvin the giant metal squid, or at the very least get them close enough to land so they could abandon ship if necessary.

Anne, Penelope, and Hiro prepared as best they could. Penelope sharpened her new sword. Hiro checked and rechecked the available spells in his catalog (after retaping it correctly). Anne polished her gauntlet but mostly sat in anticipation of the inevitable confrontation with Octo-Horse Pirate. Jeffery even wrote a few more stanzas of Anne's eulogy until she told him it was probably bad luck. He got all huffy and flew up to the crow's nest and composed a song about a lost peanut instead.

"All hands, brace for fireball travel," shouted Locke.

Everyone held on tight. Nana sucked in a lungful of air and shot out a green fireball. It surrounded the ship and flung them across the Hierarchy on a heart-stopping (not to mention completely inadvisable) trajectory. The fireball vibrated as bolts of green flame ricocheted in all directions, bouncing off the hull of the ship and exploding against the interior shell of the fireball itself. Despite everything they were facing, Anne couldn't help but smile. One way or another, she was finally going to get answers.

———◆———

Storm the castle.
Storm the castle.
Storm the caaaaaastle!
Storm the castle.

—Lyrics from the song "Storm the Castle" by
Pompf the Mime

———◆———

The Two-Plus-One Towers

As promised, Nana delivered them practically on the castle's front doorstep. Despite her miniature size, Nana's fireball was as precise as ever.

The castle had dropped low over the BGFM—so low, in fact, that waves of magick buffeted the tier as they broke against its rocky bottom. A great uneven tear on the surface of the barrier was visible in the distance, growing ever larger as the castle drew closer. It was the rift. The edges of the tear flashed purple and blue, but the center was the blackest black Anne had ever seen. Coils of black smoke poured out of it like tentacles threatening to grab anything that came too close. Dark clouds circled over it, sending out jagged bolts of lightning.

On the castle grounds themselves, all was quiet. The three towers rose like three great spikes, shadowy and menacing. There was no immediate sign of Marvin the giant squid, so Locke ordered that the ship descend and the rappelling ropes be made ready. Once the ship was directly over the castle walls, the crew lowered their ropes and dropped down. Only the helmsman and a handful of sailors stayed behind, the bare minimum needed to sail the ship should they need to retreat.

They had worked out a plan of attack and done their best to prepare for any surprises that might happen along the way. Anne, Penelope, Hiro, and Marri would investigate the towers. The pirates would provide an escort and also secure the castle grounds. Even Jeffery and Nana had been assigned special tasks should the need arise.

Marri sent out scouts to see what they were facing. The rest of the crew hunkered down and waited. Although everyone remained quiet, there was a lot of nervous shifting from one foot to the other. Penelope was practically bouncing on the balls of her feet, and Hiro was mumbling to himself, no doubt rehearsing his spells. There were butterflies in Anne's stomach, and she couldn't even begin to wonder what Marri must be thinking of the prospect of confronting her father.

Anne shielded her eyes against the early-morning sun. "How much time do you think is left?"

Marri looked at the sky. "It's hard to be precise. I'd guess an hour or so at the most. Maybe slightly more."

"One hour eleven minutes and twenty-nine seconds," said Jeffery. He tapped his foot against the black medallion. "That is, if you really trust this thing. Personally, I've always been a little iffy on master medallions. I once read this article in *Blacksmith Token* magazine, and according to them—"

"Jeffery, can we maybe discuss this some other time?" said Anne.

"Oh, sure thing," he said. "I mean, presuming we don't all die in the next hour."

The scouts returned and reported that all was clear. The crew divided into two groups. One group was assigned to escort Marri, Anne, Penelope, and Hiro to the towers. The second group had orders to take up positions around the main gate and maintain a watch.

"I don't like it," said Marri. "It's almost too quiet."

"Maybe your father didn't expect us to come back,"

said Anne. "He may not even know that we escaped from the other side of the barrier."

They proceeded down the ramp to the courtyard below and crept along the wall to the first tower. The wall was smooth and black. As soon as Anne's finger made contact, a blue grid appeared on the side, just like the one at the Infinite Tower during their first quest. It was a way to open a door. A person could type in letters and numbers. But words already appeared above the grid: INSERT KEY. Below the grid was a small opening like a keyhole.

"What key is it referring to?" asked Marri.

Anne took out the page from *The Adventurer's Guide* and studied it again. "The medallions are each pictured next to a specific tower. The first tower has the copper medallion, the one from our second quest."

"You picked up the crystal key on that quest," said Hiro.

Anne held her gauntlet-hand up again. "Activate crystal key."

A small crystal key appeared in the air above the gauntlet. Anne snatched the key out of the air and inserted it into the slot. It turned a full 180 degrees until there was a distinct click. The portion of the wall directly in front of them disappeared, forming an arched doorway. They proceeded inside. The interior of the tower looked very familiar. It was basically a hollow tube with a pillar in the center that stretched all the way to the top. A set of stairs wound around the inside wall of the tower. The steps were four feet wide and had no railing. It was like being inside a smaller version of the Infinite Tower.

Jeffery's color faded, and he became noticeably more transparent.

"Jeffery, perhaps you'd better wait in the gauntlet," said Anne.

"Sounds good to me," said Jeffery, and he disappeared.

"You might have to continue without me, too," said Marri, gazing up the spiraling staircase.

"Forget the stairs," said Penelope. "We'll just take the elevator."

"The what?"

Penelope marched over to the cylinder in the center of the tower. It would have taken ten adults standing with their hands stretched out to reach around the circumference of the pillar. Penelope touched the surface and a seam appeared. A set of double doors slid apart to reveal a small rectangular compartment inside.

"It's an Old World device," Anne explained. "It will take us to the top in a matter of seconds."

Anne, Penelope, and Hiro stepped inside the elevator, but Marri hesitated.

"Trust us," said Anne. "We've done this before."

Marri turned to the crew. "The rest of you wait outside." The pirates immediately began to protest, but she held up a hand. "I'm sure the four of us can handle whatever is up there. We need you to secure our exit. Besides, it's a tight compartment, and by the smell of things not one of you has taken a bath this month."

They sheepishly obeyed her orders.

Marri took a deep breath and pushed her chair inside. The doors closed behind her, and the elevator shuddered slightly as it began its upward journey.

"Are we sure this is a good idea?" asked Hiro nervously.

"Don't fall apart on us now, Darkflame," said Penelope. "This is your tower, remember?"

If anything, Hiro now looked even more nervous.

After half a minute, the doors opened and they exited into a long gray corridor with a door at the end. When they opened it, instead of the room Anne had been expecting, there was a ramp leading up to the next floor. They proceeded slowly and on constant alert.

The room at the top of the ramp filled the entire floor, and the outer wall was lined with windows. This was odd given that from the outside the tower didn't appear to have any windows at all. In the center stood a black column only slightly shorter and smaller around than Anne herself. Another computer terminal. The stone tiles on the floor formed three concentric circles.

Anne called for Jeffery, but he didn't appear.

"Is it the black walls again?" asked Penelope.

Anne nodded. "I was hoping he could transfer the Construct into that terminal, but I guess that will have to wait. Hopefully not for too long, though," she added as a blue line of energy crackled across her gauntlet.

"I have a bad feeling about this," said Hiro.

"Only one?" said Penelope. "Because I have at least a dozen bad feelings, and that's just about the pattern on the floor alone. Don't even get me started on the windows that only look like windows from the inside, or the computer terminal. Remember the dragon trials? This room has crazy puzzle chamber of death written all over it."

"We don't have much choice," said Anne. "We can't stand here all morning wondering what's going to happen. We'll just have to deal with whatever happens as it comes."

"Was that supposed to be encouraging?" said Hiro. "Because I don't feel encouraged."

Anne took a steadying breath and started forward. As soon as her foot touched the outer ring of the circle, fire spread around its perimeter, forcing them back.

A voice spoke to them. "Let the Darkflame approach."

"I don't feel encouraged by that, either," said Hiro.

Anne scanned the room, but there was no sign of the speaker. She held a hand toward the flames but yanked it back almost immediately. The heat was unbearable.

"Let the Darkflame approach," the voice repeated.

"She's talking to you," Penelope said to Hiro.

"I know, I know," he said. "Why are you being so pushy about it?"

Penelope cracked her knuckles. "Because Anne's the antagonist now, and I'm her enforcer. Welcome to the dark side."

Anne handed Hiro the copper medallion, and he approached the ring of fire. He held his hand toward the flames. "I don't feel anything."

Closing his eyes, he stepped through the flames to the other side. The fire didn't seem to touch him at all.

"What now?" he asked.

"Keep going," said Anne. "Check the terminal and see if you can find a way to make the flames go away." If anything, they were even hotter than before, and beads of sweat began forming on Anne's face. She, Penelope, and Marri backed up all the way to the outer wall.

Hiro walked across the first ring of tiles with slow, deliberate steps.

Nothing happened.

He walked even more slowly across the next ring.

Still nothing.

He walked across the final ring at a snail's pace.

All remained quiet.

"If you think all this nothing that's currently happening should be making us feel better, you'd be wrong," Penelope said to Marri as they pressed themselves against the walls to escape the heat. "The longer it takes to spring the trap, the worse it is."

As Hiro reached the terminal, a ghostly form appeared in front of him: an elderly man wearing the long brown robes of a wizard.

"I think it's another hologram," said Hiro.

"You are here to prevent the barrier from coming down?" asked the old wizard.

"Yes," said Hiro. "What do I need to do?"

The old wizard tapped the terminal. A seam appeared

on the top and a hatch slid aside to reveal a circular slot just large enough to hold a medallion. "Place the copper medallion in there, and then proceed to the next tower."

Hiro started toward the terminal, but the old wizard held up a hand.

"Hear me first, Hiro Darkflame," he said. "I offer you a choice. If instead you should choose to withhold the medallion, your reward would be great. Within this terminal resides the power to make you human—fully human. No longer would you have to live in fear of your true nature being discovered. No longer would your magick suffer unintended consequences. You would become the most powerful wizard ever known. What say you?"

"It can really make me entirely human?" asked Hiro.

"Yes."

"With no trace of the doppelgangers?"

"Yes."

Anne's heart skipped a beat. She knew what that must mean to Hiro, to become truly and fully human and have his magick finally work. Hiro looked down at his taped-together magick catalog. He glanced over at Anne and Penelope, and Anne could see the conflict in his eyes, could see how much he wanted to be rid of this curse.

Hiro looked back to the old wizard again. "What happens to the castle if I accept?"

"It will be permitted to continue on its course."

"Meaning it will bring down the barrier."

"Yes."

Hiro shook his head. "No, thank you."

"Think carefully, my young friend," said the old wizard. "If you refuse, there will be...consequences."

"I decline your offer," he said.

The old wizard's eyes darkened. "As you wish," he said, and he disappeared with a flourish of his robe.

Almost immediately, the ramp to the lower level sealed itself off and the ring of fire began to expand. Anne, Penelope, and Marri were forced back against the wall. Even worse, a second ring of fire appeared around the terminal, forcing Hiro back. Apparently he wasn't immune to this one.

"See?" said Penelope. "I told you. Every time it's like this."

The flames intensified, and Anne shielded her face from the heat.

"How do we stop it?" asked Penelope.

"I have something!" shouted Hiro. He flipped

through his spell catalog. "I thought I saw a spell—here it is!" He held up the page. "Blob of Water!"

"Does it involve poultry of any kind?" asked Penelope.

"It doesn't matter," said Anne. "Cast it before we're all burned to a crisp!"

The two rings of fire continued to expand, filling the space. Hiro knelt in the center circle of stones between the rings and placed the spell catalog in front of him. He studied the text, and then he closed his eyes and began chanting. A small sphere of water appeared in the air above the catalog.

"Impressive," said Penelope. "We are surely saved."

The sphere began to grow. Soon it was the size of a fist. Then the size of a person. Then the size of an iron knight. Hiro kept chanting, and the sphere continued to grow until it reached the outer ring of fire. With a great hiss of steam, it overtook the flames and extinguished them.

The blob of water continued expanding.

"That's enough!" yelled Anne. "Shut it off! Shut it off!"

The blob expanded once again and soon completely filled the room. Anne was tossed upside down as the wall of water struck her. Hiro was trying to reach the floor. He had dropped the medallion.

Anne swam to help him, but the current held her back. Just when she thought her lungs would burst, Hiro grabbed the medallion, swam over to the terminal, and pushed it into the slot. The terminal released a shockwave in all directions, flipping Anne upside down again. When the shockwave reached the outer walls, every window in the tower exploded outward. The water rushed out, and Anne and the others flopped to the floor with a thud. The terminal turned white and sank into the floor.

Anne groaned and rolled over. She counted three figures on the tiles next to her. Everyone seemed to be still alive, if only barely.

"How did you know inserting the medallion would do that?" she asked Hiro.

"I didn't. I just didn't want Penelope to be able to say I didn't finish my part."

Penelope lay sputtering on her back and raised her arm weakly. "Three cheers for the blob of water."

After taking a few minutes to catch their breath, the group rode the elevator back down. They rejoined the members of Marri's crew waiting for them outside the entrance to the tower. The crew shouted at the sight of them. Apparently, the waterfall down all sides of the tower had caused them great concern. Marri assured her crew everything was okay, and they made their way across the courtyard to the second tower. The wind had picked up, and Anne held her cloak tight around her. The rift was closer, as were the storm clouds.

As with the first, when Anne touched the outer wall of the second tower a blue grid appeared, containing the words INSERT KEY.

Anne held up her gauntlet-hand yet again. "Activate the Key You Cannot Hold."

A small golden key appeared in the air above the gauntlet, the key from their first quest and the one activated by the silver medallion. She took it swiftly and inserted it into the keyhole, and a section of wall changed into an arched doorway.

The interior of the second was identical to the first except it was twice as tall and the interior staircase wound counterclockwise instead of clockwise. They rode the elevator without a problem, and quickly up another ramp they soon found themselves at the top.

The layout was the same, with three rings of stone tiles and a computer terminal in the center. This time, however, someone was waiting for them. A knight in shining armor stood next to the terminal. Not an iron knight, but a human one. A sword was sheathed at her side, and a shield hung from her back. Her helmet rested atop the computer terminal.

"Another hologram, do you think?" asked Anne.

"Let the Shatterblade approach," said the knight.

"This one's all yours," Hiro said to Penelope.

Penelope nodded and walked to the center of the circle.

"Penelope Shatterblade," said the knight. "If you so choose, you may insert the medallion and continue on your way. But consider another option. Within this terminal lies the power to grant you what your heart most desires: to free you from the curse of your family name. You need only accept, and you shall be free to roam the Hierarchy, to study wherever you wish, and to become the greatest sword fighter in all the land."

Penelope looked stunned. "You can really do that?"

"Yes."

"You can restore my family name?"

"Yes."

"And I can study anywhere I wish? Any academy I choose?"

"They will not be able to refuse you."

As with Hiro, Anne knew how much this offer meant to Penelope. All her life, the curse of her family name had prevented her from following her dreams. If Anne had the power, this is exactly the gift she would give her friend. And she would never ask her to refuse it. She couldn't imagine how difficult the choice must be.

Penelope turned to Anne. "I did say those things to Hiro. I'm sorry I didn't tell you. I should have been honest."

Anne swallowed. "I understand."

Penelope faced the knight once again.

"Your answer?" asked the knight.

A smile spread across Penelope's face. "It's a tempting offer, but I pass. I'll just have to become famous the old-fashioned way."

"Think carefully. I am known as the Unbeatable Warrior. If you reject my offer, you will not be able to access this terminal unless you first defeat me in single combat."

"You mean like a duel?" asked Penelope.

"Correct," said the knight.

"I accept," said Penelope.

"Pen, are you sure about this?" asked Anne. The knight looked formidable. Anne wanted to stop the barrier from coming down, but maybe there was another way to prevent the corruption from spreading and infecting the entire Hierarchy.

Penelope grinned. "Having my family name back won't mean anything if I have to abandon my friends to get it. Besides, no one is unbeatable. Captain Copperhelm says it's all just hype."

"Do you mean to insult me?" asked the knight.

"No, I just don't believe anyone is that good."

The knight picked up her helmet. "Try me."

"Fine. I choose trial by footrace."

"I accept—wait, what? What do you mean, footrace?"

"One hundred laps around the inside of this room," said Penelope. "Blindfolded."

The knight frowned. "But we're supposed to fight with swords."

Penelope shook her head. "Wrong. You said it's a duel. That means you make the challenge, and I pick the weapons."

"But—but a footrace isn't a weapon."

Penelope crossed her arms. "Are you saying you forfeit?"

"No, but surely you can't expect—"

"I can expect, and I do expect. Now stop stalling and put your blindfold on. Oh, and we have to spin around ten times first."

"This is highly irregular," said the knight.

Penelope ripped two lengths of cloth from Hiro's robe (ignoring his protests) and handed one to the knight. They both moved to a position along the outer wall and tied their blindfolds on. Anne spun Penelope ten times and Hiro spun the knight.

"No cheating now," said Penelope.

"I am insulted that you would suggest I would even consider such a thing," said the knight.

"Are you ready?" asked Marri.

Both contestants nodded.

"Go!" Marri shouted.

The knight took off and immediately ran straight into the wall. She fell to the floor unconscious.

Penelope whipped off her blindfold. "Interesting. I had no idea a hologram could knock itself out. Quick, while I'm waiting for the room to stop spinning, someone put the silver medallion in that computer terminal and let's get out of here."

"You have to do it, remember?" said Anne, and she folded her arms across her chest. "But I'm not sure that was entirely on the up and up. Technically you didn't win the race."

"Who cares? We're pirates, and you're the Official Antagonist for the quest. Cheating is practically in the job description."

"It really is," said Hiro. "Section 3 Subsection F of the *Official Antagonist's Handbook*. And the *Pirate Handbook* dedicates an entire chapter to the subject."

"See?" said Penelope. "Now give me the medallion and let's get moving!"

"Fine," said Anne. "But somebody make sure the knight is okay."

Hiro removed the knight's helmet and waved his catalog back and forth over her face like a fan.

Anne handed the silver medallion to Penelope, and she walked over to the terminal and touched the top. When a hatch opened, Penelope slid the silver medallion into place, and as with the other terminal, this one turned white and sank into the floor.

"Two down and one to go," said Anne.

The knight began to stir. Hiro helped her into a sitting position.

"Did I win?" asked the knight.

"I'm afraid not," said Hiro. "But it was very close."

"Pity."

During the trip down the elevator, something occurred to Anne, and she paused as they exited the second tower.

"We might have a problem," she said. "The first two towers required a key from one of our previous quests."

"So?" said Penelope.

"The only medallion left is the gold one. If the third tower requires a key, it will be from the current quest. But we haven't come across a key yet."

"Maybe the key is in the gold medallion itself," suggested Penelope.

Anne held up her gauntlet-hand. "Activate Gold Medallion Key."

Nothing happened.

"Activate High Castle Key. Activate Third Tower Key. Activate Octo-Horse Pirate Key."

None of these commands resulted in a key appearing.

"Maybe we need the original medallion," said Marri. "Maybe the key is the one thing a master medallion can't duplicate. You know, as an extra security feature. There seem to be plenty of those on this quest."

"And I'm afraid that's where you're going to run into a bit of trouble," said a voice above them.

Octo-Horse Pirate dropped out of the sky and landed in front of the third tower in a cloud of smoke. As usual, his parrot was perched on his shoulder.

"Polly want a key?" said the parrot.

Anne shook with a mixture of fear and anger. Fear because she knew Octo-Horse Pirate was both willing and able to hurt them. Anger because she was tired of fighting self-serving villains who had no regard for anyone but themselves.

"Let us pass," she said in what she hoped was a steady voice.

Octo-Horse Pirate placed a hand on the hilt of his rapier. "And if I decide to fight you?"

"Ha!" said Penelope. "You and what army?"

"Why, this one, of course."

Octo-Horse Pirate gave a whistle. Footsteps echoed from every direction as hundreds of figures stepped out of the shadows on the walls above and filled the perimeter of the courtyard. Several walked forward and stood next to Octo-Horse Pirate. Penelope's double was there, as were the doubles of the pirate crew. Anne thought she even recognized the faces of people she'd met during her first two quests, such as the villagers in the Black Desert and some of the guards from the Sapphire Palace. Every single one of them wore a dragon stone.

Doppelgangers.

Indeed, an entire army of them.

THE EPIC GUIDE TO EPICALLY EPIC BATTLES OFFERS THE FOLLOWING EPIC WORDS:

When preparing for your epic battle, make sure to strap on your epic sword, secure your epic breastplate, put on your epic helmet of epicness, and march out epically to face your epic foe. Fight epically, with epic strength and epic endurance, for an epic amount of time. And when you finally, epically achieve your epic goal, be sure to cry aloud in epic victory, for there will be only one epic word to describe that epically epic feeling:

Very good.

18

The Battle of the Five Armies

Anne's heart sank. The doppelganger army was a hundred soldiers wide and ten ranks deep. They completely blocked any path to the third tower. Anne found it disturbing to be staring at so many faces she recognized, knowing she might have to fight them—and soon, too, for time was running short. They had reached the edge of the storm, which meant the castle must now be close to the rift itself. The temperature had dropped enough that their breath was now visible, and the wind whipped their cloaks back and forth.

"This is bad," said Hiro. "This is very, very bad."

"Can you cast another spell?" asked Penelope.

Hiro shook his head. "The blob of water soaked my catalog and made all the ink run. It's ruined."

Penelope drew her sword. "Well, I guess we'll just have to do this the hard way, then."

Anne looked to Marri. The pirate captain had her sword in hand and looked ready for a fight. Anne took a steadying breath and steeled herself for whatever might come. No matter the odds, they had to find a way through.

A rainbow-colored object streaked past them and headed straight for Octo-Horse Pirate.

"Leave my friends alone, you big bully!" Jeffery yelled.

He swooped as though to attack, but just as Octo-Horse Pirate swung, Jeffery performed a roll midair and dropped beneath his grasp. He dove for Octo-Horse Pirate's torso and snatched the bag hanging from his belt—the bag holding Marri's magick dice, the dice in which the staff of Saint Lupin's had been imprisoned. With the bag held firmly in his beak, Jeffery immediately changed direction and tried to climb, but Octo-Horse

Pirate snatched him out of the air with his gauntlet-hand and held Jeffery in a tight grip.

"Let him go!" shouted Anne.

"A little fish like this should learn to leave the sharks alone," said Octo-Horse Pirate, and he squeezed harder, causing Jeffery to let out a squeak.

With only Anne, Penelope, Hiro, and Marri and her crew, the odds weren't exactly in their favor. Anne was about to summon the Three-Handed Sword when several dozen shadows fell over the courtyard. The sky above the castle filled with hulking airships. All cannon ports were open and ready for action.

"I think reinforcements have arrived," Hiro said excitedly.

As the airships sailed closer, Anne saw the black seven-pointed star painted on each sail. Wizards' Council ships.

"Scratch that," said Hiro. "I think we're in even more trouble."

The ships came to a stop over the second tower and threw down ropes. Hundreds of robed figures descended to the ground. They were accompanied by several dozen eight-foot-tall armored knights—iron knights, to be exact. Several wizards held glass control cubes in their hands.

The council army landed in front of the second tower and formed ranks, with the iron knights taking the center. There were fewer wizards and iron knights than there were doppelgangers, but what they lacked in numbers they made up for in magickal abilities and sheer strength.

Lieutenant Formaldehyde from the Wizards' Council stepped forward and held up a piece of official-looking parchment.

"In my capacity as Acting Minister of Questing, I am hereby declaring this quest illegal," he said. "All participants are ordered to surrender their weapons and disperse in an orderly fashion. That is, everyone except for that group," he said, pointing at Anne and the others. "You may consider yourselves under arrest."

"I think we should get a card stamped every time someone tells us we're under arrest," said Penelope. "You know, like for every ten arrests we get one free. Or maybe a bag of candy."

"I get the impression you're not taking this seriously," said the lieutenant.

The courtyard darkened further as new shadows fell upon them. More airships had arrived, but these didn't belong to the Wizards' Council. It was an eclectic group of ships of various shapes and sizes. Ropes dropped from these ships as well, and hundreds of pirates rappelled to the ground.

"The pirates from the Haven have come to help us!" exclaimed Penelope.

"Not quite," said Marri. "Those ships belong to the museum guards."

Anne looked at her. "The museum guards have their own warships?"

"They're from one of the displays."

Once the guards from the Pyrate Museum had arranged themselves in front of the first tower, the chief of the museum guards stepped forward and pointed at Anne and the others.

"We're here—"

"Yeah, yeah, we know," shouted Penelope. "You and your guards are here in those ridiculous uniforms to arrest us for stealing your precious gold medallion, blah blah blah."

"And an avocado!" shouted a random guard in the back.

Penelope threw up her hands in annoyance. "Whatever! In case you haven't noticed, we're already facing two other armies here, so if you want a piece of us you're going to have to get in line!"

"Well, there's no reason to yell," said the chief. "Also, I think that crack about uniforms was uncalled for. Words hurt, you know."

Octo-Horse Pirate stepped forward and cleared his throat. All eyes turned toward him.

"Not to be 'that guy' or anything, but technically we were here first," he said. "Normally I would just let things play out, but I've invested a fair amount of time into organizing all of this, and you're sort of stepping on my moment."

The lieutenant and the chief mumbled their apologies and stepped back to stand with their respective armies.

"Thank you," said Octo-Horse Pirate, and he turned back to Anne and her group. "Anvil, Keeper of the Sparrow, Rightful Heir of Saint Lupin's, Dragon Slayer, and now Official Antagonist in the Pirate Treasure quest, also known as the Quest of the High Castle, the forces arrayed against you are vast, even if not entirely expected and/or welcome and/or in agreement with one another. Nevertheless, you cannot hope to win against any one of us, let alone all of us, and your time is running short. And so, I present you with a choice: You can stand your ground here and lose everything, or you can accept my offer of peace and my personal assurance that everyone here will be saved from the imminent catastrophe that is upon us."

The lieutenant raised his hand. "Just to clarify, to which imminent catastrophe are you referring? Because speaking only for my group, and in my capacity as a representative of the Wizards' Council, we weren't made aware of any impending disasters."

"Still my moment," growled Octo-Horse Pirate.

The lieutenant apologized again and lowered his hand.

"What about the rest of the Hierarchy?" Anne challenged. "What will the corruption do to them? Turn them all to doppelgangers? Destroy all life in the Hierarchy? Are we simply supposed to abandon millions of people to their fate?"

"Sometimes sacrifices must be made."

"I agree," said Anne. "But just who and what a person is willing to sacrifice says a lot about them, don't you think? And in any case, what gives you the right to decide how the world should be?"

"Nothing," Octo-Horse Pirate said matter-of-factly. "Nothing gives me the right. I merely have the power. When you have that, you don't need the right. Why does no one ever seem to understand that?"

"So you're just going to sit here and do nothing while the corruption spreads?"

Octo-Horse Pirate shrugged. "We can argue as long as you wish. I lose nothing by standing here. Can you say the same?" For emphasis, he held up his gauntlet-hand. Jeffery was still struggling to get free.

"You think you've planned this all so meticulously," said Anne. "But I'm afraid you've overlooked one thing."

"Are you referring to your master medallion? Because I know all about that. Suffice it to say, I'm not overly worried. You can't use it if you can't get into the tower."

"I'm not talking about that," said Anne. "I'm talking about our secret weapon. Now, Marri!"

Marri's arm arched back and snapped forward again, and a small black object flew out of her hand straight toward Octo-Horse Pirate. It struck his gauntlet dead center, causing him to release Jeffery. The little sparrow soared into the air, well out of his reach.

The black object looped around and came to a stop in front of him.

It was Nana.

Octo-Horse Pirate laughed. "This is your secret weapon? Forgive me for saying so, but however formidable her powers might be when it comes to rescuing sparrows, I think my entire army of doppelgangers can handle one tiny dragon."

"Who said anything about there being only one dragon?" growled Nana. "Hit it, Jeffery."

Jeffery's eyes began to glow, and two tiny orbs of light shot out of them into the sky, well above the tallest of the towers. The orbs joined together and expanded into a single giant dragon.

"The emergency beacon!" shouted Penelope.

Every quest was permitted one use of the emergency beacon. Anne hadn't been certain whether the beacon would activate using the master medallion, but Jeffery had assured her it would work. He had even made a few modifications.

An instant later the air was filled with the sound of flapping leather wings as hundreds of dragons appeared in the sky over the castle. Most of them circled in formation around the airships, but a handful broke off and glided down to land atop the castle walls above the main gate where the rest of Marri's pirate crew stood. In the center stood a large red dragon.

"Valerian!" Anne shouted excitedly.

She waved, and the red dragon winked at her. At the end of their last quest, in a gesture of thanks for all Anne had done for the dragon clans, Valerian had promised to come to her aid. She needed only to send out a special signal.

"Begone, foul beasts!" yelled the lieutenant. "You're interfering with the official business of the Wizards' Council, and your presence here could be construed as an act of war."

In the blink of an eye, the red dragon took the form of a human boy with dark hair wearing a red cape.

"If there is to be war, we will not shy away from our duty," said Valerian. "For let it be known, the dragons of the Hierarchy stand with Saint Lupin's!"

He raised his fist in the air, and the dragons around him let out a mighty roar.

Jeffery swooped overhead and dropped the bag of dice into Marri's waiting hands. Marri quickly opened it and dumped the dice in her lap. One was bouncing, and she picked it up between her thumb and forefinger. A blue ray of light shot out from the dice, and Sassafras appeared in front of them.

He blinked several times. "Did the bell ring already? Is class over? Is it naptime yet?"

Another began to vibrate, and a blue ray of light shot

out, depositing Captain Copperhelm in the middle of the courtyard. He surveyed the armies.

"Status update?" he asked.

"You've missed pretty much everything except for the final battle, which is happening right now," said Penelope.

Copperhelm hoisted his ax. "Sounds like good timing to me."

Rokk appeared next and looked around in what Anne took to be mild surprise. "My internal sensors indicate I have experienced a time lapse. Are we here to kick some tentacled equestrian butt?"

"Close enough," said Hiro.

Three more dice began trembling and hopping about. From these emerged Princess Whiskers, Dog, and Jocelyn. Jocelyn brushed off her vest.

"Well, that was a most unpleasant experience," she said.

Anne wrapped her arms around Jocelyn. "It's wonderful to see you. It's so good to have all of you back," she added to the others.

"Just so we're clear, I'm not a hugger," said Copperhelm.

Jocelyn surveyed the awaiting armies. "Would you care to bring us up to speed?" she asked. "Keeping in mind you will be graded on both the conciseness of your summary as well as the relevance of the details."

Anne pointed at the third tower. "The supreme leader of the pirate factions stole my quest, and now I'm the Official Antagonist. We need to get in there and stop this castle before it plunges into the rift and brings down the BGFM, which is really a magickal barrier dividing the world in two and preventing a terrible corruption trapped on the other side from infecting the entire Hierarchy."

"That . . . might be a little too concise."

The five armies faced off. Octo-Horse Pirate and his army of doppelgangers looked quick and dangerous, while the army of wizards and iron knights from the secret Wizards' Council warehouse appeared strong and menacing. The guards from the Pyrate Museum gripped their swords and seemed ready for a fight. Anne, Penelope, Hiro, and the staff from Saint Lupin's stood with Captain Marri Blackwood and her pirate crew, and a contingent of dragons led by their king, Valerian, swarmed the skies and the castle battlements.

"Oh, man, this is going to be epic!" said Penelope, twirling her sword.

"That's what I'm afraid of," said Hiro.

The time had come, and Anne felt completely calm. All her anxieties and nervousness melted away. She knew what she had to do.

Anne lifted her gauntlet-hand above her head.

"Activate Three-Handed Sword," she said, grabbing the holographic copy of the sword out of the air as soon as it appeared.

Octo-Horse Pirate raised his rapier, holding it over his head for a few seconds, and then dropped his arm.

"Attack!" he shouted.

"For Saint Lupin's!" shouted Anne.

The five armies launched themselves at one another.

The iron knights smashed through the first line of Marri's pirates, scattering them in all directions. Marri ducked a wicked blade slash and took off a knight's leg with a stroke of her own, but it wasn't enough. The sheer weight of the knights forced the pirates back to the wall. Several dragons swooped down and started plucking iron knights off the ground, flying them over the edge of the tier and releasing them into the rift.

Jocelyn leapt and twirled her way through a squad of attacking wizards. Spells flashed by her head, but she dodged every one of them, all the while blocking and slashing. Beside her, Copperhelm employed the more direct approach of charging straight at the wizards and bowling them over. Sassafras fell asleep midspell and got knocked over by a flying pirate.

Rokk led the charge against the doppelgangers. He plowed into their ranks, hacking and slashing at them with the real Three-Handed Sword, leaving trails of black smoke in his wake. Penelope was beside him, her sword in constant motion as she fought off two doppel-gangers at once. Hiro managed to scoop up a fallen wizard's spell book and started casting from that. He soon had several wizards gasping and wheezing inside a purple cloud.

One of the iron knights made the unfortunate move of stepping on the tail of Princess Whiskers. The cat tore into the knight, hissing and clawing and tearing its armor to shreds. When she finished, she left the iron knight in a heap and chased away three others.

"We could really use a few of those iron knights on our side," said Anne. "Jeffery, can you tune a few of them to my gauntlet?"

"Leave it to me," said Jeffery.

He swooped over a group of iron knights, pausing for a second or two over each one. The iron knights stopped, much to the surprise of the pirates who had been fighting them.

Anne raised her gauntlet-hand, and the iron knights responded.

"Much better," she said.

She sent the iron knights under her control running back into the ranks of the wizards. They cut a wide path, knocking scores of wizards off their feet. When they punched through the other side, Anne didn't have them turn back. Instead, she sent them into the remaining iron knights. Anne was more experienced in operating them than the wizards with their control cubes, and she sent her iron knights tearing into theirs, ripping off armor plating and chopping off heads. Soon only Anne's knights were left standing.

With the iron knights under Anne's control, the tide of the battle began to turn. The dragons and Marri's pirate crew joined Rokk and Penelope, forcing the doppelgangers toward a breach in the wall that had been created when one of Hiro's spells backfired. There was nothing on the other side but the edge of the tier.

"Don't let any of them escape," yelled Marri.

The pirates charged, and the doppelgangers were pushed through the breach. Some of them tried desperately to climb the outside wall to get away, but several dragons swooped down and flicked them off with their tails. Still, the sheer size of the doppelganger army gave them an advantage. One section broke away and flanked the pirates, and the tide of the battle shifted again, this time in their favor.

Something tugged at Anne's sleeve.

It was Dog.

He seemed to be trying to pull her in the direction of the third tower.

"Right," said Anne. "Thanks for the reminder."

Anne scanned the courtyard for any sign of Octo-Horse Pirate, but he was lost in the fray. She didn't have time to go searching for him. Neither Penelope nor Hiro was nearby, but she spotted Captain Copperhelm and ran over to him. Dog tagged along.

"I need to get inside that tower," said Anne.

"Do you need someone to go with you?" asked Copperhelm.

Anne looked around the courtyard. "I think the best way to help would be to keep everyone else out."

"Say no more," said Copperhelm. He grabbed Sassafras by the collar, hauled him to his feet, and shook him awake. "We need a path cleared from here to that tower. I'll cover you."

Sassafras raised his hands and started chanting immediately. Museum guards rushed in from all directions, but none of them got near Sassafras—Copperhelm swatted them away like flies.

Sassafras finished the spell, and a tiny ball of light appeared—accompanied by a rhinoceros. With a flick of his wrist, Sassafras sent the ball of light hurtling toward the tower. The rhinoceros followed, mowing down anyone unfortunate enough to be in its path. Anne hurried along behind it, with Dog at her side. When the rhinoceros reached the tower, it veered away, but Anne ran directly up and slapped her palm against the wall. The blue grid appeared, along with the expected INSERT KEY.

Jeffery landed on her shoulder. "Did you find a way in?"

"Not yet, but in the other quests there was always a clue in the quest riddle. In the first quest, the riddle explicitly said to find the Key You Cannot Hold. In the second quest, the riddle said to find the Three-Handed Sword, which is where the key was located."

"So you think the riddle for this quest contains a clue?" said Jeffery. "But the only location it mentions is the High Castle."

"The location of the key might not be a place," said Anne. "It could be inside an object."

"Like the rose?"

"I was thinking more about the legend's power," said Anne, and she pulled the jade cylinder seal from her pocket.

"You think there's some clue hidden in that thing?"

"The lines of a riddle can have more than one meaning. What's another name for legend?"

"A key!" cried Jeffery.

"Activate key," said Anne.

A jade key appeared in the air over the cylinder seal. Anne carefully reached for it with her gauntlet-hand. When she touched the key, it disappeared.

She held up her gauntlet-hand. "Activate Jade Key."

The key appeared again and Anne grabbed it. She jammed it into the slot in the wall of the tower, and an archway appeared. Anne wasted no time and ran inside.

"I don't think I'm going to be able to follow," said Jeffery, and even as he spoke he began to fade.

"That's okay," said Anne. "I need you to let Penelope, Hiro, and Marri know that we found a way into the third tower. Tell them to come right away!"

"Will do!" said Jeffery, and he shot back out through the archway.

Dog was no longer with her, but Anne didn't have time to go looking for him. She rode the elevator to the top of the tower. The doors opened to reveal yet another long gray corridor. Anne stepped out hesitantly, but there didn't appear to be anyone around. At the far end of the corridor was a single door bearing the faded image of a dragon. Anne walked to the door and stopped. A rectangular spot on the wall next to the door was lighter in color, as though something that had hung there for a long time had been removed.

Anne turned the knob and opened the door.

It was the same room as the one in her dreams, yet different. For one thing, there was no Oswald, although she hadn't really expected him to be there. Also, there was a ramp along the back wall leading to the next level. Anne climbed the ramp. The room at the top was identical to the other two towers, complete with a black computer terminal in the center.

And then she remembered.

Only a Daisywheel could activate the gold medallion. She needed Jocelyn.

How could they have overlooked that?

She turned to head back down the ramp, only to discover someone coming up. It was Octo-Horse Pirate, still with the parrot on his shoulder. He stopped at the top of the ramp and blocked the way.

"You have a habit of showing up where you're not wanted," he said to her.

"How would you know?" asked Anne.

"I know more than you realize."

Octo-Horse Pirate began to spin, but it wasn't an attack. He spun faster and faster until his body became a blur. His tentacles formed themselves into two groups and melded together, and his head changed shape. When the spinning stopped, he had undergone a complete transformation. The tentacles had become two human legs wearing a pair of gray pants and black leather boots. The armor had changed to a charcoal tunic with a midnight black cape slung over one shoulder. And the parrot had become a crow.

The gauntlet remained on his right hand.

Most important, instead of the horse-shaped helmet

there was a man's head, with tanned white skin, a firm square jaw, and dark wavy hair graying at the temples.

Anne stumbled back in shock. "Lord Greystone?!"

Lord Greystone smiled back at her. "Welcome to the end of the world."

THE INSTRUCTIONAL GUIDE *HOW TO SPOT A FAKE BEARD* OFFERS THE FOLLOWING TIPS ON HOW TO DETERMINE IF SOMEONE YOU'RE TALKING TO IS WEARING A DISGUISE:

1) Ask "Are you wearing a disguise?"

2) Pull on their beard if they have one. (If it's fake, it'll come off; if it's not fake, though, you're in big trouble.)

3) Tell a very long and detailed story about your last vacation. When they fall asleep due to boredom, they'll drool all over themselves. This won't tell you whether or not they're wearing a disguise, but it'll be really funny.

19

The Legend and the Lady

Anne could hardly believe what she was seeing. Octo-Horse Pirate—Marri's father—was actually Lord Greystone, the Minister of Questing.

"But—when—where—how?" she stammered.

"All succinct and articulate questions," said Greystone.

"I was expecting someone else."

"I'm sorry to disappoint you."

Anne was at a complete loss. She had been certain that Octo-Horse Pirate was really Oswald Grey. Hadn't he used his blood to activate the castle along with hers?

Didn't he know all about her dreams and the creation of the world? What did this mean? Had it been some sort of trick on the part of Greystone all along?

She was finally able to gather her thoughts. "We need to stop this castle."

"It's restoring the world to its original form," said Greystone. "Surely you don't object to that."

"If you let it bring down the barrier, the corruption will spread and infect everything. I can't imagine even *you* would want that to happen."

His expression became deadly serious. "On the contrary, that's exactly what I want to happen."

Anne couldn't believe what she was hearing. "But why?"

"I have my reasons."

Anne clenched her jaw. "I'm not going to let you do this."

"But you already have. The wheels are in motion. All I have to do is wait here until the castle reaches its destination—which, incidentally, should be in just a few minutes. I think it's safe to say I've won this time."

"Don't be so sure," said Anne. "Your doppelganger army is nearly defeated, and I have another medallion.

And any minute now the rest of my group is going to come running in here, and then we'll see who wins."

"Ah, yes, the master medallion," said Greystone. "Thank you for reminding me." He turned to the crow. "Neeva, a little assistance, if you please."

The crow launched from his shoulder and dove straight at Anne. She tried to duck, but Neeva latched on to her gauntlet. Before Anne realized what was happening, the crow had ripped the black medallion out of its slot and flown back to Greystone.

Neeva landed on Greystone's shoulder and dropped the black medallion into his hand.

Greystone shook his head. "Tsk, tsk. Some people never learn."

"Give that back!" said Anne.

"A bit of trivia: Genuine quest medallions are nearly indestructible, which makes sense, given what they have to endure. Unfortunately, in order to remain adaptable, that's the one quality a master medallion cannot duplicate."

Greystone squeezed his gauntlet-hand into a fist.

"No!" yelled Anne.

When Greystone opened the gauntlet again, all that

remained was a pile of black powder. He turned his palm over and let the particles scatter.

Brushing the dust from his hands, he looked back to Anne. "Now we're back to just the one."

Anne stretched out her gauntlet-hand. "Transfer gold medallion!"

Nothing happened.

Greystone chuckled. "Nice try. Our gauntlets might be twins, but mine has received a few upgrades. I'm afraid that little trick isn't going to work."

Anne couldn't stop the castle without a medallion, and time was almost up. She needed to gain possession of the gold medallion quickly. Too bad it wouldn't simply decide to fly to her gauntlet on its own as in the first two quests. But maybe that was it! A wild plan formed in her head. It was risky, but the time for caution was long past. Her gauntlet might not be powerful enough to beat Greystone's, but perhaps the medallion itself was.

"I challenge you to a duel for leadership of the pirates," said Anne in a clear, strong voice, hoping she sounded convincing. She had no hope of defeating Greystone with a sword, but if her plan worked she wouldn't actually have to fight.

Greystone chuckled. "Sorry, but I'm afraid that only works if you're a pirate under my command."

Anne pulled her pirate token from her pocket and held it up for him to see. "But I am one. Marri had Penelope, Hiro, and me sign the contracts yesterday morning back at Saint Lupin's. We were officially part of her crew, but then she surrendered her ship to you yesterday. Technically, that makes you its captain."

Greystone stared at the pirate token. "And what exactly do you think winning a duel will gain you?"

"I'll be the leader. Then you'll have to follow my orders."

Greystone laughed. He obviously thought the idea of a duel was ridiculous, which was exactly what Anne was hoping for.

"Well?" she pressed.

He shook his head. "I'm not dueling with you."

Anne did her best to mask her excitement. "Does that mean you forfeit?"

"Call it whatever you want, I'm not—"

Greystone paused as realization dawned on him. He shook a finger at her. "Nice try."

Anne swallowed. "What do you mean?"

"Pirate law. If I refuse to duel, I forfeit all my possessions to you, including the medallion."

"What would it matter?" said Anne. "It's not like I could force you to give it to me."

He patted his gauntlet. "True, but these medallions of yours seem to have a mind of their own. Was that your plan? Hope I would forfeit and then the medallion might jump back to its new owner?"

"It might not," said Anne.

"That's not a risk I can afford to take," he said, clearly annoyed. "You've given me no choice, but let's make this brief, shall we? I have more important matters to attend to." Greystone raised his gauntlet-hand. "As the person challenged, I get to choose the weapons. And I choose gauntlets."

The plan had backfired. Not only had Anne lost the opportunity for the medallion to return on its own, but if she lost to Greystone, he would win all her possessions, including her gauntlet.

She raised her gauntlet-hand and did her best to keep it from trembling. "Activate Three-Handed Sword of the Guardian."

The Three-Handed Sword appeared above her gauntlet, and she grabbed it out of the air. As always, despite its immense size, she had no trouble wielding it. She didn't know any fancy flourishes as Penelope did, but she hoped the sheer size of it might give her an edge. Unfortunately, Greystone didn't seem overly surprised or concerned by the appearance of the sword. If anything, she got the sense he'd been expecting it. After a moment's pause, he held out his own gauntlet-hand.

"Activate Three-Handed Sword of the Guardian," he said.

Another Three-Handed Sword appeared in the air above his gauntlet, the exact twin of the one Anne was holding, complete with a dragon stone in its cross guard. Greystone reached up and grasped the hilt.

Anne's jaw fell open. "Where did you get that?"

Greystone grinned. "This gauntlet is the twin of yours, remember? In fact, it's more like its successor. Everything yours can do, mine can do better, and it even has a few extra features yours doesn't. Also, if we're going to play pirates—"

He spun in a blur once again and transformed back into Octo-Horse Pirate.

"—then I should probably dress the part."

Lord Greystone was formidable enough in his human form. In his Octo-Horse Pirate form, in his armored power suit, he was well over seven feet tall. The metal was smooth and polished, and the dragon stone in the center of his chest plate shone brightly. His tentacles swished and slithered on the floor. He spun his sword around in a few arcs, leaving no doubt as to his own sword-fighting abilities.

The rift loomed large in the windows. The castle had almost arrived at its destination, and the entire tier shook as the storm intensified. Anne's thoughts flitted briefly to the battle below, and she wondered how it was going. Were her friends winning? If she lost here, then it wouldn't matter. She couldn't let them down, and she gripped the hilt of her sword and took several steadying breaths.

Greystone advanced on her, and Neeva took to the air, still in crow form. For some reason, he hadn't changed back into a parrot this time.

"What's the matter?" said Greystone. "Change your mind? Bitten off more than you can chew? Well, I warned you numerous times that you had no idea what you were getting yourself into and that sooner or later your antics would get you killed. It appears now is that time."

Anne looked over to the ramp, but it was sealed. She

couldn't get out, but worse, it meant no one could get in to help her.

"It's just the two of us, I'm afraid," said Greystone.

He charged at her and swung his sword.

Anne ducked and rolled under the sweeping blade. The sword cut a wide gash into the wall exactly where her head would have been. Leaping to her feet, Anne aimed a swing at his torso, but Neeva came swooping in. Anne was forced to abandon her attack and dodged the crow's talons instead. She shuffled sideways and moved toward the center of the room. Anne was no sword fighter at the best of times, and she definitely hadn't anticipated having to deal with two opponents.

Greystone laughed. "Run all you want! You're only wasting your own time."

He charged at her a second time and swung wildly. Anne dodged again, even managing to deflect his blade slightly with her own. But Neeva dove at her and yet again cut off any possibility of a counterattack. She retreated behind the computer terminal, but Greystone's tentacles carried him up and over the black column without breaking stride. Neeva circled above, ready to strike at any moment.

Anne kept moving back until she reached the outer wall and found herself pressed directly against one of the windows. Greystone towered over her, his sword raised above his head, poised to strike.

"Well, shiver me timbers, it looks like you lose," he said.

Anne formulated a quick plan, but the timing would have to be perfect. She held her sword in front, as though bracing for the blow. Just as Greystone swung, however, she ducked low and rolled in the other direction. Greystone's blade struck the window, and it exploded in a shower of glass. The shards flew in all directions, and a great gust of wind from the storm sent him stumbling back.

As soon as Anne was back on her feet, she raised her gauntlet-hand. "Activate GPS!"

Jeffery appeared in a burst of light. He was still a bit faded, but at least he was there.

Anne nearly collapsed with relief.

"You're cutting it close, you know," said Jeffery. "Although I do like a dramatic entrance."

As if to emphasize the point, a bolt of lightning lit up the sky.

"Well, now that you're here, I could use some help

dealing with that crow," Anne yelled over the crash of thunder.

Jeffery stared at Neeva circling above them. "I'll handle him. But two things first. One, I need to transfer the Construct to a computer terminal now or we're going to lose her."

Anne pointed to the terminal in the middle of the room. "Can you use that one?"

Jeffery nodded.

An arc of energy shot out from the gauntlet and connected with the terminal. The Construct appeared next to it on the floor. She was almost completely transparent and lay unmoving. Unfortunately, there wasn't anything they could do to help her right at that moment.

"And the other thing?" asked Anne, fully aware that Greystone had recovered.

"I brought you a present. Hold it in your gauntlet-hand and activate it." He opened his claw and a small object dropped into Anne's hand. It was one of the glass cubes the wizards had used to control the iron knights.

With that, Jeffery shot straight into the air. Neeva banked away and flew to the other end of the room, and Jeffery gave chase. They swooped and rolled and dove with such speed that they looked like two blurs, one black and one rainbow colored, ricocheting around the room.

Greystone was advancing on her once again.

What exactly had Jeffery meant by "activate it"? Anne could only think of one thing.

"Activate iron knight," she said.

Her feet were lifted from the floor as a holographic iron knight formed around her. She took control and swept up the Three-Handed Sword using the hand of the knight.

She turned to face Greystone.

"I believe we have a duel to finish," she said.

Anne launched the iron knight at him in a full charge. He barely raised his own sword in time. The blades came together in an explosion of sparks. Anne twirled and immediately attacked again from a different angle. Greystone's tentacles twisted him around to meet her. They crossed swords again in a quick series of blows, sending out arcs of energy.

Greystone launched a counterattack. Anne retreated several steps and ducked an especially vicious blow, but then she launched another attack of her own. She put the weight of the iron knight into her blows, and she soon had the upper hand again.

After several more exchanges, Greystone leapt back, clearly winded, but Anne wasn't going to give him time to catch his breath. She continued forward, swinging left and right in great sweeping arcs. Greystone managed to parry the blows, but his movements had slowed considerably. He stumbled into the computer terminal and nearly fell over, dropping his guard. Anne pressed her advantage. She crashed her sword into his armor again and again.

Finally, she kicked out with the iron knight and caught Greystone in the chest. He went crashing to the floor and his sword disappeared. The light from his dragon stone flickered. The blow had cracked it down the middle. As he struggled to regain his feet, Anne knew what she had to do. She raised her sword over her head.

"This is for everything," she said.

And she swung.

The blade struck the dragon stone dead center, and there was a blinding eruption of light as the stone shattered into a million pieces. Greystone collapsed in a heap and lay unmoving. With the dragon stone destroyed, his armor was without power.

Anne didn't waste any time. She knelt beside him and slid the gauntlet from his hand. As soon as it was free, it transformed in front of her eyes, becoming smooth and metallic. She recognized it immediately: It was the Matron's metal hand! Greystone's suit must have disguised its true form as well.

She bent to remove the gold medallion, but before she touched it, a black streak swooped out of the air and snatched the medallion out of the metal arm.

It was Neeva.

"Hey!" shouted Anne.

The crow soared back into the air and hovered near the ceiling.

"Who *are* you?" asked Anne.

Jeffery landed on her gauntlet. "He's the GPS from the other gauntlet."

"That's GPC, thank you very much," said Neeva. "General Pathfinder Crow. Much superior to those ridiculous sparrows."

Anne gasped. "You can talk?"

"Of course I can talk!" said Neeva, sounding offended.

"I'll show you who's superior," said Jeffery, and he launched himself at the crow.

Twin beams of light shot from Neeva's eyes and slammed into Jeffery. He dropped like a stone and crashed to the floor. Anne rushed over. His feathers were ruffled, their edges singed.

"Are you okay?" asked Anne.

"Never better," he croaked. "But I think I'm going to need an upgrade."

Jeffery hopped onto Anne's gauntlet and plucked the glass control cube from her gauntlet-hand. "I just need to borrow this for a minute."

He flew into the air.

"Activate iron knight!" he yelled, and the holographic iron knight formed around him.

"Ha-ha! Now that's more like it!" Jeffery exclaimed. "This upgrade is the best thing ever!"

Neeva took off again, bobbing and weaving all over the room. Despite the acrobatics, however, Jeffery managed to stay with him. The iron knight jumped and lunged and even cartwheeled. The knight's sword was a constant blur, cutting off Neeva's every path of escape, especially keeping him away from the broken window. Finally, the sword caught the crow broadside and sent him spinning into the wall. The gold medallion fell from his talons and clattered across the floor.

"Score one for the good guys!" said Jeffery.

His iron knight picked up the medallion. He started

toward Anne, but a whistle brought him up short. Neeva was perched atop the metal arm.

"Remember Greystone's warning," he said. "'Anything yours can do, mine can do better.' Activate iron knight!"

A holographic knight formed around the crow. It was bigger and more heavily armored then Jeffery's. Neeva charged at him. Jeffery tried to block him, but his iron knight was much too slow. The larger iron knight barreled into his and knocked it to the ground. Then it straddled Jeffery's knight and rained blows down upon it, smashing through the armor and tearing it to pieces. With a final blow, Jeffery's iron knight exploded in a blast of light.

Jeffery lay on the floor, unmoving. Anne watched in horror as Neeva's knight lifted its foot and brought it down heavily on the tiny sparrow: once, twice, thrice.

"Stop it!" screamed Anne.

Anne tried to reach Jeffery, but Neeva's iron knight stood in her way. It towered over her with its sword raised above its head.

She looked up.

"Just so you know," said Neeva, "this is completely personal."

But it didn't swing at her. Instead, the iron knight

turned and swung at something on the floor. The gold medallion. There was nothing Anne could do. The sword struck the medallion dead center.

And the medallion exploded.

This time for real.

Anne was unsure how much time had passed. When she finally uncurled her aching body, she discovered that she had been thrown back several yards. Her head was throbbing, and her eyes were playing tricks on her. In the distance, the blurry outline of a bird seemed to transform itself into the blurry outline of a man. She blinked several times, but when she looked again the outline was gone.

Both Greystone and the Construct were still unmoving.

As Anne sat up, her arm brushed against something on the floor. It was the other gauntlet, the Matron's metal hand. Its surface had been singed from the explosion, but it seemed otherwise undamaged. She looked down at her own gauntlet then. It too had been hit by the explosion, but it hadn't fared nearly as well. Many of the metal strips had been torn clean off, and there was a gaping tear along the seam of the leather glove. The inset on the cuff was dangling from a single wire.

Jeffery still lay unmoving on the floor. Anne crawled over and scooped him up in her hands. His body hung lifeless. She lightly stroked his feathers, but there was no response. Then, slowly, in a rainbow of glittering color, he crumbled to dust and sifted through her fingers.

"No!" she gasped.

She scrabbled at the tiles, trying to save the shimmering pieces, but each one she touched faded to nothing. Tears flowed freely down her cheeks. Of all the things, she was crying over a little bird—a ridiculous, crazy, sarcastic, wonderful, brave, heroic companion.

She held up the gauntlet. "Activate GPS," she whispered.

Nothing happened.

"Activate GPS!" she shouted.

Still nothing.

She held back a sob.

"Jeffery, please come back to me."

There was no response.

Anne gently slid the gauntlet from her hand and placed it carefully, almost reverently, on the floor. It was destroyed beyond repair. She knew it in her heart. And

Jeffery was gone with it. His final act had been to protect her.

"Hello, Anne."

At the sound of the voice, Anne leapt to her feet and spun around. A thin young man with pale white skin and unruly dark hair, dressed in a white lab coat and brown loafers, stood next to the computer terminal.

"You're—you're Oswald," said Anne.

"Yes," said the young man.

Anne blinked several times to make sure she was really seeing him. "But how can you be here? You lived over ten thousand years ago, before the world was even created."

Oswald smiled. "Perhaps I've just aged really well." He reached a hand toward the terminal as though to touch it, but his hand passed through. "Or perhaps not."

Anne gasped. "You're a hologram?"

"Something like that."

"Wait. Did I just see you transform? Were you Neeva all along?"

"Playing the role of a gauntlet GPS was a convenient way to keep an eye on things without being too conspicuous, but that role has served its purpose. I've now transferred myself out of the gauntlet and into this terminal. You have no idea how long it's taken me to reach this place."

Anne's head was spinning. With the loss of her gauntlet and Jeffery, it was difficult to process what she was seeing. But she forced herself to focus on the moment. Her gut told her this wasn't over yet.

"You just called me Anne," she said.

"Of course," said the Oswald Hologram. "That is your name, isn't it?"

"Yes, but I just—someone gave me the impression that I might be...Zarala."

The Oswald Hologram tilted his head. "Well, the resemblance is unmistakable. But then, that's to be expected."

"I don't understand."

"All will be revealed in due time."

Anne glanced out the window. Strangely, the air was completely still. The storm was gone, or else something was holding it back. The rift threatened to swallow the entire tier. They had minutes left at most.

"The castle!" she cried. "We have to stop it!"

The Oswald Hologram began pacing. "We could do that. But first I'd like you to consider my offer. I can give you a home and a family. Someplace safe and warm, with people who love you. Just what you've always wanted. But even more than that, I can grant you the power to create worlds of your own, whatever you wish. Just imagine the adventures you could have."

Anne looked again at the computer terminal and noted that Oswald never strayed very far from it even while pacing around the room.

"Are you the guardian of this terminal?" she asked. "Like the old wizard and the knight in the other towers?"

"Oh, I think you'll find I'm much more than just a mere guardian. Zarala didn't see it that way, of course, but I had other plans. Oswald made sure of that when he programmed me."

"*Oswald* programmed you?"

"Oh, yes. He had wonderful plans for me, too. Plans to rule this world and as many others as he could create. But those plans came to naught after the war, after the world shattered and the barrier was put in place. I have to admit, Zarala made it nearly impossible for me to escape, and I'm not ashamed to say there were times I considered giving up altogether. It's taken me nearly ten thousand years to regain control of the computer, but I believe I've finally found a way."

"That's why you're doing this? To take control? To rule the world?"

The Oswald Hologram shrugged. "What can I say? I admit it's a bit predictable, but it's how I was programmed. I'm a two-dimensional villain in a three-dimensional holographic body."

All the time he was speaking, the Oswald Hologram had been turning something over in his hand. Anne finally caught a glimpse of it. It was a small green object.

She stuck her hand in her pocket. The jade cylinder wasn't there. She checked her other pockets, but it was nowhere to be found. It had still been in her possession when she reached the top of the tower, but in all the kerfuffle it must have fallen out. Or else someone had taken it.

Oswald held out the seal. "Are you looking for this?"

Something about seeing the Oswald Hologram holding the jade cylinder seal made Anne uneasy. Hadn't the seal already fulfilled its function by helping them read the map and providing the key to enter the tower? What further use could it possibly have on this quest?

"Can I have it back, please?" asked Anne as politely as possible.

"Certainly," said the Oswald Hologram. But instead of handing it to her, he suddenly hurled it at the floor, where it shattered into pieces, scattering in all directions.

"What did you do that for?" she demanded.

The Oswald Hologram ignored her and began searching among the debris.

While the hologram was distracted, Anne looked around for anything she might use as a weapon. The only thing close was the Matron's metal hand. Moving slowly so as not to draw attention to herself, Anne bent down to retrieve it. It wasn't that she expected to be able to do anything with it, but she felt better holding something rather than nothing. When she picked it up, she noticed writing around the cuff: ANTAGONIST/ VILLAIN. Those two words reminded Anne of something the Matron had said early on in their first quest, about how being the antagonist didn't necessarily make someone the villain. Anne also noticed that some of the letters were thicker than the rest: the AN of ANTAGONIST, and the VIL of VILLAIN.

AN.

VIL.

ANVIL.

Seeing her name shocked her to her core, but what could it possibly mean? And even more important, how could it help?

"Ah, there you are," said the Oswald Hologram, bringing Anne back to the present.

He picked up a piece of the shattered cylinder. Except it wasn't a jade shard. It was a small gray square. He held it up for Anne to see. There was a small z painted on it.

"What's that?" asked Anne.

"Something I've been wanting to acquire for a very long time."

He walked over to the terminal and spoke. "Activate physical keyboard."

A rectangular seam appeared in the side of the terminal, and a hatch slid away. A thin gray rectangular block extended. The surface of the block contained dozens of small gray squares similar to the one the Oswald Hologram was holding, except they all had a different letter, number, or symbol. It reminded Anne of the blue grid. There was a small gap in one of the rows, and it was into this gap that the Oswald Hologram placed the z square. The square clicked into place, and the terminal beeped as though acknowledging its return.

"That ought to do it," he said.

He began typing, but he continued speaking as he did so. "You people are so gullible. You believed everything Lord Greystone told you, just as he believed everything he read in that ridiculous journal I gave him. The medallions and their quests were Zarala's. Her mistake, of course, was in assuming Oswald didn't know about them. Quite the opposite, in fact. He feigned ignorance, all the while working in secret to ensure that the true object of this quest was me. I was trapped in the terminal down in the courtyard, but blocked by Zarala from accessing this tower, meaning I could never reach my full potential. The rose that never bloomed, as it were. You rightly deciphered the legend as a key, but in my case, it referred not to the jade key but rather a physical key hidden inside the hollow cylinder. A keyboard key. The one letter without which I could not enter Zarala's user name.

"But now I have everything I need. Once I access her account, I will have complete control over the computer. Then I will be the one to decide what worlds to make and what worlds to crush under my feet."

The Oswald Hologram tapped a symbol on the keyboard, and LOGIN appeared on the side of the terminal. He then entered Zarala's name, typing slowly, as though relishing every keystroke. He pressed another key, and PASSWORD appeared on the screen.

"And now Zarala's failure is complete," said the Oswald Hologram.

He typed five keys, all numbers: 6-5-5-3-5.

It took a moment for the numbers to register, but Anne recognized them. Together, they comprised her orphan identification number. It couldn't be a coincidence. None of it could. Zarala had left a clear trail of clues leading Anne to this place. And now Anne was holding yet another piece of the puzzle, an item she had always loathed but which nevertheless seemed to form some integral part in everything. It was time to embrace who she was, and if that meant becoming the antagonist by choice, then so be it. After all, becoming the antagonist just meant being an opponent. Which of them was truly the "bad guy" remained to be seen.

Anne slid the metal hand over her own. It morphed around her and fit like a glove. It didn't burn or hurt at all. More than anything, it felt like it belonged.

Anne stretched out her right metal hand. "Stop what you're doing, or I'll be forced to destroy you."

"You can try," he said.

Anne willed the hand to do something, anything, but nothing happened.

The Oswald Hologram shook his head. "Poor Anne. Zarala is out of tricks, I'm afraid. There's no one left to help you."

Anne forced herself to think. What had Oswald said

about the gauntlet? Something about playing the role of the GPS? But if he was only playing the role, didn't that suggest that he wasn't the original GPS? And if he had transferred himself out of the gauntlet, did that mean the real GPS, whoever it was, was still in there? If that was true, then...

Oswald tapped a final key, and several more words appeared on the screen:

WELCOME BACK USER ZARALA

The Oswald Hologram threw back his head and laughed. "After all this time, I actually did it! I can't believe it! I can already feel the power coursing through me. The computer is mine. All hail Oswald, King of the Holograms, Master of Worlds, Lord of the Universe. My name shall be forever etched in the heavens. No one will ever—"

Anne stretched out the metal hand once again.

"Activate GPS!" she yelled.

A dark streak shot out of the metal hand with such force that it nearly knocked Anne off her feet. The streak smashed through the center of the Oswald Hologram.

"Ah, fiddlesticks," he said.

The Oswald Hologram shattered into a million pieces.

The black blur whirred around in a wide arc and stopped in front of Anne. It was a fire lizard, two feet from snout to tail. It had black scales and wings. Its eyes were bright green.

"Dog?" said Anne, incredulous. She knelt down and gave his head a pat. "Dog, is that really you? But—how—what...?"

Dog nudged her metal hand with his snout.

She laughed. "Sorry, but I don't have biscuits for you right now."

Dog persisted, and she got the sense he wasn't after a snack. He kept bumping the Matron's metal hand.

Anne wrinkled her nose. "What do you want with that?"

Dog flew over next to the prone form of the Construct and lay down next to her missing arm.

Anne began to catch on.

She pulled off the metal hand and positioned it where the Construct's hand had been severed. The metal hand connected to the Construct with a bright crackle of energy, such that Anne had to shield her eyes. When she looked again, the Construct was no longer lying on the floor. Instead, she was floating in the air. Her clothes were no longer tattered and dirty. In fact, gone were the lab coat, shirt, and pants. In their place, the Construct wore an emerald-green gown that glowed softly. And the metal hand was attached to her, as if it had always been a part of her.

Moreover, her body had changed. Now it was smooth and gleaming, as though it were made of dark crystal.

The Lady of Glass!

The Construct stretched out a hand. A small cloud of dust gathered around it and slowly formed itself into a small object: the black medallion. She offered it to Anne.

"Would you like to do the honors?" she asked.

"But it won't work," said Anne. "I'm not a Daisywheel."

The Construct winked at her. "Let's try it anyway, shall we?"

Anne took the medallion and walked to the center of the room. She tapped the computer terminal, and a slot opened up. With no small amount of trepidation, she placed the black medallion into the slot. There was a brief click.

"Full computer access granted," said a voice from nowhere in particular. "Do you wish to proceed with barrier removal?"

"No!" shouted Anne. "I mean, please leave the barrier in place."

"Acknowledged."

The floor shuddered as the castle stopped just above the rift opening.

Anne let out a sigh of relief.

"Congratulations," said the Construct. "You have completed your mission."

The Construct stretched out her arms. A sphere of light appeared and expanded to encompass the entire room. Anne's feet left the floor, and she floated in the air. Greystone's unconscious body, still in the form of Octo-Horse Pirate, was lifted as well. The sphere of light carried them through the window and out of the tower.

THE ADVENTURER'S GUIDE TO STORY ENDINGS OFFERS THE FOLLOWING GUIDELINES FOR TYING UP THE LOOSE THREADS OF ANY QUEST:

1) Actually finish the quest.

2) Leave several minor plot threads uncompleted to drive people crazy.

3) Don't forget to thank the squirrels.

20

The Rogue Keeper

Anne floated over the battlefield in a bubble of pure light. The fighting had ceased. The ground was littered with broken weapons and pieces of smashed iron knights. There wasn't a single doppelganger in sight; presumably all were either destroyed or driven off the side of the tier back into the BGFM. The armies from the Wizards' Council and the Pyrate Museum had returned to their airships and were retreating to a safe distance, not in the least because the dragons were patrolling the skies and keeping everyone well back. The *Leaky Mermaid* hovered high in the air just beyond the edge of the tier.

The sphere of light deposited them on the airship and disappeared. Anne landed between Penelope and Hiro, with the unconscious Greystone a few feet away. Marri immediately ordered two of the pirate crew to carry her father into her cabin and went with them. Anne was relieved to see everyone had made it back aboard safe and sound.

Penelope pulled Anne into a body-smooshing hug, and Hiro as well. The staff from Saint Lupin's gathered around them, as did the pirate crew. There were many hugs and cries of joy.

Jocelyn beamed at Anne. "Well done, Anne. I knew you could do it."

Anne smiled at the compliment. "Not without the rest of the group."

"Well, I'm very impressed with all of you."

"Where's your gauntlet?" asked Hiro. "Where's Jeffery?"

Anne's smile faltered, and a well of emotion threatened to overtake her. In all the excitement, she had momentarily forgotten. She couldn't bring herself to tell them Jeffery was gone, couldn't bear to speak the words.

Penelope must have read something in her expression. She put her arm around Anne's shoulders.

"What happened?" asked Penelope.

Suddenly the Construct was in their midst. "Why, Anne saved the world yet again, of course."

Anne sniffed. "What about the barrier? And the corruption?"

"The barrier is safe and secure once again, and now that I have full access to the computer I have corrected the error that caused the corruption. Its influence has been completely removed from the doppelganger world as well, and they are free to build their own society as they see fit."

"So, it's finally over, then?" asked Anne.

"Not quite," said the Construct. "I believe you still have some questions regarding your origins."

Anne swallowed. This wasn't Greystone telling her half-baked stories he read in some ten-thousand-year-old journal. This was what she had waited for her whole life: the truth.

"Am I Zarala?" she asked.

"No and yes."

"Well, *that's* not cryptic or anything," said Hiro.

The Construct smiled indulgently. "You are not the original Zarala, but you are her clone."

"Hey, Anne is not a clown!" shouted Penelope. "You take that back!"

Hiro placed a hand on Penelope's shoulder. "She said *clone*, not *clown*," he explained. "A clone is like an exact copy of a person."

Penelope's eyes widened. "Anne is a doppelganger?"

"It's a very different process, I assure you," said the Construct. "Also, a doppelganger tries to replace the original person. A clone exists alongside them. As you have probably guessed by now, it was Oswald, not Zarala, who sabotaged the computer. Zarala realized something had gone terribly wrong, but she also knew she wouldn't be able to fix it within her lifetime. She created you, Anvil, and placed you as an infant in cryostasis in the hopes that one day you would awaken at a time when the error could be fixed and the corruption eradicated. She also created the three medallions to grant you the necessary access to the computer, medallions that could only be activated using Zarala's gauntlet."

"Why three?"

"The quests were designed to work together: the gold medallion to lower the barrier, the silver medallion to correct the error, and the copper medallion to ensure the integrity of the data. And all three together could be used to gain full computer access."

"She couldn't have just left a note or something?" asked Anne.

"The computer contains incredible power and carries with it a tremendous responsibility. She could not risk making it too easy."

"No danger there," muttered Hiro.

"Unfortunately, Oswald refused to cooperate with Zarala, and the barrier remained in place for the rest of their lives. And then, after many more generations, people simply forgot what the medallions were for. The three families guarded them closely, but no one remembered their true purpose."

"What woke me, then?" asked Anne.

"To explain that, first you must understand how the computer operates. Due to a physical limitation in its design, it can only measure time using four digits. Thus it can only count to the year 9999 before having to reset. Furthermore, in the Old World each year consisted of three hundred sixty-five and one quarter days. But in this world, each year has only three hundred sixty days exactly. Over the course of ten thousand years, the difference between those two systems of counting adds up to around one hundred and fifty years."

"Let me guess," said Penelope. "When our world hit its ten-thousand-year mark, it caused a rift to form in the barrier. And then one hundred and fifty or so years later when the computer hit ten thousand years by the Old World's way of reckoning, it opened the rift again."

"Precisely."

Hiro looked impressed.

"What?" said Penelope. "Sometimes I actually pay attention."

The Construct continued. "Since the second rift was tied directly to the computer, it woke you, Anne. Evelyn Daisywheel knew how to access the laboratory beneath Saint Lupin's, and she found you and brought you to the orphanage. But after she was killed during the expedition to the other side of the barrier, her doppelganger returned and took over."

"Why were *you* on the other side of the barrier?" asked Anne.

"When the first rift happened, I contacted Hieronymus Darkflame, since his family had possession of the gold medallion that could control the barrier. Using my metal hand, which is really Zarala's second gauntlet, one she created specifically for me, we successfully activated the quest...."

"But I thought my gauntlet originally activated the medallion."

The Construct shook her head. "Because the gauntlets are twins, the medallion could be activated by either one. Doing so brought us in close proximity to the High Castle, however, and the Oswald Hologram took the opportunity to attack us. He wrested the medallion from the gauntlet, resulting in an explosion. I lost my hand, and Hieronymus was killed. I fell through the rift before it closed, and my metal hand went with me. The doppelgangers found the hand before I did. Since the hand is what granted me my autonomy, without it I was forced to attach myself to the first computer terminal I could find, the one you found me near. But it had been corrupted by the error, and my program began to degrade almost immediately. It wasn't long before I couldn't remember who or what I was."

"Is that why you weren't solid?"

"Yes."

"Wait. If you've been on the other side of the barrier for one hundred and fifty years, then who was the Construct we met on our quests?"

"Those were emergency backups. With me missing, the computer still needed an interface and so created copies in my absence. Unfortunately, they had limited abilities and the terminals where they appeared had also suffered varying degrees of corruption."

"Because they were located on dead tiers?" asked Anne.

"Yes. When a high-level quest fails, it opens a temporary rift to the other side, allowing the corruption to seep through and kill the tier. For this reason, dead tiers are connected to the corruption's influence, even from this side of the barrier. That's why they're drawn to the High Castle—because of its connection to the other side."

"What about him?" asked Anne.

The Construct's expression became grave. "Just as you are Zarala's clone, Lord Greystone is Oswald's clone. He was also placed in cryosleep, but he awoke during the first rift. Hence the difference in age, and the fact that he has a daughter."

"And let me guess: All clones have yellow eyes."

"That is correct."

"But Lord Greystone's eyes aren't yellow," said Penelope.

"His appearance as Lord Greystone was a holographic disguise provided by the suit. His eyes could be whatever color he wished them to be. Likewise, he used the suit to disguise the true appearance of my metal hand."

Anne had no family—at least, not in the true sense. She was merely a copy of someone else. For just an instant she regretted that she had rejected the Oswald Hologram's offer of a home and a family.

"You're saying Greystone is over one hundred and fifty years old?" asked Hiro.

"Using Old World technology, he found ways to extend his life," said the Construct.

"But why was he trying to destroy this world?" asked Penelope.

The Construct's expression softened. "That is his story to tell. I suggest you hear him out, and try not to judge too harshly."

Penelope frowned. "If you're suggesting we simply forgive him for everything he's done, don't count on it."

"What you decide to do is up to you, but be careful not to counter hate with hate. That path only ever leads to destruction."

A gleam of light caught Anne's eye. It was the sun reflecting off the Matron's—or rather, the Construct's—metal hand. She reached out hesitantly and touched it.

"And what about this?" she asked.

"Ah, yes," said the Construct, holding up the arm. "The hidden meaning of the riddle. The High Castle was the name of the laboratory where Zarala and Oswald conducted their research. Zarala designed me after herself, but of course I couldn't grow, hence the rose that never bloomed. The legend's power referred to an upgrade intended for the gauntlet to grant me full access to the computer so I could deal with the corruption. It activated the gold medallion, but of course I lost the hand soon after, before I could act."

Anne pointed to the words ANTAGONIST/VILLAIN, still visible on the metal hand. "Why that inscription?"

The Construct gave a grim smile. "I was suspicious of Oswald early on, but Zarala thought it was simply a glitch in my programming. After his betrayal, of course, she realized I had been right all along. She also realized how dangerous it was to have all her power centralized in one place, and that if Oswald ever got his hands on her original gauntlet there would be nothing to stop him. So she created this hand for me to provide more of a balance, and the inscription was a reminder that sometimes it's good to challenge one's beliefs."

"But why make that my name?"

"Because in the same spirit, she didn't just want a

copy of herself. She wanted you to become your own person, to make your own choices, even if that meant opposing some of hers. And in that regard, I know she would be proud of who you've become."

Anne blushed. "Okay, that makes sense, I guess, but it's still a weird name."

"Oh, I don't know. Originally she wanted to name you Lady Wynter Snookums Fufu Butterscotch, after her pet squirrel."

Penelope opened her mouth, but Anne clamped a firm hand over it before she could say anything. "That's okay. Anvil is fine."

"But how did the Matron get possession of the hand?" asked Hiro.

"The Evelyn doppelganger, whom you knew as the Matron, was the one who found it. Since it wasn't designed for humans, she was unable to fully access its power, but it was enough to bring her through the barrier, from the doppelganger world into this one."

"But what about Anne's gauntlet?" asked Jocelyn. "Why did my parents have it?"

"Because Zarala entrusted the gauntlet to a very ancient family, of which you and your sister are the most recent descendants."

Anne frowned. "What family?"

"Why, her own family, of course. Zarala lived long enough in this world to have a son who then carried on the family line."

Penelope's eyes widened. "But wouldn't that make Anne...sort of...Jocelyn's great-great-great-times-a-hundred-grandmother or something?"

Jocelyn coughed.

Anne felt her cheeks grow warm. "She already said I'm not Zarala."

Penelope crossed her arms. "She said you're her exact duplicate."

"I'm not anyone's great-great-anything."

Dog glided over and stopped beside the Construct.

"And he's the GPS for the gauntlet, correct?" said Anne.

"Wait, Dog is a GPS?" said Penelope. "But he's—he's—he's Dog!"

"He has a little more autonomy than most GPSs," the Construct explained. "He couldn't act as long as the Oswald Hologram had control of my hand, but once he left, Dog was free to return. And speaking of GPSs and gauntlets, there was one final thing."

The Construct raised her metal hand and the pieces of Anne's gauntlet appeared on the deck. A blue sphere of light encircled them, and they glowed so brightly that everyone was forced to look away. When the sphere disappeared, the gauntlet was whole once more. The Construct took it and handed it to Anne.

Anne held it tentatively, not daring to hope for too much. "Activate GPS," she said, her voice shaking.

A tiny rainbow-colored sparrow appeared in a burst of light.

"Jeffery!" she exclaimed.

He landed on the gauntlet and began to check himself over. "Okay, just for the record, being dead sucks," he said. "But on the upside, I can cross resurrection off my bucket list."

"Dying and being resurrected was on your bucket list?" said Hiro.

"Hey, you do you and I'll do me." Jeffery examined the gauntlet. "Wow! It's like it's brand-new."

The Construct patted Jeffery on the head. "I removed your access to the computer, since no GPS should have that kind of power, but in recognition of your bravery I also removed the block. You can appear whenever you want, whether you're on a quest or not."

"Oh, wow, this is going to be great!" he said. "Just think of all the late-night talks we can have now."

Anne sighed, but contentedly.

All was well with the world once again, and she was finally home.

An hour later, Anne, Penelope, Hiro, and Jocelyn had gathered along with Marri in the captain's cabin. Greystone was lying in the bunk, still in Octo-Horse Pirate form. With the dragon stone destroyed, he was unable to transform. The slit in his helmet was open, but his eyes remained closed. Marri moved her chair closer to the bed, while the others stayed back. She took her father's hand in her own.

Greystone stirred and opened his eyes—his bright yellow eyes. He surveyed those gathered in the room. "I suppose you're... here to arrest me," he wheezed. His voice sounded weak and shaky.

Anne resisted the urge to lash out at him. The Construct had asked them to listen to his story, and she would do so, through gritted teeth if that's what it took.

"We just want answers," said Marri. "Why did you do this?"

He tried to lift his hands to his head but didn't have the strength.

"Remove...my helmet," he said.

Marri reached over and slid the horse-shaped helmet from his head. As soon as the helmet was off, his body transformed before them, although without the spinning this time. The tentacles disappeared, leaving behind one twisted human leg and one that was completely missing below the knee. Both his arms were intact, but one hand was missing all its fingers. The left side of his face was covered in heavy scar tissue, but not so bad that Anne didn't recognize him.

"You look exactly like him," she said.

"Like who?" asked Marri.

"Oswald Grey, the scientist who worked with Zarala."

Marri turned the helmet over in her hands. "Why did you disguise yourself with this?"

Greystone coughed. "The expedition. My body... was broken. I needed...power...to make things right."

"What happened to you?" asked Jocelyn.

Greystone took a deep, shuddering breath before he spoke. "I was a member of the expedition group that went to the other side of the barrier," he began, his voice a little steadier. "We had formed a special adventure group for the Wizards' Council and were ready to take on the world. We had talent, no question, but I was eager, too eager as it turns out, to prove myself. I led them on a quest that was far too dangerous. I should have known better. I did know better, in fact. I just ignored the warning bells in my head. It ended...badly. That was...eleven years ago."

Eleven years. Anne felt like that number had significance, but before she could place it Penelope stepped forward.

"*You* were the leader?" asked Penelope, her voice near to cracking.

"Yes, I was the Keeper," said Greystone. "The other members were...Siri Greystone, my wife and Marri's mother...Evelyn Daisywheel...and Rachael and Constantine Shatterblade."

Jocelyn gasped at the mention of her sister, but Penelope continued, her whole body shaking as she did.

"And you—you let people think it was my parents' fault all this time? You let *me* think that? That they had caused the quest to fail and killed all those people? You let everyone think all those terrible things about our family?"

"I...needed time...to fix it. I justified it...told myself they would have understood...the necessity. I'm...truly sorry."

Penelope said nothing more, but she turned and left

the room, slamming the door behind her. Hiro followed her out, presumably to ensure she was okay.

"Why the gold medallion?" asked Anne. "If you knew the dangers, why did you want to bring down the barrier?"

He choked back a sob. "Because—because it was my one best chance...of bringing her back."

"Who?" asked Marri.

Greystone stared into her eyes. "Your mother." He turned and stared straight ahead, as though looking at someone who wasn't in the room. "Our quest took us to the doppelganger world.... She was killed by the corruption...but I never found her copy. Her doppelganger. The Oswald Hologram appeared to me... gave me the journal...hinted that if the barrier were removed...and the worlds reunited...she might return to me. To us. And then I saw the metal hand...down in the laboratory...after your first quest...and I knew...I knew I had a chance."

Anne's stomach twisted into a knot. Her disgust for everything Greystone had done remained, but it was tempered by a great sense of loss—for Penelope, for Jocelyn, for Marri, and even in some small way for Greystone himself.

Greystone closed his eyes and lapsed back into

unconsciousness. There was so much more Anne wanted to ask, but she knew she would never get enough answers to mend all the hurt and confusion she felt.

Jocelyn left the cabin, but Anne remained by the door, unable to tear herself away.

Marri sat by her father's side, holding his hand in silence. Anne wasn't sure how long they stayed there—whether it was just a few minutes or a few hours—watching the slow rise and fall of Greystone's chest, until finally he breathed his last.

And then Anne wept.

Marri's crew gave Greystone a proper pirate burial. For whatever else he might have been in life, to them he was the supreme leader of the pirates and, at least for a short time, their captain. They wrapped his body in long strips of cloth and lowered it on ropes into the BGFM. They sent his helmet with him.

After the funeral, Anne wandered to the stern and leaned against the railing. Eventually Jocelyn joined her.

"That's...not what I was expecting," said Anne. "None of it."

"It rarely is," said Jocelyn.

They stood there together for a while, watching schools of flying fish soar past and enjoying the afternoon breeze. Eventually, though, Jocelyn placed a hand over Anne's.

"We should probably talk about your plans," she said.

Anne looked at her. "What do you mean?"

"The school is in shambles, and with everything that's happened, I suspect the Wizards' Council isn't likely to allow you back into the quest academy, even with Lord Greystone gone."

"That's okay," said Anne. "I lost my blacksmith token anyway."

"If I still had a school, I would give you your certificate now. Goodness knows you've earned it. You've accomplished more in these past few months than most adventurers do in a lifetime. I just wish I could have prepared you better."

An idea struck Anne. It was perfect, perhaps the most perfect idea she'd ever had, and it would at least make sense of something amid the confusing jumble that was her current life.

She gripped Jocelyn's hand. "You should have Saint Lupin's."

Jocelyn looked stunned. "I couldn't possibly."

"Yes, you could," said Anne. "It belongs to your

family, to Zarala's family. I want you to reopen the quest academy and fill it with students. I want everyone to know what a wonderful place it is and what a wonderful teacher you are. And Captain Copperhelm and Sassafras, too. I think Zarala would want it that way."

At first Anne thought Jocelyn would protest, but instead she gave Anne a hug. "Thank you, Anne. I promise we'll do just that. But what about you and the others?"

Anne smiled. "I'm sure we'll figure something out."

Anne joined Penelope and Hiro near the mainmast. They seemed in much better spirits and were arguing over who had done a better job dealing with the castle's tower security: Hiro against the firewall with his blob of water, or Penelope against the knight with her footrace.

Anne filled them in on her talk with Jocelyn.

"So," she concluded, "I guess that means we're not going to be students anymore."

"If you really think about it, technically we never were students," said Hiro. "We didn't even make it through one class that whole time."

"Marri said we're more than welcome to stay aboard

the *Leaky Mermaid*," said Penelope. "We still have the pirate tokens, and it *is* what we always talked about."

Anne recalled all their conversations back at the orphanage about becoming pirates and hunting for Old World treasure. In a roundabout way, all of it had come true.

"Maybe," said Anne. She examined her shiny new gauntlet. "It's too bad I never got to try this out, though."

Hiro shifted uncomfortably.

"What is it?" said Anne.

"I don't really want to say," said Hiro.

Penelope cracked her knuckles. "You've already started, so finish."

Hiro sighed. "While it's true most Keepers are trained in proper quest academies, there is such a thing as an independent adventurer. They're known as Rogues. You can sign with one of their guilds. All they require is proof of practical experience, but in this case I can't see that being a problem. It's not as prestigious as working for the Wizards' Council, but under the circumstances..."

Anne brightened. "That's—that's fantastic!"

Penelope eyed Hiro suspiciously. "Why didn't you tell us about this earlier?"

Hiro hesitated. "Because you still have to have a minimum of three people in your group."

"Well, Anne's obviously in," said Penelope. "And I'm in for sure."

They looked expectantly at Hiro.

"It's not that I don't want to..." he started.

Penelope leaned closer.

"You know how I am about regulations and rules. I would just drive you both crazy. Plus, with the whole business about the doppelgangers and the barrier being out in the open now, who knows what kind of trouble that could bring us if people find out, you know, about me."

Penelope leaned in until they were almost nose to nose.

He threw up his hands. "Okay, fine, I'm in, too."

Penelope pumped her fist in the air. "Woo-hoo! We're going to be adventurers!"

Hiro shook his head. "My mother is going to kill me."

"Your mom is going to love it," said Penelope. "And if she doesn't, we'll straighten her out."

Anne gazed out over the passing tiers. "Rogue Keeper," she said, testing out the title. "I think I like the sound of that."

Penelope clapped a hand on her shoulder. "See, it turns out you're the thief of the group after all."

Later that night, after everyone had gone to bed, Anne lay in her hammock in her cabin. Penelope was fast asleep in the hammock next to her, snoring away, but Anne was still wide awake and thinking about all that had happened.

She glanced at her gauntlet. Its metal strips gleamed in the candlelight.

"Jeffery," she whispered.

Jeffery appeared in a flash of light. "Hey, how's it going?"

Anne shrugged, which is a very difficult thing to do in a hammock. "Okay, I guess. I still feel angry about a lot of things. And a little sad. But I'm also happy that the Construct is whole again and that Jocelyn is going to return to Saint Lupin's and that we still get to go on adventures. Do you think it's weird to feel all those things at once?"

Jeffery landed on her pillow. "No, I think it sounds about right. That's just life, and it's going to be messy and complicated and confusing at times, but also wonderful and full of joy and surprises. I don't think you get to have one without the other."

Anne reflected on this. Life was indeed all those things, and she strongly suspected it wasn't going to change anytime soon. Still, for the first time in *her* life, she knew where she came from and where she was going, and at least that was something.

"I guess you're right," she said, and she reached over and patted Jeffery on the head. "Thank you for everything, by the way. I never could have done it without you."

"No problem," he said. "That's what I'm here for."

He gave her a salute with his tiny wing and disappeared.

Then he reappeared. "I'm also here for delicious books. Just in case there was any doubt."

He disappeared again.

Then he reappeared yet again. "Just checking to see if this coming-out-of-the-gauntlet-whenever-I-want thing really works. This is going to be fun!"

Yes, Anne decided, it was.

It was going to be very fun indeed.

THE END
(IN ALL LIKELIHOOD)

Avast, Here Be an Epilogue

And so Anne became a Rogue Keeper, and Penelope and Hiro joined her as a sword for hire and a wandering wizard, respectively.

Jocelyn returned to Saint Lupin's. After completing repairs, she opened its doors at the beginning of the next school year and filled the campus with students. Rokk became a professor and taught a course in Old World mythology, and Princess Whiskers taught Combat 101.

After turning one thousand and two years old, Sassafras finally retired to his wizard's tower and promptly blew it sky high, leaving a sizable dent in the surrounding countryside. Local authorities took him into protective custody (their protection, not his) and eventually transferred him to the Asylum for the Magickally Insane. He wasn't technically insane, of course, but it proved to be a good fit nevertheless.

Captain Copperhelm was offered a position with the Wizards' Council that involved tracking down sassy bards and giving them a good thumping. This also proved to be a good fit.

Nana severed her contract with Fireball Travel Incorporated and remained aboard the *Leaky Mermaid* with Marri and Locke to search for a cure for her shrunken condition. Only one sailor made the mistake of referring to her as the captain's new parrot. The crew nicknamed him Mr. Flambé.

As for Anne, Penelope, and Hiro, they signed with a group called the Independent Adventurers' Guild. Their first assignment involved hunting down a five-ton squirrel that was terrorizing a small village. They defeated it, but they required three weeks to recover afterward.

They also kept their pirate tokens handy.

Just in case.

'Tis the Secretest of Epilogues

An undetermined amount of time after these events, across a computer screen of undetermined location, appeared the following:

LOGIN NAME: ZARALA
PASSWORD: *****

M70: WELCOME BACK USER ZARALA...

SUPPLEMENT TO THE SUPPLEMENTARY READING LIST FOR WOULD-BE ADVENTURERS

(only to be read by those students who have at least two pirate accessories and are seriously considering joining a pirate crew)

＊＊＊◆◆◆＊＊＊

QUESTING 301

- *One Thousand Quests for the Armchair Adventurer*
- *101 Quests That Ended in Complete and Utter Disaster*
- *Kelley's Guide to Bizarre Taverns of the Hierarchy*
- *Famous Keepers and Their Untrimmed Nose Hair*
- *Quests That Never Happened*

HISTORY OF ADVENTURING 301

- *A Complete History of Pirates and Their Severed Limbs*
- *A History of Everything Important That Has Ever Happened at Precisely Three Forty-Six on a Sunday Afternoon*
- *A Long History of Adventuring (Written in Very Short Sentences)*
- *The Historical Guide to the Future: Prophecy vs. Prediction vs. Flipping a Coin vs. Outright Guessing*

COMBAT 301

- *Pirate Combat, Volume 1: How to Lose an Eye in Sixty Seconds*
- *Pirate Combat, Volume 2: How to Swash Your Buckle*
- *Gauntlet vs. Gauntlet*
- *The Game of Checkers: Tips and Tricks for Mortal Combat*
- *Water Squirrels: Scourge of the High Seas*

MAGICK 301

- *Magick for Pirates*
- *Magick for Nonpirates*
- *Pirate Spells: A Compendium*
- *Magickal Ingredients Every Wizard Has on Their Shelf but Never Uses*

DRAGONS 301

- *Twenty-Seven Dragons Who Ate Things They Probably Shouldn't Have and Regretted It Later*
- *Famous Dragon Sayings*
- *Dragons Who Said They Were Sorry (and Other Myths)*
- *Why You Should Never Refer to a Dragon as a Parrot*

ACKNOWLEDGMENTS

It's hard to believe that with the release of this book I now have a trilogy out in the world. And to think, just over two short years ago I wasn't even a published author yet! This truly has been a dream job.

Thanks to Elizabeth Kaplan, my wonderful agent, who continues to be a steady guide and adviser and who keeps an ever-vigilant eye on all the business stuff related to writing that a head-in-the-clouds writer might overlook.

Thanks to Lisa Yoskowitz, my editor at Little, Brown, who has championed each book in this series. Her passion for this story and these characters has been greatly appreciated, and every page has benefited from her keen editing.

My thanks as well to the rest of the team at Little, Brown for all their hard work, including (but by no means limited to) Kheryn Callender, Jeff Campbell, Jackie Engel, Shawn Foster, Karina Granda, Jen Graham, Mike Heuer, Katharine McAnarney, Hannah Milton, Emilie Polster, Jessica Shoffel, Victoria Stapleton, Megan Tingley, and Karen Torres. Also, thanks to folks at Hachette Book Group Canada, especially Dominique Delmas, and to Jacques Filippi from Canadian Manda Group.

Thanks to Mariano Epelbaum, who created the art for all three books. I was captivated by his work the moment I first laid eyes on his portfolio, and I couldn't be more thrilled with his illustrations. He has captured the heart of this story, and readers always give high compliments to the artwork everywhere I go.

Many thanks to the hardworking booksellers who have gone above and beyond to support and promote this series.

A special thanks to Lee Gjertsen Malone, Janet Johnson, Patrick Samphire, and Phillip White, all fabulous writers in their own right, for their insightful critiques of an early draft of the book. It is unquestionably stronger for having received their input. And thanks as well to Wendy McLeod MacKnight and Casey Lyall, my fellow Canadian writers and sometimes school tour partners, for their support over the past several years.

Thanks to my wife, Wendy, for her love and support and encouragement and wisdom, and to our three boys for their ongoing enthusiasm for (and occasional contributions to) these stories. Thanks also to our cat, Ariel, who inspired one of the characters in the series (Princess Whiskers) and whose picture continues to delight students at all the schools I visit.

And finally, thanks to the many readers who have enjoyed and supported these books. Your letters and pictures inspire me to continue writing.